ALL HE'LL EVER NEED

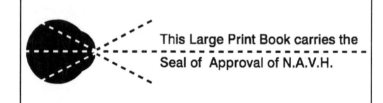

This Large Print Book carries the
Seal of Approval of N.A.V.H.

ALL HE'LL EVER NEED

LOREE LOUGH

THORNDIKE PRESS
A part of Gale, a Cengage Company

Farmington Hills, Mich • San Francisco • New York • Waterville, Maine
Meriden, Conn • Mason, Ohio • Chicago

LIBRARY OF CONGRESS CIP DATA ON FILE.
CATALOGUING IN PUBLICATION FOR THIS BOOK
IS AVAILABLE FROM THE LIBRARY OF CONGRESS

ISBN-13: 978-1-4328-7157-4 (hardcover alk. paper)

Published in 2019 by arrangement with Zebra Books, an imprint of
Kensington Publishing Corp.

Printed in Mexico
1 2 3 4 5 6 7 23 22 21 20 19

This novel is dedicated to my beloved husband, whose steadfast support has allowed me to dedicate countless hours to researching and writing;

to my daughters, who've long been my cheerleaders and best friends;

to my "grandorables," who've served as living, breathing examples for the "brighter than average" kids that appear in my books;

to readers, who stay in touch through social networking sites and plain old snail mail to let me know that they're looking forward to my next release;

and last but not least,

to God,

for blessing me with the ideas and creativity that inspired every story I have written

ACKNOWLEDGMENTS

My heartfelt thanks to my new Amish friends for sharing insights and details about your beliefs and way of life. (By now, you know that I wasn't kidding when I told you I'd be back . . . often . . . so thanks for welcoming me, every time, with open arms!) Thanks, too, to Jody Teets, longtime resident of Oakland, MD, for providing me with details about the town that even a frequent visitor doesn't have access to!

PROLOGUE

"Is your little boy all right, Mr. Baker? He's as white as a bedsheet."

Phillip glanced down at his son, the light of his life . . .

. . . and watched as the boy sank to the floor of the auto supply store like a marionette whose strings had been cut.

Heart pounding, he dropped his billfold on the counter and, gripping Gabe's upper arms, went down with him. Phillip cradled the boy to his chest and did his best to ignore other patrons who had encircled them. Gently he combed his fingers through his son's golden-brown locks, searching for a bump — or worse, blood. Finding neither, Phillip breathed a sigh of relief.

The clerk hid behind her hands. "Oh my. Oh dear. Oh goodness gracious!" She peeked between two fingers. "Should I call nine-one-one?"

"I already did," barked the man to Phillip's left.

An ambulance . . .

Phillip remembered the day, several years earlier, when Gustafson fell from the barn loft. His wife called an ambulance, and without insurance, it had taken the elderly couple more than a year to pay the invoice. Like most residents of the community, he didn't have health insurance, either. But that was a worry for another day. He'd find a way to pay the bill, even if it meant working eighty hours a week instead of fifty. Anything for his Gabe. *Anything.*

"Why does he look upset?" the wife asked. "He should be thanking you for your quick thinking!"

From the corner of his eye, Phillip saw the husband frown.

"He's *Amish,* that's why," the man said. "Those people will spend big bucks to care for their cows and horses, even pigs! But their kids?" He expelled an angry snort.

Those people, Phillip wanted to retort, did *not* care more about livestock than their children. Living Plain was a concept very few Englishers fully understood. The lifestyle was, at times, difficult for *him* to understand. Phillip shrugged it off, as he had every other time someone in town passed judgment on his way of life. It didn't matter what others thought. Gabe mattered, and nothing else.

The ear-piercing wail of a siren grew louder, and so did the murmurings of those gathered. Then, silence as the boxy red-and-white vehicle lurched to a stop out front.

Two burly first responders leapt from the cab, raced around to the back, threw open the doors, and shoved a gurney into the auto supply store.

"What's the trouble here?" the taller one wanted to know.

"I'm the one who called you guys," the big man offered. "This kid here." He pointed at Gabe. "He fell, just like that." He snapped his fingers.

"Fainted is more like it," his wife corrected.

Phillip wished they'd both just stop talking. "He's my son," he said. His voice trembled, exactly as it had on the night he'd lost Rebecca. He cleared his throat. "He . . . he collapsed."

The men made quick work of easing Gabe onto the gurney. It wasn't until they unbuttoned his dark wool jacket that tears filled the boy's eyes.

"What are they doing, Dad?"

"It's okay, Son. These good men are here to help you."

11

A shallow, shaky breath issued from Gabe's bluish lips as he blinked the tears away.

"What's his name, sir?" The man's name tag said MATTHEWS. His partner's read WHITE.

"Gabe. Gabriel Baker."

Stethoscope in place, Matthews listened to Gabe's chest while White gripped the child's pale, narrow wrist.

"Thready pulse," White said. Then, leaning closer to Gabe's face, "Gabriel? Can you hear us?"

The boy nodded.

Matthews clamped a device onto Gabe's forefinger.

"What is that?" Phillip asked.

"An oximeter. It measures the oxygen in his blood." He turned to the boy. "How old are you, Gabe?"

"Four."

Phillip's heart clenched when his boy held up four tiny fingers and sent a wan smile his way.

"Wow. Four, huh! I have a five-year-old daughter." He held a thermometer under Gabe's tongue. "Ninety-nine point five," he said after it beeped. Then, "When will you turn five?"

"July fourth."

"No kiddin'! Lucky kid! Fireworks *and* a cake!"

A slight furrow creased Gabe's pale brow. Was he remembering last summer's community celebration, when his aunt Hannah tripped over a tree root, carrying the birthday cake, and splattered it across the lawn? No, it had probably been the baseball game that inspired the frown. Gabe, so busy waving at his grandmother during the ninth inning that he'd nearly missed the ball. It bobbled in the tiny, made-by-Phillip mitt, and when at last he got control, the ball sailed right past the first baseman. The error cost his team the win, and it had been pretty much all Gabe talked about for the remainder of the day, even as bright, colorful fireworks painted the inky sky with star- and waterfall-shaped explosions.

Matthews pricked Gabe's finger. The boy flinched, but only slightly. "Sorry, kiddo. I should have given you a heads-up about that." He met Phillip's eyes. "This is just to rule out diabetes, sir."

"He isn't diabetic."

"It's a disorder that can present itself quickly." He touched a small card to the dot of blood and directed his attention to Gabe. "Are you thirsty a lot, Gabe?"

The boy shook his head.

"Headaches?"

"Sometimes . . ."

He looked over at Phillip. "Has he lost weight lately?"

"No. Not that I know of. Gabe has never been . . . hefty."

"Noted. So tell me, Gabe, do you find yourself feeling tired easily?" Meeting Phillip's eyes again, Matthews said, "If he is diabetic, it could explain what happened today."

"Yes, I do get tired, but only if I run a lot."

White stepped up. "So who's your favorite superhero, kiddo? Spider-Man? Batman? Ant-Man?"

"We're Amish," Phillip said. "He doesn't know anything about those —"

"I know about Snoopy. Can he be a super-hero?"

"Sure he can." White wrapped a colorful bandage around Gabe's tiny finger and squeezed his shoulder.

Matthews met Phillip's eyes. "Has he had a cold lately? The flu? Any long-standing medical issues we should know about?"

"Issues?" Phillip echoed.

"Like heart disease. Cancer. Diabetes."

"No, no, thank the good Lord. Nothing like that. He's never been as sturdy as other boys his age, but until recently, he hasn't been weak and pale, either."

"Are you in pain, Gabe?" White asked.

"No, just dizzy."

"Dizzy, huh? How often do you feel this way? Every day?"

"Yes, but not the whole day. As I told you, usually just when I run, or climb the stairs too fast."

The paramedics exchanged a glance. Phillip didn't like the concern on their faces.

"Well," Matthews said, "you're a brave boy. Your dad must be real proud of you."

Gabe zeroed in on Phillip's face.

"Yes." He gave Gabe's hand a light squeeze. "As proud as a father can be."

Matthews covered Gabe with a blanket while White fastened the security straps over the boy's chest, waist, and thighs.

White asked, "Did he hit his head when he fell?"

"No, I don't believe so. I checked for a bump, and blood, but didn't find either."

White turned Gabe's head, just enough to comb gloved fingers through the boy's hair. "I don't see anything, either. But don't worry. They'll have a closer look in the ER."

With that, the small crowd parted as the partners wheeled the cot toward the exit.

"We're taking him to Garrett Regional."

Locking the gurney into place on the ambulance floor, Matthews added, "You can meet us there, sir."

Phillip and his neighbors in Pleasant Valley were New Order Amish, and many drove gas-powered vehicles. His '99 pickup looked every bit its age and had earned its nickname. Yes, Old Reliable would get him to the hospital, but he had no intention of following the ambulance. "I promised not to leave him alone," he announced. "I'm going with you."

Matthews perched on the narrow bench beside the gurney. "Okay, but it's gonna be tight in here." He pointed at the other end of the seat. "Park it and try to stay out of the way."

The clerk raced up to the still-open rear doors. "Mr. Baker!" she hollered, an oversized bag dangling from one hand, waving Phillip's wallet with the other. "Mr. Baker, don't forget these!"

Phillip could have hugged her. "Thank you. I totally forgot."

"Under the circumstances, that's perfectly understandable." She handed him the plastic bag of spark plugs, air and oil filters, and other assorted parts he'd purchased to repair the assortment of lawn mowers, small earth movers, and miscellaneous farm equipment awaiting his attention at the shop. "Your receipt is in the bag. Good luck with your little boy."

"Thank you," he said again, and climbed in beside Matthews.

From the driver's seat, White called over his shoulder. "Puttin' her into gear and headin' out. Everybody buckled up?"

Seconds later, siren blaring and lights flashing, the vehicle maneuvered in and out of traffic on Route 219.

"I think we set a record," White said, parking alongside the hospital's ER entrance. "Six minutes flat."

Seemed more like an hour to Phillip, especially as he watched his nearly unconscious son struggle to keep his eyes open.

Inside, the first responders wheeled Gabe into an exam cubicle, and Phillip dogged their heels.

"The ladies at the desk are gonna want some info from you," White said, nodding toward the admitting counter.

"It can wait. I promised to stay with him, remember?" There wasn't much to tell, anyway: name, age, birth date. Besides, he couldn't risk having them turn Gabe away when they learned he was uninsured.

"By law, they have to treat your boy, even if you're not insured," Matthews said reassuringly.

White added, "They'll see him sooner once they have what they need."

Torn between setting things in motion and leaving Gabe alone, Phillip shifted his weight from one foot to the other.

"Okay with you, Gabe, if we hang out with you while your dad fills out some paperwork?"

A weak nod was his answer.

Phillip squeezed his son's hand again. "I won't be long."

It took less than five minutes to provide the necessary information, and to his great relief, the woman barely reacted when he explained his lack of insurance. Upon returning to Gabe's cubicle, White greeted him with a grin. "You're in luck. My sister's on duty. She's one of the best diagnosticians in the state."

A *female* doctor? Phillip didn't know how to feel about that.

All it took was a pathetic moan from Gabe to shift his attitude: If she could help his boy, it didn't matter that she was a woman.

Right?

CHAPTER ONE

Emily stepped up to her patient's bed. She'd read his chart before entering the cubicle, added the data to what her paramedic brother and his partner had scribbled in their report: low blood pressure, low-grade fever, low blood sugar, shallow breaths . . . She'd order a full workup, starting with X-rays to rule out a concussion. Based solely on the pallor of his skin, she'd order extensive bloodwork, too.

Grasping the boy's thin wrist, she smiled. "My name is Dr. White. What's yours?"

"Gabriel Baker. But you can call me Gabe."

"Gabe. Simple and strong. I like it." Silently she concentrated on her watch face: seventy pulse beats instead of the normal eighty to one hundred twenty.

"I'm his father. Phillip Baker."

How she'd overlooked him, Emily couldn't say. He stood no less than six foot two and likely weighed in at two hundred pounds of raw, broad-shouldered muscle.

"I'll need your permission to run some tests on little Gabe here."

"Of course. Anything. Whatever you need. Whatever *he* needs."

He'd tried to mask it, but she heard the unease in his voice, noted the "deer in the headlights" glint in his eyes — gray-blue eyes that reminded her of a pre-storm sky. His obvious distress surprised her, because Amish males were, in her experience, stoical.

Emily softened her tone. "If either of you have questions, please feel free to ask them, and I'll explain everything in words Gabe can understand. And whenever possible, you're welcome to stay with him."

"Good, good."

She looked past the boy's small, inactive body, where her brother stood, pecking the small keyboard of his tablet. "Where's Al?"

White looked up from the device. "He had to leave." Grinning, then rolling his eyes, he added, "Didn't want to be late for Sheila's birthday party."

Over the years, she'd heard many stories about his partner's demanding wife.

"Can't say I blame him," White admitted.

"And you stayed behind because . . . ?"

"Because I promised this li'l dude I'd stick around while the intake lady grills his dad."

How like Pete to make such an offer. She'd never admit it aloud, but he'd always been her favorite sibling. When Miranda blamed Emily for breaking their mother's crystal bud vase, Pete stepped up and confessed to a crime he hadn't committed. And on that terrifying, stormy night when Joe thought it would be funny to lock her in the basement? It had been Pete who'd climbed through a veil of spiderwebs covering the ground-level window to set her free. When his first love dumped him for the school's quarterback, it had been Emily he'd turned to for comfort. Quirky and daring, Pete often terrified her with risky antics, like diving from one of the tallest trees on the banks of Lake Kittamaqundi, to firing off kit-made rockets, swallowing live goldfish, and eating thumb-sized beetles.

"I'm not surprised that you stayed."

Pete's cheeks reddened a bit. "Yeah, well," he said around a playful grin. "What're *you* still doin' here? I thought this was your weekend off."

Emily had volunteered to stand in for Dr. Cartwright, who'd volunteered to chaperone his son's camping trip. To admit it would start a flurry of questions: What had

21

Cartwright promised in return? When would she get some downtime? How many patient charts — hers and Cartwright's — was she juggling? Truth was, she'd rather deal with a crazy-busy schedule than go home alone to think about her dismal social life.

"Weekend off?" She forced a laugh. "What's that?"

He walked around to her side of the bed and gave her a sideways hug. "What was it ol' Abe Lincoln said about fooling people?"

Emily, who'd minored in history, didn't bother pointing out that no written evidence existed to prove exactly what the sixteenth president had said, or if he'd said it at all.

"Call me when you finally decide to leave this disinfectant-scented place. I'll buy ya a pizza at Tominetti's."

Standing on tiptoe, she kissed his cheek. "Sounds good."

"Promise?"

"Promise."

On his way into the hall, he extended his hand to Mr. Baker. "Good luck. That's some great kid you've got there."

"Yes. Yes, he is. And thanks for staying with him."

The instant Pete turned the corner, Emily unpocketed her stethoscope and leaned closer to the Amishman's son. Slow, irregular heartbeats concerned her, especially in one so young.

"Let's sit you up," she said with a confidence she didn't feel, "so I can listen to your lungs."

It took every bit of the child's strength to comply. His father must have noticed, too, for he moved closer to help support the boy's narrow back.

"Nice deep breath in, okay?"

Gabe inhaled and exhaled another half dozen times. Satisfied that she didn't hear the typical crackle or wheeze that signaled pneumonia, Emily helped him ease back onto the pillows and pressed the diaphragm to his chest once again, hoping something had changed since the last check.

It had not.

"What's wrong?" Mr. Baker asked.

Gabe fixed his big-eyed gaze on her face, waiting for her reply.

"We don't know that anything is wrong," she said, choosing her words carefully. "I'll have more answers for you once the test results come in."

His quick nod told her that he got it: She didn't want to speculate and risk frightening his son.

She repocketed her stethoscope and parted the partition curtain. "I'll be back just as soon as I've ordered those tests."

A furrow formed between the man's well-arched eyebrows, a sure indicator that a hundred questions churned in his mind. She didn't know why, but it was difficult to leave him — and his little boy — on their own.

"Is your wife on her way to the hospital?"

"We, ah, Gabe and I, we lost her some years back."

If this wasn't one of those "wish the floor would swallow me" moments, she didn't know what was. "Oh. I'm sorry. So sorry to hear that." She couldn't imagine going through something this traumatic alone.

She motioned for him to join her in the hall. And when he hesitated, she said, "Just a few questions, and we'll leave the curtain open, so you can keep an eye on him."

Even with that assurance, Baker seemed uncertain. But he followed and stood facing her, arms crossed over that broad chest, feet shoulder-width apart.

"How often does Gabriel experience these bouts of dizziness?"

He shook his head. "He isn't one to complain, so I honestly don't know."

No surprise there, either. In her experience, Amish parents didn't like admitting that something regarding their spouses, parents, or children had slipped their notice.

Baker's gray-blue eyes narrowed. He licked his lips. Clamped his teeth together so tightly that it caused his jaw muscles to bulge. It couldn't be easy, raising a small boy all by himself. When he'd greeted her earlier, she'd felt thick calluses on his palm, proof that he worked long, hard hours providing for his son.

"Is Gabe your only child?"

"Yes."

Ah, she thought, a man of few words. At times like these, Emily didn't know whether to classify the trait as good or bad. She felt sorry for him. But sympathy wasn't doing Gabriel any good. Wasn't doing his nervous father any good, either.

"I'll send in a nurse to take some blood. As I said, we'll have a better idea what's causing his problems once the lab reports come in." She'd let him wrap his mind around that before letting him know there would be other tests: EKG, EEG, X-rays, scans . . .

"How much . . ." He swallowed. "How much time will all of that take?"

Emily got the feeling his latest concern, spawned by her list, was what it would all cost. That answer would have to wait. Typically, although the tests could be completed in a few hours, it might take days to get the results. Longer, if the lab was backed up. From what she'd seen so far, this patient couldn't wait days. "I'll call in a few favors to speed things up," she said, as much to herself as to Baker.

He drove a hand through thick sandy-blond waves. "All right. Thank you."

Emily waited until he returned to his son's side. She barely knew him, so why did it hurt to watch his shoulders slump under this extra burden? *Good thing there are rules about doctors fraternizing with patients and family members because . . .*

Forcing the very idea from her mind, she made her way toward the nurses' station. After typing up the orders for a full blood workup, she wheeled the desk chair away from the computer. "Hey, Jody, this little boy — Gabriel Baker — is Amish. Four years old. No experience with needles, and you're so good with blood draws. . . ."

"Say no more," the nurse said. "I'll give him plenty of extra TLC." She leaned in close and whispered, "Are the parents hoverers?"

"The mom died a few years ago." She remembered the way Baker had looked and sounded when he'd shared that bit of information. If she had to guess, Emily

26

would say he loved his wife, still. "Mr. Baker is concerned, understandably, but seems reasonable."

"In general? Or for an Amish guy?"

"Both, I guess."

"Good. Because — and I don't mean to complain, or demean them in any way — but those people can be tough to work with."

Emily understood. Perfectly. Facing the computer again, she typed in a request to put a rush on Gabriel's tests and labs, remembering that her last Amish patient had been the middle-aged mother of three small boys. The woman refused to explain why she'd ingested nearly a whole bar of caustic lye soap, until Emily sent her husband to the cafeteria. He wasn't out of earshot a minute when the woman's confession spilled out: Upon learning she didn't want any more children, he'd started abusing her. Marital relations, he'd insisted, were part of her wifely duties, whether or not they resulted in a child. Since the Amish didn't believe in oral contraceptives or medical procedures and devices to prevent pregnancy, Emily had suggested natural methods, such as tracking her menstrual cycle. The very idea had put the woman on the verge of hysteria. When the last doctor

27

had recommended that course of action, she'd told Emily, her husband refused to cooperate with even those short periods of abstinence. Now, as he returned carrying only one Styrofoam cup of coffee, the wife withdrew again, trembling and avoiding his eyes. Emily knew that the husband's behavior was the exception, not the rule in the community. She'd taken an oath to respect her patients' wishes, especially those stemming from religious beliefs. But she hadn't promised to overlook assault. While a nurse pumped the wife's stomach, Emily backed the husband against a wall and made it clear that the contusions and abrasions she'd found during the initial exam were clear evidence of spousal abuse. Abuse, she'd stressed, that, if reported, would result in arrest and jail time. Abuse that, by law, she was required to report. Nothing could have pleased her more than the terror flickering in *his* eyes. She hadn't seen the couple since, hopefully because her threat had been enough to put a stop to the beatings.

Based solely on Baker's interactions with Gabriel and the gloom that had shrouded him when speaking of his wife's passing, Emily concluded that he had never raised an angry hand against Gabe or his mother. Yes, his "only the facts" responses had been borderline gruff, but the fear of losing his little boy likely explained his reticence. That, and worries about how he'd pay for it all.

Fingers curved over the computer's keyboard, she typed "Amish" into the Religion space. Treating this child would no doubt be a challenge, compounded by the Amish old-world view of medicine and female practitioners.

She hit Enter to save the file. Hit it harder than intended, drawing the attention of two nurses in the station.

Diagnosed with dyslexia during junior high, Emily had faced numerous challenges in college and med school. Her family — everyone but Pete, that is — had tried to talk her into choosing an easier career path. She'd proven all of them wrong, outpacing and outproducing many of her male classmates, and graduating at the top of her class at Johns Hopkins School of Medicine.

She would prove herself to Mr. Phillip Baker, too.

Don't be so self-centered, she chided herself. *You'll do it for the little boy's sake, not to gain his father's approval!*

Still, it would be satisfying, once she'd diagnosed and treated Gabriel, to see relief *and* approval in his father's eyes.

His big, long-lashed, blue-gray eyes . . .

CHAPTER TWO

It was barely dawn when another call put Pete back in the ER.

"Where's Emily?"

"Seeing other patients, I expect," Phillip said.

"How's Gabe?"

"To quote your sister, we won't know anything until the test results come back."

"Well, good that he fell asleep. Place like this? You grab a few z's whenever you can."

It was good, seeing that Gabe had dozed off.

"He's in good hands," Pete said, "so if you want me to drive you back to the hardware store to get your truck . . ."

Phillip almost declined. But he had much to do at home. His only dilemma, whether or not to wake Gabe to let him know he'd be back, soon.

As if the EMT had mind-reading talents, he said, "No need to wake the poor kid. The nurses will explain where you are, and that you won't be away long."

It made sense. "Thank you, Mr. White."

Pete held up a hand. "Hey. Mr. White is my dad's name." Extending the hand to grasp Phillip's, he said, "It's Pete."

While walking toward Pete's vehicle, Phillip began compiling a short list of things he'd need to do upon arriving at home: update his family about Gabe's condition; check his answering machine messages and make some calls to customers, explaining why it might take a while to finish repairing the motors still in his shop. It was good, knowing he'd hear only supportive responses.

The men rode in silence for several minutes, Phillip trying his best to see the beauty in the red-gold sunlight shimmering on the clouds. His wife had painted similar vistas, some on cloth squares that his mother added to quilts, some on old milk cans, and half a dozen or more on scrap wood. What a struggle it had been for her to pretend she wasn't proud of her God-given talent! He shook his head to clear the memory.

"You can quit worrying. I wasn't kidding when I said that Emily is the best."

Pete had mistaken Phillip's silence for concern about his sister's abilities, which, in

Phillip's opinion, still remained to be seen. "That's good to hear."

"Can I ask you a question, Phil?"

"I can't promise to answer, but you're free to ask."

"All the other Amish I've met speak with some kind of German accent or something. . . ."

"Pennsylvania Dutch."

"Yeah, that. They rarely use contractions. The men wear suspenders, not leather belts. Beards. Straw hats. You don't do any of that. So what's the story? You only part Amish or something?"

At fourteen, he'd had a long talk with the bishop, and after explaining what he hoped to do for a living, Fisher gave him permission to look for work in town. As it turned out, none of the auto mechanics in Oakland were hiring, but a local contractor was, and he'd joined the crew within minutes of filling out his employment application.

"I worked for a home builder as a teen. Found it was easier to imitate the other men's speech and clothing than defend mine." Not many in the community had made the same decisions, and those who still abided by the old ways made no secret of their disapproval. There were enough, though, who seemed to share his opinion . . .

that as long as he stayed right with the Almighty, the others' opinions shouldn't matter.

"Kids can be mean," Pete said. "And adults can be meaner. They've had more time to practice."

He remembered well how, during that first meeting with Buzz Myers, the boss had challenged Phillip by asking him to identify every instrument stored in the shoulder-height toolbox, lying on the long workbench beside it, and hanging from the pegboards above it. Phillip had passed the test, despite having to guess at the names of several power tools. By week's end, his coworkers — most old enough to be his father — approved of his work ethic to the point that they'd willingly shared tricks of the trade that had taken them years to hone.

"Then we're not that different, after all," Pete said. "I spent a couple summers working for a Baltimore home builder." He laughed. "Learned some colorful language from those guys, let me tell you! Learned still more during my years as an Army medic. Between the two, I knew what I wanted to do with my life. Driving ambos pays the bills, and I build stuff in my spare time."

Funny, Phillip thought, that his positive

experience with Myers hadn't changed his desire to work with motors. If anything, the job had only underscored his desire to fix broken things.

Pete navigated his boxy SUV into the parking space beside Phillip's pickup.

"How many miles have you racked up on that old beast?"

"She just turned over 155,000. Still runs like new, though."

"Man." Pete whistled. "Amazing." He patted the steering wheel. "This thing is only a year old. Not even twelve thousand miles on her, and she's been in the shop twice." He shook his head. "Who does your tune-ups?"

Phillip opened the passenger door. "That'd be me. It's how I earn a living."

Extending his right hand, Pete grinned. "I might just be in touch when my warranty runs out."

"I'll appreciate the business. And thanks for the lift," he said, stepping onto the blacktop. "Thanks for everything you did for my boy, too."

"Hey. All part of the job."

Phillip wasn't buying it but kept it to himself.

"Happy to be of service. He's a great kid. If I ever have a son, I'll consider myself blessed if he's anything like Gabe."

"Thanks." It seemed dishonest to take any credit for Gabe's temperament. Everything good about that boy came by way of his mother.

"One last thing, Phil . . . I know you people aren't in favor of women in positions of authority, but you can bet on this: My sister's the best. She'll take good care of Gabe. I'd stake my life on it."

"We don't have problems with women in positions of authority. Provided, of course, the women in question have their priorities straight."

"In other words . . . husband, kids, house first, then job-related duties?"

"Close." Phillip smiled. "God goes at the top of the list." He thanked Pete again and closed the passenger door. He couldn't wait to get back to the house he'd built, board by board and brick by brick, as a wedding gift for Rebecca. Couldn't wait to eat a decent meal, shower and change into fresh clothes, update his family and customers, and head back to the hospital. The image of Gabe, all alone in that room, looking small and vulnerable and afraid, would shadow him until he returned.

His mother must have heard the truck's tires grinding over the gravel drive as he pulled in beside the house. The instant his feet hit the ground, she enfolded him in a crushing hug.

"Oh, thank the good Lord!" Sarah said. "I have been frantic since Micah told me what happened in town."

Word traveled fast in a community the size of Pleasant Valley. The clerk must have made a few calls, and considering the human tendency to dramatize things, no telling how much she'd embellished the story. He shuddered to think how much it might have changed by the time word reached his mother.

She'd probably been up all night, praying and pacing, doing her best to press worry to the back of her mind while whispering verses to remind herself that God was in charge, that whatever happened was His will. Red-rimmed eyes told him she'd been crying, too, and he felt terrible about that. A plain black rotary dial phone hung on the wall of his shop. He'd rebuilt an old answering machine, but leaving a message would have been futile since Sarah refused to let him teach her how to use it.

As she led him inside, he said, "Sorry I couldn't get word to you, directly."

"Never mind that." She pulled out the chair at the head of the table, then tightened the belt of her white apron. "You look more weary than when . . ."

Her voice trailed off, and Phillip knew exactly why: His mother remembered the way he'd behaved after Rebecca passed, and how, after the humble funeral, he'd locked himself in the workshop and buried himself in work, hoping to blot those memories, too, from his mind: a half dozen neighbor men, emptying the parlor of its furnishings to make room for the fifty-dollar unlined wooden casket; Hannah and Rebecca's mother, tenderly garbing his beautiful young wife in a pale gray dress, white apron, and cap — the same clothes she'd worn on their wedding day. He pictured the row of horse-drawn black buggies and plain jalopies lined up on the front lawn. And black-garbed mourners trooping slowly by the casket to pay their last respects. After the burial, as he let each visitor clasp his hand, Phillip could barely speak, because his mind seemed frozen on the small white tombstone. REBECCA, WIFE OF PHILLIP, MOTHER OF GABRIEL, it said. She'd deserved a large, ornate marker, like the ones he'd seen in cemeteries on his way to Baltimore, something engraved with angels and daisies — her flower of choice — to represent the beautiful, loving life she'd lived. If the community had been Old Order, the stonemason would have carved nothing but a number into the limestone that marked her place in the cemetery. *At least you can give thanks for that. . . .*

"Sit," Sarah said, interrupting his thoughts, "and I will prepare for you something to eat."

"Thank you."

Sarah began assembling ingredients for a sandwich and, her back to him, said, "Now, tell me everything." She sliced a loaf of home-baked bread. "Do not leave out a single detail."

Phillip inhaled a deep breath, let it out slowly. Should he describe the way Gabe had melted to the floor? The terror in his eyes as the ambulance sped to the hospital? The enormous, forbidding machines that aimed peculiar, glowing red cross–shaped lines on his frail body? Or the nurse's deft fingers, sliding a needle into a vein in the bend of Gabe's little arm, then filling and labeling five finger-sized vials with his lifeblood?

"He doesn't have a concussion, but that's all they know for sure. At least for the time being."

Sarah whirled around so quickly that her apron ties slapped silently against her hip.

"What do you mean, that is all they know? You were there all through the night, and it is morning now!" She shook a maternal digit in his direction. "Do not keep things from me, Son. I want the truth."

He shrugged, feeling numb and helpless. Stupid, too, for not asking more questions while he'd had the chance to demand additional information.

"The doctor says it takes time, sometimes a few days, for the lab techs to deliver the test results."

"Days!" she all but shouted.

How could he explain what he didn't understand himself?

She slapped ham and cheese onto a slice of buttered bread. "What else did he say, this *doctor* with his fancy degrees?"

"Her brother drove the ambulance to the hospital. Drove me back to the auto supply store to retrieve the truck, too," he said. "He says his sister is the best diagnostician in the area, so we shouldn't worry."

The plate hit the table with a ceramic *thunk*. "*Handt dunna,*" she ordered, and automatically, Phillip placed his hands in his lap, bowed his head, and eyes closed, silently recited the prayer she'd taught him as a small boy: "You provide every animal with food and every flower with water, and

39

you have never forgotten us, either. Heavenly Father, we thank you . . ."

He'd barely completed the "amen" when she sat beside him and hid behind her hands. "All right, son of mine, tell me more about this . . . this diag . . ." She waved her hand, frustrated at her inability to repeat the title. ". . . this woman who is caring for our precious Gabe. What are your thoughts about her?"

She wasn't asking for a physical description. Phillip knew that. And yet, all he could think of was Dr. White's quick-to-smile, expressive face. Hair the color of chestnuts that escaped her bun and curled beside her freckled cheeks. Eyes that couldn't decide if they were brown or green.

Phillip took a huge bite of the sandwich, as much to avoid answering his mother's question as to extinguish his guilt. He'd vowed to love Rebecca to his dying day. What business did he have noticing such things about another woman!

"I am pleased to see that you enjoy the sandwich, Phillip, but it is not good to eat so quickly."

"Sorry, *Maemm,*" he said around the bite.

She rose, filled a tumbler with fresh-squeezed lemonade, and placed it beside his plate.

"I added more sugar than usual," she said, returning to her chair.

"Oh? Why's that?"

"I thought you might need a little extra sweetness after what you have been through."

Smiling, he patted her hand. "You're truly a blessing to me. To Gabe, too."

Her brow furrowed. "You are frightening me, Phillip. I can tell you are keeping something from me."

He studied her face. Concern about Gabe — that sort of fear was expected. But what had *he* done to frighten her?

"It is not like you to keep things from me. Not since you have come into manhood, that is."

Once, he and his best friend had gotten lost on the way back from a new fishing hole, and another time, he'd let Caleb talk him into hitchhiking to town to check out the new ice cream parlor. Both adventures put them home long past dark, and knowing it would have terrified his mother to hear that her only son had gotten into *two* cars with total strangers, *and* teetered on the banks of the Youghiogheny River, known far and wide for its wild whitewater rafting rides . . . better to suffer the consequences, he'd decided, for not 'fessing up: extra chores and no dessert for two weeks.

"Phillip Baker. Look at me."

He met her stern gaze.

"Do you trust this doctor?"

"Yes. Yes, I do." He'd said it without hesitation, and that surprised him a bit.

Sarah took a sip of his lemonade. "That is good enough for me, then." She winked. "I baked pies last night to pass the time."

He surveyed the rolling cart beside the stove, where no fewer than ten pies lined the shelves. "I can see that. An order for Hannah's shop?"

Sarah shrugged. "I suppose." She stood beside him. "Let me get for you a slice."

Good as that sounded, Phillip wanted nothing more than to shower, change, and get back to the hospital.

As he'd walked inside earlier, Phillip had noticed a short stack of empty fruit baskets on the porch. "Apple pies?"

"Amos stopped by with a few bushels."

She wasn't fooling him. Apple pie was his favorite. Gabe's, too. She could have canned a few jars instead of baking.

"I know you are in a hurry, but would you mind stopping at Hannah's on your way back to town? She can sell a few of these for me. I will use the money to buy some yardage for my next quilt." Grinning, she added, "If they stay here, I will need longer ties to hold up my apron!"

Phillip grinned, too, and reached for his billfold. "How much do you need? For your quilting supplies, I mean."

Sarah, hand raised like a traffic cop, stopped him. "I will pay for them myself."

"But —"

"Hush. It makes me feel good to spend money I have myself earned." A short pause punctuated her statement. "But I will understand if you feel you do not have time to stop at your sister's."

"No, no, I don't mind." God willing, Hannah would be busy with customers at Threads of Faith, and not at home when he called. Because what he didn't have time for was Hannah's lecture about all the reasons city doctors, hospitals, and medicine were ungodly.

"Stop looking so worried." Sarah playfully poked his chest. "I happen to know that Eli is alone with the boys today. And that means Hannah is in the shop."

He exhaled an exaggerated sigh of relief and made quick work of finishing the pie. "Delicious, as always, *Maemm.*"

"Mueller came by this morning to ask about his tractor."

Phillip slapped a hand to the back of his

neck. He'd just paid for the needed parts when Gabe passed out. "I have everything I need to make the repairs in his engine." *Everything but the time it'll take to do the work.*

"Yoder stopped by, too, asking about . . . you know? I forget what he said he had left for you to fix."

He sighed again. "A lawn mower."

"You say it will be several days until the doctor knows what is wrong with Gabe?"

He put his empty plates and tumbler into the sink.

"I know you, Phillip. You are afraid to leave him alone in that big hospital. But you have a business to run. Let me go there with you, sit beside him in your place. By the time the reports are in, you will have finished your work here, most of it, anyway. Then you can return to the hospital with peace of mind."

It wasn't a half-bad idea. "All right. He'll be glad to see you. You might want to pack a bag, though. No telling how long you'll be there."

"Pie for Gabe?"

Phillip shook his head. "They're limiting his diet."

"Why?"

He saw no point in protecting her from his worst fear. "In case the test results require surgery."

Fingertips pressed to her lips, Sarah gasped quietly. Tears puddled in her eyes, too, but to her credit, she got hold of herself quickly.

"Go," she said, giving him a gentle push. "Clean yourself up. By the time you are ready, I will have packed a bag for both of us and put the pies onto the back seat of your truck."

Phillip drew her close and pressed a kiss to her forehead. "Have I told you lately that I love you?"

"Yes, but I never tire of hearing it."

She shoved him again, and this time, he left the room.

After showering, shaving, and donning clean black trousers and a crisp white shirt, Phillip half ran down the stairs. He was buckling his black leather belt when he stepped into the kitchen.

"That awful thing," Sarah said. "It makes noise. Yet another reason suspenders are better."

Rather than defend his reasons for not wearing them, he motioned toward the bags, standing near the door. "As always, you've made sure everything is ready. You must be as eager to get to Gabe as I am."

She walked silently toward the truck, and

if asked to guess, Phillip would say she wanted to add that his belt wasn't her only complaint. She probably wanted to comment on the way he spoke more like an Englisher than an Amishman, too. He helped her into the pickup's cab, and Sarah said nothing. She remained quiet during the short drive to his sister's place. Hannah's sons, upon noticing Phillip's truck, leapt from their rope swings and raced down the short, narrow drive. Their young voices harmonized as they shouted, "*Grossmammi! Onkle* Phil!"

"Now, now," Sarah said, chuckling, "step back, *Kleinzoons,* or I will not be able to open the door."

"I have never been fond of *kleinzoons,*" the taller boy said. "Can't you call us grandsons, instead?"

"Better still," his brother chimed in, "how about calling us John and Paul!"

"I will not. And if you complain, I will not give you the pie I baked for you!"

They studied her face, and seeing that she was teasing, began jumping up and down.

"Cherry pie?"

"Apple." She opened the passenger door. "And you will not complain about that, either, you hear!"

Phillip loved his nephews' exuberance,

and wondered if Gabe would ever be as robust and energetic. The thought of his boy, lying alone in the sea-green-painted room, woke a yearning to check on him immediately.

Reaching into the back seat, he lifted one of the cardboard boxes that held his mother's pies.

The boys peered around him. "Are all of those for us?" John asked.

"No, just one," their grandmother answered. "The rest are for your mother to sell at the shop."

Paul stamped a small black-booted foot. "May I choose the one that is to be ours?"

"They are all alike." Sarah's left eyebrow rose. "But all right."

"That way," the boy whispered to his brother, "I can choose the one that is fullest of apples."

"Smart!" said John.

"You will be smart, too, little brother, when you are nine."

Pouting, John said, "Three whole years before I get smart? I cannot wait that long!"

"Ah," their grandmother said, "do not wish your lives away, my sweet grandsons. One day all too soon, you will wake up with gray hair and wrinkles, just like me!"

John's eyes grew wide. "Did you hear,

little brother? She did not call us *klein-zoons*!"

Paul giggled as their father descended the porch steps and peeked into the top box. "More pies for Hannah's shop?" Eli asked.

Sarah smiled at her son-in-law. "And one for you and the boys, of course."

"Marrying Hannah was the smartest thing I ever did. You are my favorite *shoonmoder*!"

"Your one and only *shoonmoder*!" she said, and reached up to pinch his cheek.

"Your daughter is busy with bookkeeping at the shop," he said as his older son held open the door. "You are welcome to come in and wait. She promised to be home by noon. She left stew and bread. There is more than enough for you two."

"Thanks anyway," Phillip said, "but we're in a rush to get back to the hospital."

"Hospital?" Paul sounded every bit as worried as he looked.

"Gabe fainted again," his brother said. "I heard Mama say so before she left this morning."

Paul shook his head. "Poor Gabe." He turned to Phillip. "I hope the doctors and nurses can fix whatever is wrong with him. Then he can do all the things we do for fun. We could have a race, and the winner would get —"

48

"A piece of pie!" John bellowed.

Eli stopped laughing long enough to say, "Brother-in-law, I wonder if you would mind doing me a favor . . ."

His sister's husband was about to ask him to bring the pies to Hannah's shop to save Eli the trip.

And sure enough, Eli said, "Since the shop is right on your way, would you mind —"

"Any other day," Sarah broke in, "we would do it, happily. But Gabe has already been alone for far too long. Now, I love my daughter, you know I do, but . . ."

"But she has a tendency to go on and on, and you could be there until well past noon."

"*Daed* is right," John said. "*Maemm* does love to talk!"

Paul feigned shock. "I will tell her you said so!"

"You will do no such thing." Eli finger-combed his dark beard. "It would sadden her to hear that you think she talks too much. And why would either of you want that?"

Eyes wide, John's mouth formed a tiny O. "I would not want that. I love her!"

Phillip felt the same way and gave his young nephews credit for loving his sister, flaws and all. Funny, he thought, the way

49

love teaches people to tolerate imperfections in those they care about most. Even before the rainy Tuesday when Rebecca became his wife, he'd overlooked how quickly she tired, and the way every movement seemed painfully slow. It wasn't until shortly before pneumonia took her from him that he learned that, for years, she'd been masking symptoms of multiple sclerosis.

Paul tugged at his father's sleeve. "Why does Onkle Phillip look so sad?" he whispered.

"I think because he is missing Gabe."

But the empathetic glint in his eyes told a different story. What had he heard to inspire it?

"Time to go, Phillip." Sarah led the way down the walk.

He didn't waste a second, falling into step beside her.

Paul caught up with them. "Will you tell Gabe that we miss him?"

"I will," he promised, tousling the boy's hair.

"And tell him that we will pray that he comes home soon, all healthy?" said his brother.

Crouching to make himself boy-sized, Phillip drew them into a hug. His nephews were well known as the community's most notorious mischief-makers, lantern-breakers, and cooling-pie takers. But their hearts were pure, and he cared deeply for them.

"Of course," he told them. Mostly, because any other outcome was unthinkable.

CHAPTER THREE

The lab techs rarely made mistakes. In the case of little Gabriel Baker, Emily hoped they'd erred in a big way.

After reading the initial reports, she'd pressed the lab to repeat the studies . . . twice more. After three identical reports, she sent his file to a friend at the Mayo Clinic, who agreed that an electrocardio-gram with meds should be next on the tests list. When she'd presented the findings to Phillip Baker, he'd asked for time to think and pray. Upon returning half an hour later, he said, "You have my permission to do whatever is needed to help Gabe."

So she ordered the electrocardiogram, which verified her worst fear: an extremely rare and potentially fatal condition known as Brugada syndrome. Knowing that Baker had already lost his wife, Emily wasn't look-ing forward to delivering the news.

She'd spent the equivalent of thirty hours

reading up on the disorder and interviewing the cardiac specialists who'd written about Brugada in well-respected medical journals and textbooks. Armed with her thick file of facts and figures, Emily made her way to the pediatric ward and found Gabe sitting up in bed, enjoying his first meal in three days. To his right sat an elderly woman. To his left, Phillip Baker.

"A burger and fries," Emily said, forcing a smile. "Bet that tastes good!"

"Oh, yes. I especially like the chocolate milk."

Baker stood. "Dr. White, I'd like you to meet my mother, Sarah."

The older woman nodded. "You have brought to us good news, I hope."

Emily had never believed in giving false hope. But she didn't believe in causing unnecessary worry, either. Especially with Gabe right there in earshot. She chose her words carefully and adopted her all-business façade: Stand tall. Chin up. Voice firm but friendly. "We believe we've identified Gabe's problem."

The grandmother sat up straighter. "You *believe*? After all this time, after starving our boy and subjecting him to needles and wires and big, noisy machines, *you* still *are not sure*?"

53

Gabe must have described his hospital experiences to her in great detail. He put down his burger and looked from his grandmother to Emily. She didn't know him well, but it was clear that this bright little boy wanted answers, too.

Unfortunately, we are *sure,* Emily thought, tightening her grip on the folder.

Baker picked up on the seriousness of the situation. "Where can you and I discuss this, Dr. White?"

Not in front of my mother and son, his stern expression said.

"There's a family area just down the hall. It's quiet there."

"Good." And to his mother and son, he said, "We won't be long."

Once situated in the small, pleasantly decorated lounge, Baker helped himself to a cup of coffee. "May I pour some for you, Doctor?"

"No, thanks. I've had my daily quota." In truth, she'd consumed a full pot, trying to stay awake while investigating Gabe's illness during the wee hours.

He sat across from her, elbows on knees and big hands nervously turning the Styrofoam cup.

"Well?"

Now, looking into his expectant, worried-dad face, Emily wished she'd accepted his offer of coffee, so she could take a sip and put off the inevitable, at least for a moment.

"Gabe has Brugada syndrome."

His well-arched brows dipped low on his forehead as he echoed the words. "Brugada syndrome. What is it?"

"It's a condition that causes a disruption of the heart's normal rhythm, causing irregular heartbeats . . . ventricular arrhythmia. It's responsible for his lightheadedness, and why he passes out. It can also cause seizures, but I believe we can prevent that by implanting a cardioverterdefibrillator to monitor his heart's rhythm and —"

"Meaning, an operation."

"Yes." She'd explain the details once he gave his consent.

"How rare is this . . ."

". . . Brugada syndrome," she finished for him. "Five people in ten thousand have it."

"And what caused it?"

"To put it simply, gene mutations."

"Inherited?"

"Your signature on the forms gave me permission to study your wife's chart, and I took the liberty of doing so. Unfortunately, I found nothing in her doctors' notes to indicate the likelihood of Brugada."

He nodded. Slowly. Sitting back, he shook

55

his head, stared at some unknown spot on the wall behind her. "She was always so pale. Grew tired so easily. Fainted from time to time. But they blamed it all on the MS." Meeting her eyes, Baker said, "Is it possible she had Brugada *and* MS?"

"I wish I could give you a definitive answer, Mr. Baker, but since she wasn't given the tests that are standard for diagnosing Brugada, there's nothing in her file to answer your question."

He sat, quiet and stone-still for several minutes, and Emily could only imagine all the questions that must be circulating in his mind.

"Will it kill him?" he ground out.

This. *This* was the information she most dreaded delivering. Emily held her breath, determined to get the words out in a truthful but kind manner.

"After surgery, we'll follow the rules. Keep him out of the heat. Take his temperature often and avoid exposure to colds and flu, and other childhood illnesses that cause fevers. Make sure he's always well hydrated. And, with the defibrillator in place, proper drug maintenance, and regular checkups, I believe Gabriel can live a long, mostly normal life." Later, she'd explain that studies didn't include patients under sixteen, and that Brugada, despite its rarity, was most prevalent in men over forty. Right now, Baker only needed to hear and cope with the basics.

He took a long draw of the coffee and swallowed. Hard. "Let me see if I'm understanding this correctly. My boy could die of heart failure at any time, whether or not he has surgery."

The simple answer? Yes. But she said, "We'll do everything we can to prevent that."

Placing the cup on the table beside his chair, Baker scrubbed a hand over his face. "How soon will this operation take place?"

She quoted her former Johns Hopkins classmate: "The sooner, the better."

Again, he fell silent. He didn't seem the type to reject surgery. From what she'd heard, the majority of Pleasant Valley residents had relaxed many of the Old Order rules. Gas-powered vehicles, electricity, and plumbing were permitted. While many still held fast to the "trust God, not medicine" rules, many saw doctors on a regular basis. Perhaps his concerns were financial.

"I'm sure you're wondering what all of this will cost. I can put you in touch with agencies that can help defray —"

"I'll pay my own way," he all but barked.

Again, Emily wished she had coffee, water, *some*thing to sip that would hide her discomfort.

"I'm sorry for shouting. None of this is your doing."

"No apology necessary."

But, as if she hadn't spoken, Baker continued. "My hesitancy . . . You see, my parents were raised in the old ways. Decisions like this would have been easy for them."

"They'd simply say no, and trust God's will."

"Exactly."

"But Mr. Baker, you don't speak like those who follow Old Order Amish ways. You don't wear the clothes, or the beard and hat. You drive a pickup truck. And agreed to let me run a battery of tests on Gabe. Forgive me if I seem obtuse, but —"

His impatience was evident as he silenced her with the wave of a hand. "Before I consent to this, I'll need more information. Lots more. About this disorder and how it progresses, *if* it progresses. How invasive it is. . . ." He studied her with a sidelong glance. "Will *you* perform the operation?"

"No, a colleague has agreed to do it. He has an excellent reputation."

"Then I'll want details about that reputation." He paused, drove a hand through his hair. "Details about . . . how many patients have survived this surgery, and how many haven't. I want to know about the operation itself. How long will Gabe be in the operating room, and what's involved afterward, as he recovers?" Another pause as he stared at that unknown spot again. "I want to know if something . . . I mean, once he's home, is it possible that he'll relapse?"

Like many others in the Pleasant Valley community, he'd chosen a far more contemporary lifestyle than his parents, grandparents, and some current neighbors. Still, even if he had access to the Internet — and something told her he didn't — it wasn't likely he'd have time to scroll through hundreds of sites, looking for answers to his questions.

"I've taken the liberty of compiling some data that I think will help you better understand everything." She held out the folder, and he accepted it. "I'm hoping you'll agree to meet with me this evening. That'll give you some time to take a look at the file, and then we can discuss Gabe's case in detail. You can ask questions and I'll —"

"Meet with you?"

Unless she was mistaken, he'd stopped himself from completing the question with *alone*?

"There's a quiet little café about a block from here. Close enough to walk. We can talk over supper."

She'd heard the phrase *tongue-tied,* but until now, hadn't witnessed it. Emily felt a little guilty for putting him on the spot.

"I signed up for the night shift, so I'll need a decent meal to hold me until morning. I hate to eat by myself. You'd be doing me a favor, joining me. We'll bring back something delicious for your mom. . . ."

Baker took a moment to mull it over. He got to his feet and, after dropping the white cup into the trash can near the coffee counter, tucked the folder under one arm.

"All right. I will read this material as soon as I get to Gabe's room. When were you planning to leave for the restaurant?"

She glanced at her watch. "It's one thirty. I'll stop by his room at about five, give him a quick exam, and we can leave right after."

Emily didn't think a man could look more uncomfortable. Was he worried that his mother wouldn't approve of him spending time alone with a woman — a woman who wasn't Amish?

"Tell you what," she said. "I'll meet you at the café instead. It's easy to find. Turn right when you exit the hospital's main entrance and walk a block. You can't miss it. The sign says 'Ella's Café and Bakery.' "

Instantly his shoulders and taut facial features relaxed. Not much, but enough to tell her she'd guessed correctly.

For a reason she couldn't explain, Emily was already looking forward to spending time with him, away from the hospital, away from staff, to focus on his little boy's condition and treatment.

Oh, who are you kidding? You're looking forward to getting to know Phillip Baker, Amish man, better!

Now Emily wished she hadn't made the suggestion. Nothing in the Hippocratic oath forbade a personal relationship with patients' family members, but she'd read several articles in the *Code of Medical Ethics* that openly disapproved of the practice. It made sense, because . . .

Talk about putting the cart before the horse, she thought. He was a loving son and father. Single-handedly ran a successful business. Had a mind of his own, as evidenced by the decisions he'd made that didn't wholly conform to his community's codes. Handsome, strong, soft-spoken . . . Surely one of his female Amish neighbors had captured his attention. Was she the reason Baker seemed reluctant to accept her supper invitation?

61

Maybe dining alone would be better, after all. She'd use the time to call Alex, firm up his surgery schedule. With a little luck, she could also remind herself of the reasons she'd decided to focus solely on work, instead of a social life.

"We can leave Gabe's room together," he said, surprising her. "While you're doing his once-over exam, I'll take my mother aside, explain that we need a quiet, private place to discuss Gabe's case. She'll understand. It'll be easy."

And if she didn't, his tone and stance said, he'd handle it.

Well, you've officially crossed the line, Em.

Something told her that an hour or two alone with this charming, caring man would be a lot of things, but *easy* wasn't one of them.

CHAPTER FOUR

If it had been up to Phillip, plain roller shades would hang in his shop's windows. But Sarah wouldn't hear of it. "As much time as you spend out there," she'd said, "you need something nice. Something to remind you that good things, like family, are waiting for you *in*side!"

This afternoon, her hand-sewn curtains fluttered in the warm spring breeze. Between each lift and fall of the pale blue fabric, sunlight painted butter-yellow streaks on the small wooden *mummy schtool* that stood against the wall. She'd insisted he build it so that Gabe could stand beside him, reciting the names of every tool hanging from the pegboard above the workbench. Sarah had also insisted that he make one for the kitchen, because the boy enjoyed helping her by cracking eggs for cake batter or breakfast.

He missed hearing his son's angelic voice.

And the way Gabe's eyes lit up when he figured out, all on his own, whether a job required a hammer, a wrench, or pliers. For the longest time, he believed the Phillips-head screwdriver had been named after his father. The memory still had the power to make Phillip chuckle, even now.

"It is good to see you, Phillip."

If he hadn't been woolgathering, he might have heard the bishop's boots crunching up the gravel path. Might have seen the big man's shadow stretch across the wood-planked floor.

"I'd greet you with a handshake," he said, hands extended toward the older man, "but as you can see, I'm up to my elbows in axle grease and motor oil."

Micah Fisher laughed, a big sound that filled the space. "Then we will shake twice when next we meet." He removed his broad-brimmed black hat, pressed it to his sus-pendered chest as a somber, concerned expression darkened his eyes. "Any news on Gabriel's condition?"

"The doctor is waiting for test results." He delivered an abbreviated version of Bru-gada syndrome, adding, "Gabe might need an operation."

Fisher stroked his beard. "Might?"

"From all I've gathered, it's more likely

than not."

"And you have given your consent to this."

A statement, he noticed, not a question. "Not yet, but if it comes to that, of course I'll consent."

"This means you have already asked for God's guidance, then."

Another statement. He saw no purpose in admitting that he hadn't done much praying since Rebecca's funeral. Oh, he still believed in God, but after losing her despite months and months of pleading, well, if letting a young wife and mother die was part of His will . . .

"I'm Gabe's father, and as such, I'll do whatever is necessary, whatever is best for him."

"So." Fisher tapped the brim of his hat. "You are still angry with the Almighty, are you? You realize, do you not, how futile is your mindset."

Phillip wouldn't describe his mindset as *angry*. But he'd put his faith in God when his father fell ill. When his brother struggled to live. And when prayers to God hadn't protected Rebecca —

"Even as a small boy, you were stubborn. Always ready with an answer, even before a question was asked." Like a disappointed father, he shook his head.

Blue eyes, magnified by the lenses of round, wire-rimmed glasses, narrowed. Unless Phillip was mistaken, the bishop was about to launch into a long-winded lecture, citing all the reasons doctors, hospitals, and operations went against the Almighty's will.

"This doctor . . . you trust her?"

So, Phillip realized, he'd talked with Sarah before stopping by the workshop. How else could the bishop have known that Gabe's doctor was a woman?

Her image flashed through his mind, brief as a blink . . . but more than long enough to remind him of dark, gleaming hair and thick-lashed, pale-brown eyes. He licked his lips. Swallowed. Cleared his throat. In his mind — and in his heart — such thoughts were wholly inappropriate, especially in the presence of Bishop Micah Fisher! He had just one thing in common with the doctor: Gabe. And once his boy's health improved . . .

He concentrated on Noah Nielsen's generator motor. Once he completed this, and two more small jobs, he'd have almost made up for the time lost while at the hospital. Amos Bontrager's big round-baler engine could wait. On the day Amos dropped it off, he'd thanked God for keeping the old thing going until he'd harvested his largest field. "I will need it by late June, though," he'd said, handing Phillip a crisp one-hundred-dollar bill, "when I will bring in the second crop."

The bishop rapped on the workbench. "You are not fooling anyone, Phillip Baker. I know the look of smitten when I see it."

That got Phillip's full attention. "Smitten." He couldn't help but chuckle. *Me?*

"Your dear mother told me of her concerns, that you are investing too much of yourself and your time in this . . . this *Dr. White*."

She'd said as much to him when he'd mentioned his dinner plans, but Phillip had no intention of admitting it.

"I heartily regret the community's decision to modernize," Fisher said. "When we left the old ways behind, we opened the door to temptation. Too many temptations. Perhaps if things hadn't changed, I'd still have my Esther."

Esther. The daughter he'd shunned so many years ago for no reason other than she'd fallen in love with the wrong man.

The wrong man. It made him wonder where things could possibly go with Emily.

With Dr. White, *you fool!*

"You are even less Amish than the rest of us. Possibly the least Amish of us all!"

Fisher pointed at his brass belt buckle. "You own suspenders. I remember well the last time you wore them to church." He sniffed. "A place where, I might add, I have not seen you in weeks."

He could defend himself with the truth: If he hoped to meet all his customers' needs, it sometimes required working on Sundays.

"I know what you are thinking. That missing services is a less grievous sin than not providing for Sarah and Gabriel."

Phillip added mind reader to the man's numerous talents. *If only people skills was among them!*

"If you truly believed in His will, you would believe He will provide, even if you do not work on Sundays. And that He will heal Gabriel! Your faith in the Almighty is weak, Phillip. Weak!"

Well, the bishop had him dead to rights, there. *But with good reason,* he added.

"Whether you realize it or not," Fisher continued, "you are setting an example for the boys and younger men. They look up to you. What sort of role model is a man who values money over the Word!"

Phillip put down his tools and picked up a scrap of white cloth. "You're right, of course."

The bishop threw back his shoulders and

lifted his chin. Phillip had seen that look before, too many times to count: The older man believed his dressing-down had hit the intended target . . . and made a difference. Should he challenge the belief with one of his own, that such an opinion was, in effect, a sin of pride?

Phillip could think of no reason to upset the elderly bishop. Yes, his unwelcome counsel could sting, but he meant well. And as often as not, his advice helped. Eventually. So Phillip said, "Maybe we'd both make better use of our prayer time if we asked the Almighty to lead those young men to emulate someone more suitable than the likes of me."

Fisher's frown deepened and sarcasm rang loud in his voice when he said, "What we should pray for is that it is God's will for this . . . this *Dr. White* . . . to help Gabriel. And that He will bless you, Phillip Baker, with common sense."

The rise and fall of the curtains slowed as a cloud passed overhead, blocking the sunlight that had brightened the *mummy schtool's* surface. Phillip was bone-tired. Hungry. And more than a little fed up with being told he didn't measure up — as a member of the community, as a son, as a father. He flattened both palms on the

69

workbench's rough-hewn surface.

"Perhaps," he slowly ground out, "if my mother had displayed some common sense, she would have summoned a doctor to tend to my father and brother. If she had, they'd both likely still be with us. And maybe," he continued, voice rising slightly, "if you hadn't made me feel like a Judas for wanting to get Rebecca to a doctor sooner, Gabe would still have a mother and I'd still have a wife. Have you ever stopped to consider that it was *God* who blessed doctors with every skill they need to find out what's wrong with a patient, then do everything possible to fix it . . . to research new cures that provide life-saving medications? And who but God could inspire inventors to create machines that assist in detecting dangerous diseases and disorders? Who but God could motivate designers to build hospitals where the sick aren't just diagnosed, but healed!"

The bishop's mouth formed a thin line, telling Phillip that this time, *he'd* hit the intended target. He hadn't started out to insult the man. Hadn't meant to sound disrespectful, or hurt his feelings, either. But now, the pained look on Fisher's face made it clear he'd done both.

With a snap of his suspenders, the bishop

turned on his heel, stopping in the doorway long enough to make a statement that chilled Phillip to the soles of his boots:

"I believe it is time to assemble a meeting of the elders, to discuss your personal feelings toward Dr. White . . . *who is not Amish.*"

"There's nothing personal between the doctor and me!"

"You allow your son to read books not approved by the elders. Books about history and science. I have seen him in town, too, reading newspapers stacked on the corner. At his age, he should not even know how to read, and yet, he can quote headlines! I have also seen him, walking and talking and laughing with his cousins — even as they pass the church building, they show no respect. All three boys need a lesson in the old ways. Sarah and I have discussed this at length, and she is as confounded by their actions as I."

"They are children, Bishop. There should be joy in their lives!"

"All joy should come from the Lord, even the joy of children."

Apparently, the bishop had said his piece and was now finished. He put the wide-brimmed hat onto his head with such force that the fabric squeaked. Then he left the shop, mumbling things like ". . . I must pray for his change of heart . . ."; ". . . let the Almighty open his eyes . . ."; and ". . . guide him, O Lord, to become a better father . . ."

Anger roiled in Phillip's gut. He wanted to go after the bishop. Grab him by the shoulders and force him to listen to reason. He'd worked hard. Had done everything in his power to provide well for his mother, for Gabe. On the nights when bad dreams woke the boy, he'd gone without sleep to comfort him, to show him affection and attention. And how dare Fisher declare, with nothing to go on but Sarah's assessment, that his relationship with Emily was anything but professional!

Sunlight flashed from the claw end of his best hammer. He picked it up . . . and slammed its face onto the worktable. Screws and nails, nuts and bolts rattled in their jars as screwdrivers and drill bits bounced a time or two on the worn wooden surface. Why did it matter so much what Fisher thought of him, what any of the elders thought, for that matter!

Then, unwelcome reality hit him like a punch to the gut: If the men agreed with the bishop, they'd visit daily to lecture, to read Scripture with him, reiterate his transgressions, and urge repentance. If he didn't mend his ways . . .

Since Rebecca's death, he'd obeyed fewer and fewer of the community's rubrics. But whom had his behavior harmed? No one! And yet Fisher had implied that if he resisted those rules, he could be forced to leave Pleasant Valley.

"Pleasant indeed," he complained.

It wasn't always easy, submitting to the Amish ways. But those ways had protected members for generations, had protected them all the way back to the 1690s. But if he didn't like being judged — as an ineffective parent, an unruly son, a disobedient Christian — because he saw things differently, what right did he have to judge others who drew comfort from the Plain lifestyle?

Perhaps he should dig out his old clothes, let his beard grow, stop talking like an Englisher. At least then, naysayers would see him as cooperative. It was also possible that the trusting feelings he'd known as a youngster would return.

But clothes didn't make the man; if he changed the outside but not the inside, he'd be living a lie. God surely wouldn't approve of that.

A lot would depend on Gabe's future.

CHAPTER FIVE

"I am very happy to see you, Dr. White. Very happy!"

"It's good to see you, too, sweetie."

Emily stood at her little patient's bedside, wondering how to pass the time until Phillip returned. She'd checked Gabe's vitals. Scanned his chart. Asked all the customary questions: "Any pain?" "Did you get any sleep last night?" "When was the last time you ate?"

After adding the latest information to his computer file, she glanced at her watch. Five fifteen. It wasn't like Gabe's dad to be late. Had he changed his mind about discussing the case over dinner? The possibility changed her mood from upbeat to sad.

"Do not worry," his mother said. "He will be here."

Had her thoughts been that obvious? Emily hit the file's Save button.

"Have you ordered a meal, Mrs. Baker, so

you can have dinner with Gabe?"

The woman shook her head. "We have our big meal of the day — dinner — at noon. The evening meal is lighter, and we call it supper. But yes, I will eat with my grandson."

Gabe's grandmother crossed her ankles. "I would like to thank you, Dr. White, for making our boy feel at ease here. Normally, he is a quiet, shy boy who rarely speaks around strangers. With you, he talks a blue streak."

The information inspired a smile, and the warmth of happiness swirled within her. As she searched her mind for a suitable reply, Mr. Baker — Phillip — entered the room.

He'd changed into rugged brown work boots, dark suspenders, and a collarless white shirt. He held a straw hat along with the file she'd given him. There hadn't been time to grow a beard, but if there had been, something told her he'd be sporting that, too. He'd only been home for a few hours. What had happened in that short time to inspire the perceptible changes?

"Dad!" Gabe said, eyes bright and arms extended.

It only took three long strides to put Phillip beside the bed. Seated on the edge of the mattress, he gathered his son close, all but blocking Gabe from her view.

The boy peered over his father's broad shoulder and grinned at Emily. "Is it true, Doctor? Are you taking my father to a fancy restaurant to eat?"

The question took her by surprise. She avoided Mrs. Baker's eyes. "Why, yes. Yes, I am. But the restaurant is hardly fancy!"

Sitting back, Gabe inclined his head. "Why are you eating in a restaurant, instead of here, in my room?"

"Because," his father answered, "Dr. White is going to help me better understand what's wrong with you, and how she hopes to fix it. It will take time for her to explain things in non-hospital terms. You need to use that time to rest, so you will be ready for the operation."

Gabe sank back into his pillows and took a deep breath. "I would very much like for you to fix my heart."

She wanted that, too. Although Emily had only spent a few hours with this precious little boy, she'd grown fond of him. She could pretend it had nothing to do with his father, but that would be a lie. Emily tried to ease her discomfort by telling herself anyone would feel affection for the bright, articulate child . . . especially since he'd made no secret of his affection for her!

"What time is it, Dad?"

"I, ah, I left my watch at home."

"Why?"

"Because neither my shirt nor my trousers have pockets."

Gabe looked as confused by his father's new look as she felt.

"Why are Amish clothes made without them?"

"Because," Sarah said, "they are not plain. They signify worldly things that are not pleasing to God."

The answer didn't satisfy her young patient's question, and judging by Baker's stern expression, it displeased his father.

"It's a little after five," Emily said.

The boy glanced at his grandmother. "Dad's stomach will rumble if he doesn't have supper soon."

The older woman nodded. "Yes, this is true."

"They should go to the restaurant then, should they not, because the sooner they leave, the sooner they will eat, and the sooner they eat, the sooner they will get back." He aimed a big-eyed stare at Emily. "And when you do get back, will you tell me what is wrong with me, and how you will fix it?"

Telling the little boy the truth would terrify him. Avoiding it would, too. She said a little prayer that, by the time she and Phillip returned, God would have provided a suitable answer.

Sarah clucked her tongue. "She is good at asking questions, but not so good at answering them."

If there had been any doubt about the woman's opinion of women in the medical profession — any profession, for that matter — they were quashed by her cutting words. Had her attitude toward Phillip's non-Amish conduct inspired the change in his speech and clothes?

"The information I've gathered in the file will provide answers to most, if not all, of your questions, Mrs. Baker. You're more than welcome to read it. And I'm more than happy to answer any that I haven't already addressed."

She shuddered under Sarah's intense scrutiny. Blue eyes that had glowed with loving warmth when looking at her son and grandson turned icy, like the glacier waters in the Gulf of Alaska.

"Gabe makes a good point," Phillip said. Facing his mother, he added, "Once Gabe is settled for the night, I will drive you home. There, you can get a bath and a decent night's sleep."

Now Sarah fixed that frosty glare on her son. "I will sleep when Gabriel is well again."

"Now, *Maemm,* that isn't healthy. What good will you be to Gabe if you get sick?"

At the mention of his name, the boy opened drowsy eyes. "I have a question, Dr. White . . ."

Emily moved closer, rested a hand on his forearm. "What is it, Gabe?"

"When *can* I go home?"

He was listless, slightly feverish, with aches and pains. If the complaints signaled an infection, surgery would be postponed. Indefinitely. Alex had made it clear that he'd called in favors to squeeze Gabe into his already overcrowded surgical schedule, and that in a few weeks, he'd leave on a world cruise that would make him unavailable for nearly three months. Even if nothing went wrong, the boy's hospital stay could be lengthy.

She summoned her best bedside manner smile. "I wish I had a good, easy answer for you, sweetie." *Sweetie? Again? Stop it! Just stop it!* "Everyone here at the hospital is going to do everything we can to make sure you're home again just as soon as possible."

The grandmother replied with a cynical snort. Phillip looked as skeptical as Sarah had sounded.

"It is getting late," he said. "Perhaps Gabe is right, and we should go."

Emily agreed. But first things first.

After withdrawing a business card from her bag, she held it up so that Sarah was sure to see it. "My cell phone number," she explained, placing it on Gabe's bedside table. "If you need me, for any reason, feel free to call." The nurses had the number, too, but perhaps this direct invitation would help quell the woman's mistrust.

Gabe sent her a sheepish grin. "If your bag is heavy, Dad can carry it for you."

She'd made a habit of carrying her wallet and keys in her well-organized medical bag. Even stocked with a pulse oximeter, wrapped tongue depressors, alcohol wipes, gloves, and masks, the waterproof, zippered case was as lightweight as any purse she'd ever carried. Emily tucked her stethoscope into a side pocket and secured the latch. Smiling, she slung its strap over her right shoulder.

"I'm sure he would, but I've been lugging this old thing around for years. I'm used to it." She gave it a pat. "We won't be long."

Emily wasted no time making her way to the elevators, and when Phillip caught up to her, he thumbed the Down button. "For someone with such short legs, you walk pretty fast."

The fluorescent bulb overhead drew her attention to the whiskers that shadowed his upper lip, cheeks, and chin. "I thought all Amish men were required to wear beards."

"Only the married ones."

What about the widowers? she wondered.

The gleaming aluminum doors opened with a quiet hiss. Alone in the car, they stood side by side. She averted her eyes from his brawny biceps. Pretended not to notice that he towered over her. Ignored the way his long lashes shimmered under the flickering light.

"I have not eaten spinach in days."

The suddenness of his deep voice startled her. "Spinach?"

"I thought maybe that's why you were staring . . . spinach in my teeth."

His wide smile sent her heart into over-drive. Rather than admit he'd been right — that she *had* been studying him from the corner of her eye — Emily said, "You have a wonderful smile. I think it's sad that you don't show it more often."

That inspired a quiet chuckle. "Have you not heard? We Amish shy away from any-thing that draws attention to us."

"That can't be true."

"Oh?"

"Your clothes and accent, that's what draws attention."

He nodded.

"Besides, I've treated many Pleasant Valley residents, and can't recall one as serious as you. Even those who were injured or ill managed to joke and smile, at least a little."

Eyebrows raised, he shrugged. "If I were a betting man, I would wager *you* inspired those smiles."

The elevator stopped on the first floor, and as they exited the car, he continued. "You have a way of making others feel calm, even in the midst of chaos and concern. A good quality in a person. Especially a person tasked with the care of others."

"Why, thank you, Mr. Baker." She'd heard that before, too, but from this man . . . Emily cleared her throat. "That's good to hear."

They stepped outside, where traffic beyond the parking lot whizzed past. Horns blared. Sirens wailed. A helicopter hovered overhead, preparing to position itself on the big red *X* on the hospital roof.

"I wish you would call me Phillip." He moved to her left side, putting himself between Emily and the curb. "Unless it violates some sort of doctor–patient's family rule."

"All right, but only if you'll call me Emily."

Extending his right hand, he smiled again. "We have a deal."

The rasp of his palm against hers reminded Emily of her grandfather. For forty years, Dutton White Sr. had spent his days — and more than a few nights — as a building contractor. The grueling labor had given him hard, bulging muscles and built thick calluses on both hands, just like Phillip's. Once, a few years before his retirement, she'd asked her grandfather why he worked so hard when, as owner of the White and Son Design-Build, he could have assigned the strenuous tasks to his employees. "I'm no better than my men," he'd replied. "Besides, it feels good knowing that I provided a good life for your grandmother and your aunt and uncle with my own two hands." The comparison gave Emily yet another reason to like and respect Phillip.

"You remind me of my father's father."

"Oh? How so?"

She described the way Dutton had devoted himself to his wife and children, how he'd taught her to fish, and drive a nail with a single hammer blow. "And he had hardworking hands, just like yours."

By now, they'd reached Ella's Café. He

wrapped his fingers around the weather-dulled brass door handle, then stepped aside as Emily entered.

"Dr. White!" said the girl at the cash register. "Must be a busy week. Haven't seen you in days and days. We've missed you!"

"You too, Cindy."

"Table or booth?"

"A booth would be great. One in the back would be even better."

Winking, Cindy grabbed two menus and led the way to the rear of the café. "How's this?"

"Perfect." Emily slid onto the red vinyl bench facing the entry and put her bag beside her.

Phillip sat across from her as the young woman said, "I'm pullin' double duty this evening, as usual. Hostess, waitress, bussing tables . . . What can I bring you two to drink?"

"How about some of your famous lemonade."

"Sounds good," Phillip said. "Make it two."

Once Cindy left them, Emily said, "Let's eat first, and discuss Gabe over dessert and coffee." She watched him open his menu.

One brawny shoulder lifted in a half

shrug. "You're the doctor. I will go along with whatever you think is best." Phillip took a moment to scan the entrees, then met her eyes. "You have eaten here before. What do you recommend?"

"I'm partial to the veal Parmesan. It's just the right amount of crunchy, and Hobert serves it with roasted red potatoes and salad with dressing that beats any I've ever tasted."

"Hobert?"

"The chef. He keeps threatening to retire. And I keep threatening to stop eating here if he does." Laughing, she tacked on, "His son Matt owns the place now, and insists the recipes won't change, no matter what."

"But you don't believe it?"

It was her turn to shrug. "You know the way it is with fathers and sons . . . one always trying to outdo the other."

"That was not my experience, but then, my father lived in Pleasant Valley."

Lived. Emily wondered if an ailment similar to Gabe's had taken Phillip's father.

"Meaning, you had a friendly, tolerant dad? Or disagreeing with parents is frowned upon in the community?"

One side of his mouth lifted in a wry grin. "Little of both, I suppose."

He'd reverted to what the hospital staff

referred to as Amish-speak, slipping only now and then. "Can I ask a personal question?"

"I'll tell you what I told your brother when he asked the same question. You can ask, but I may not be able to answer."

"Why the change? From Englisher clothes and speech patterns back to the Amish ways?"

His eyes darkened and his upper body stiffened. "I have my reasons."

And they're none of your business, she thought.

Cindy appeared, balancing two tumblers of lemonade on a small round tray. "Here you go, folks." Her order pad open on the tray, she gave her red ballpoint a click. "Ready to order? Or do you need a few more minutes?"

"We'll have two veal Parmesan dinners."

"As if I didn't know," she said, scribbling as she spoke. "One check or two?"

Phillip answered before Emily had a chance to. "Just one."

Cindy walked away, and as Emily started to protest, he held up a hand to silence her.

"It's the least I can do. Something Cindy said earlier makes me think that you make a practice — pardon the pun — of bringing patients' family members here to discuss

86

things in a relaxing environment." Phillip unwrapped his silverware. "It must be a false rumor, then, that doctors are required to maintain an emotional distance from patients."

And their family members . . .

"As long as we don't allow the attachment to cloud our medical judgment," she said, "I see no harm in sustaining a, ah, a certain closeness."

He sipped his lemonade and met her eyes over the tumbler's rim.

Oh, to read the thoughts that caused one corner of his mouth to lift in an appealing smile!

Chapter Six

"Tell me, what childhood event made you want to become a doctor?"

"How did you know it was a childhood event? Maybe I watched a lot of doctor shows on TV. Or had a crush on my pediatrician."

"You don't strike me as the type who spent a lot of time in front of the television, or makes lifelong decisions based on youthful infatuation."

Emily's pediatrician remained handsome well into his seventies. Not the kind of handsome that inspires girlish dreams, but handsome nonetheless. And she'd always preferred reading, sketching, making beaded bracelets over sitting in front of the TV. But how had Phillip known that?

"My mom was a Type One diabetic. Her whole life, it seemed, revolved around doctors' appointments, medications and test strips, a strict diet . . . At first, I thought I'd go into research, to find out what caused the condition, in the hope the discovery might lead to a cure. But midway through med school, I realized I didn't like being closed up in a sterile lab, that I'd rather work directly with patients. A fellow student — a, ah, a friend, actually — helped me realize that diagnostics was a better fit."

She'd said her mother *was* a diabetic. Had some diabetes-related disorder caused her death? And the way she'd said "friend" made Phillip think that the fellow student had been more than a friend. Much more. If she felt like sharing details, so be it. If not —

"One thing led to another," she continued, "and the specialty branched out when I transferred here."

"Transferred to Oakland? From where?"

"Baltimore."

Even the city's name seemed difficult for her to say. Had the so-called friend inspired the transfer?

"How long have you been with Garrett Regional?"

"Almost two years." Her forefinger traced the rim of the glass, which emitted a quiet *zinging* sound. "My brother had already moved here. Work, and distance, makes it hard to see my dad and other siblings as often as I'd like, but at least Pete is nearby. He's the best big brother, ever."

He'd spent enough time with the man to believe it. "Your other siblings . . . brothers? Sisters?"

"There are four of us. Pete is the oldest. Next came Joe. Then Miranda." She leaned forward and whispered conspiratorially, "I'd never tell them, of course, but Pete's my favorite. Always has been. Always will be. Without him, I don't know how Dad would have made it when we lost Mom. Pete chose the casket. Ordered the headstone. Wrote the obituary. Organized the service. After the customary get-together at the house, he cleaned the place, top to bottom, then took Dad on a cross-country drive. They were gone nearly three months. And when they came home, well, let's just say that time away made it a bit easier for Dad to adjust to life without Mom."

"Three months." Phillip watched as she sipped her lemonade. "He must have had an understanding boss."

"Actually, the captain made it clear that he didn't approve of Pete's time off. That's how he ended up here in Western Maryland, working as a paramedic for a private ambulance service instead of a firefighter."

"Based on his partner's behavior, I would

say he is well liked by coworkers."

Emily laughed softly. "I've never met anyone who doesn't love him. And if I did? I wouldn't trust that person!"

It was obvious she cared deeply for her family, Pete in particular. Cared deeply for her patients, too. He admired her loyalty. *Dis*loyalty had been at the root of his every major argument with Rebecca. Regardless of subject matter, or whether he'd been in the right, not once did she take his side. In the privacy of their house, it might not have cut as deeply. But at church? In her parents' home? In his shop, in front of customers? As the midwife brought Gabe into the world? He hadn't understood it then, and if he allowed himself to dwell on the memory, it still irked him.

Emily sat forward again, looking concerned. "What's wrong?"

He'd never been much good at hiding his feelings. His mother, the bishop and the other elders, even young Gabe often teased him about the way his face revealed his every thought and emotion. He didn't like the uncontrollable, angry thoughts that surfaced about Rebecca. She'd been quiet. Frail. Sickly. Her mood swings weren't entirely her fault.

He gripped the tumbler. "Just wondering

how Gabe is doing. He looked paler than usual when we left. And then the low-grade fever . . ." A necessary lie, he told himself, blended with a bit of truth.

Smiling sweetly, she patted his hand. "Don't worry, Phillip. He's safe, and in good hands. By the time we get back, the test results I ordered will be in. And his grandmother is with him, don't forget."

He might have said something flattering about his mother if Cindy hadn't returned, this time balancing a large oval tray on her shoulder. After delivering their plates, she told Emily that Hobert said "hey," and that he'd stop by in a bit to collect his weekly hug.

"If you need anything, anything at all," the girl added, "just holler." And with that, she returned to the hostess stand.

If he'd blinked, Phillip might have missed the way Emily paused and, hands folded on the table's edge, closed her eyes. Afterward, she wasted no time picking up her knife, cutting off a bite-sized chunk of veal. Deep down, he knew that he ought to follow suit. He was about to when she said, "It's so good, isn't it?"

He quickly took a bite, hoping that he could agree. Truth was, he'd taken better meals in the comfort of his own kitchen, expertly prepared by his mother. But "Yeah, it's pretty good" was what he said.

"I'm not eating all of this." She glanced toward the kitchen, then leaned forward to say, "I need to save room for Hobert's spectacular cheesecake."

"He's a chef and a baker, too?"

Small talk. He didn't hate many things, but idle chitchat was high on the list. Hopefully, she wasn't one to dawdle over a meal, because Phillip wanted to hear more about Gabe's condition, and return to the hospital, ASAP. If she didn't get to the point soon, he'd have no choice but to reintroduce her to it.

"This is a small place. Most of Hobe's staff pulls double duty. Cindy waits tables, and as you heard, she's a hostess and busboy, too." Emily pointed to the middle-aged man behind the bar, and he waved. "Robert serves drinks, and when things are slow, he's a dishwasher."

Cindy had greeted her by name. And Hobert intended to visit the table to collect a customary hug. If the bartender's wide grin was any indicator, he thought highly of Emily, too. How many meals had she eaten here to have earned "like family" status? Phillip knew little to nothing about her personal life. If she had a steady beau, he must be a doctor. Who else would tolerate her crazy schedule? Or allow a woman as wonderful — and gorgeous — as Emily to spend so much time alone?

Cindy paused on her way to a nearby table. "Everything all right, folks?"

"It's delicious, as usual. We'd like cheesecake and cappuccino. No rush. Just whenever you get a chance."

"With caffeine, of course," the girl said, winking. She met Phillip's eyes. "Decaf for you?"

Although Emily didn't speak, he heard her unasked question: *"Are the Amish* allowed *to drink caffeine?"*

Oh, how tiresome it was, watching and listening to the erroneous conclusions of others! But who was he to talk? God hadn't gifted him with mind-reading talents, yet he'd lumped her in with "the others," though she'd never said or done anything to earn it. *You're a hypocrite,* he told himself, because since losing Rebecca, he'd broken just about every Amish rule.

And yet, he felt protective of the people in Pleasant Valley, whose quiet lives harmed no one.

"No decaf for me," he said, eyes locked on Emily's. "I want to be alert for our, ah, discussion."

Cindy's eyebrows disappeared behind purple-dyed bangs. "Aw, don't tell me you two are breakin' up. That'd be a major bummer, 'cause you look so good together!"

"Breaking up?" he and Emily said together. Nervous laughter punctuated their harmony.

"Sorry. You know me . . . always jumping to conclusions." Cindy giggled. "I just assumed that since you weren't discussing some weird illness or an operation, that you two were, well, y'know, a couple."

Later, after driving his mother home and Gabe was fast asleep, he'd try to figure out if he'd said or done anything to give the girl such an idea. For now, he said, "My little boy is Dr. White's patient."

"Mr. Baker is right." A cool tone replaced the warmth in Emily's usually musical voice. "We're mostly here to discuss how we'll proceed with his son's care."

Mr. Baker. Again. And *mostly*?

He blamed lack of sleep or concern about Gabe for the strange questions swirling in his mind: Had Emily expected him to admit that he saw her as something more than Gabe's doctor? Was that what had caused the sudden shift in her manner? His heart did a wacky little leap at the possibility. That, alone, puzzled him. He'd never felt anything like it, not even the first time he'd kissed Rebecca.

He pretended to listen as Cindy described her preparations for life in a college dorm. Her enthusiasm proved that she appreciated the new experiences awaiting her. Experiences the girls at Pleasant Valley would never know. A good thing, in his estimation, since the community protected them from the disappointments and dangers so prevalent in the cities and towns beyond their borders. He leaned in, hoping it would appear that he was listening to their conversation. Despite his best efforts, memories of Adam Bontrager seeped past the edge of his consciousness. Adam, who twenty years ago, had been forced to choose between everyone in Pleasant Valley and the Grantsville divorcée who'd hired him to paint her duplex. He thought of Esther, too, who'd suffered banishment a decade later when her father — the community's bishop — caught her in a passionate embrace with a bachelor who frequented the Fishers' vegetable stand. Both had known the consequences of their actions. But Phillip couldn't help but wonder . . . had the choices they'd made for love been worth sacrificing everything — and everyone — else?

Shunning seemed innocuous, until one

considered how many lives it altered. Parents, siblings, other relatives and friends knew better than to speak of the "gone person" except in hushed tones. It was one of the reasons he'd kept quiet about the many times *he'd* considered moving to Grantsville or Deer Park, to build a new life that didn't include the tired "Faith cures all ills and eases all pain" sermon. These days, the thoughts hammered at him on a daily basis, because after the operation, Gabe would need easy access to a decent pediatric heart center. No such thing existed in Western Maryland, but in Baltimore . . .

Again he wondered, *Would it be worth it?*

Emily's soft, sweet laughter brought him back to the here and now.

"You'll have to send me your address," she was saying. And handing Cindy a business card, she added, "Once you're settled in at Frostburg State, give me a call or drop me an e-mail. I'd love to hear how things are going."

"I'll do that." The young woman tucked the card into her apron pocket and, grinning, hugged Emily. "You're the best!" she said, and headed for the kitchen.

Emily waited until she was out of earshot to say, "Where were *you* a few minutes ago?"

Clearly, he'd never make it as an actor, not if he couldn't even hide the thoughts that had taken him far from her exchange with Cindy. "Just thinking about Gabe's future." Not the whole truth, but not another necessary lie, either.

She opened the big black bag on the bench beside her and withdrew a thick folder. Had she made duplicate copies? Earlier, he'd given the pages in the first file a cursory glance, and placed it on Gabe's bedside table, thinking to give the material a more thorough read once Sarah was home and Gabe was asleep. Or had she tucked the original file into her medical bag when he wasn't looking?

"Before we get started, I just want to say . . . I don't know why you decided to go back to wearing Amish clothes and speaking Pennsylvania Dutch. But when we're alone, you and I, I hope you'll feel free to let down your guard. No need to add to your stress when it's just the two of us."

Yes, he admired her caring nature, but didn't she realize that by making such a genuine offer, she'd made his decision even harder?

"I appreciate the offer," he admitted, "but switching back and forth will prove more stressful than choosing one or the other.

For now, at least, I must get back to basics. For my mother's sake. For Gabe's."

She smiled, and he couldn't decide if sympathy or understanding prompted it.

"You'll see that I've gathered a lot more information, new information," she said, sliding several loose pages closer to his elbow. "I also took the liberty of discussing Gabe's case with a . . ." Blinking rapidly, Emily looked toward the restaurant's entrance. "With a friend who specializes in pediatric cardiology."

The same friend she'd referred to earlier? *That* got his full attention. "He's here? In Oakland?"

She shook her head. "I'm afraid not. He's in Baltimore. At Johns Hopkins."

Some time ago, he'd read an article touting the hospital as one of the best in the world. If this friend could arrange for Gabe to see a top surgeon . . .

"Alex, I mean, Dr. Williams says he can add Gabe onto his surgery schedule if we get him to Baltimore by Monday."

So. The friend performed heart surgery. Phillip swallowed his disappointment and decided to focus on the bright side: No way he could compete with a big-city surgeon, which solved the problem of putting a safe emotional distance between him and Emily.

"Monday," he echoed. "But . . . but today is Thursday. . . ." Now, Phillip focused on a newly written mental to-do list: time at his shop, completing small jobs; reaching out to customers who expected him to repair additional engines and motors; talk with Hannah about keeping an eye on their mother; could he trust his old truck to make the four-hour trip east, and back again?

"I'll help you any way I can."

Emily's offer, he believed, was sincere. She'd earned his admiration for sensing what had caused his hesitation. But even if she could help alleviate the financial burdens associated with Gabe's care, he couldn't in good conscience ask for *or* accept her aid.

He analyzed the new pages, saw immediately that she hadn't exaggerated. They contained many details not included in the material he'd already read. What he didn't see, however, were specifics about the operation itself.

"How long will Gabe be in the operating room?"

"Several hours, if everything goes according to plan."

"What are the chances they will not?"

"Slim to none. Dr. Williams is one of the best in the world."

Gabe might buy into such empty promises, but Phillip found no comfort in her words.

"What about afterward? Do you expect complications?"

She shook her head. "There's no reason to expect that."

"How long will your, ah, *friend* keep him in the hospital?"

Had she heard the sarcasm in his voice? Was that why it took a full second or two before she said, "That's an excellent question, one you should ask Dr. Williams. He agreed to make time in his schedule for a pre-op consult. That's when he'll evaluate Gabe in person. And during the exam, you can ask any questions you might have."

"Help me understand. Why this Dr. Williams instead of you?"

"I'm not a surgeon."

She looked down, her long lashes dusting her cheeks. Why hadn't he noticed the light sprinkling of freckles before?

"It's a delicate operation, and Dr. Williams is one of the best. Just as important, Hopkins has the best and latest equipment. Experienced surgical teams. Skilled nurses."

"If you had the equipment, and people in the surgical suite with the right skills here in Oakland, *then* could you perform the operation?"

Eyes wide, Emily blinked. Blinked again. "No, I'm afraid not. My specialty — if I can claim one — is diagnostics. I identify problems, then connect patients with doctors most likely to solve them."

An answer, but he still wasn't satisfied.

Elbows on the table, she leaned forward. "Look. Phillip. Dr. Williams asked me to assist. That means I'll be in the OR with Gabe the entire time."

Why would this *Williams* fellow extend such an invitation? Surely he was aware that Emily's expertise was *outside* the operating room. "Assist," he repeated. "What does that mean, exactly?"

"It means I can help, with clamps and suction and whatnot, in the event the surgical team is busy with other, ah, tasks."

In other words, Phillip thought, if something went wrong?

"And Dr. Williams, he knows about your specialty?" He couldn't bring himself to say *medical limitations.*

"Oh, yeah . . ."

She rolled her eyes. Her big, long-lashed eyes.

". . . he's aware all right."

Her tone confirmed his suspicions that she and Williams had been romantically involved. Phillip didn't know how he felt about that. How he *ought* to feel about it. Despite the interest she'd shown in him — which had probably been the product of wishful thinking — she was an Englisher, and whatever his current doubts, he was Amish. Outsiders didn't last long within the community. Of the Amish who left by choice, then returned by choice, some found their time away made it easier to live the Plain life. But a few didn't do well, waiting for others' scrutiny to end. Which would he be, if he walked away from Pleasant Valley? One thing was certain, if she kept staring into his eyes that way, waiting for him to react to her Williams comment, he might close the one-foot gap between them, take her lovely face in his hands and —

"He believes it'll be good for Gabe to see me, a familiar face, before the anesthesia kicks in."

She's only in your life because of your boy's imperfect little heart. And yet he said, "You said yes, I hope. You will be there? To assist?"

"Of course."

His heartbeat quickened when she licked her lips. Her full, perfectly shaped rosy lips. Twelve inches, he told himself. Just twelve inches . . .

"I've grown quite fond of that kid of yours."

Now, she smiled, and sent his heart into overdrive. Could she hear it, beating double time, from her side of the table?

What was *wrong* with him! Had he completely lost his mind . . . or his soul? How else was he to explain that, instead of focusing solely on Gabe's health, these notions kept pummeling him!

"It is a long drive to Baltimore," he managed to say.

"Yes, I'm aware. I have family there, remember?"

Good. A change of subject, and hopefully, a change of mood.

"You will stay with them for a few days, then?"

"No, I'll set up a lunch or dinner, so we can catch up in person, but I'll grab a cot in one of the residents' rooms. I can probably scare one up for you, too."

Amazing, Phillip thought, the way she could make ordinary sentences sound like music. He loved watching her talk, too, big eyes alight, dainty hands accentuating words like "in person" and "you too."

Distance, Baker. Keep your distance.

"Thanks, but I will pass." He hadn't intended for his words to sound hard and ungrateful. He smiled, hoping to make up for it. "I will probably be exhausted enough to sleep standing up."

Relief brightened her pretty face and she giggled. *Giggled!* He loved the sound of that, too.

"Like a horse?"

He grinned. "My mother claims I eat like one, so why not?"

Hands folded on the table again, Emily shook her head and stared as a smirk lifted one corner of her mouth.

"What . . . ?"

"That smile again. It's . . . just . . . I don't understand why you try so hard to hide it."

"I don't." *Do I?*

"Oh, but you do. I've lost track of how many times it seems you're about to smile, but you hold back."

His cheeks grew hot as her eyes bored into his. Part of him was flattered that she'd noticed such a thing. Mostly, though, he felt annoyed. She wasn't a parent, so he couldn't expect her to understand that it wasn't easy, acknowledging the possibility that in a few days, his only child could die in the operating room. That without the surgery, he'd almost certainly die.

Gabe's big, innocent blue eyes flashed in his mind. Shining golden curls that surrounded his beautiful, too-pale face. The "I love you!" smile that had the power to brighten his mood, even after hours of back-breaking, knuckle-abrading labor. The thought of life without his son hit harder even than when his mother-in-law had announced, "Our Rebecca is gone, Phillip. It is the will of *Gott.*"

One perfect eyebrow disappeared behind her bangs. Bangs the color of the chestnuts that fell from the big tree behind his house. If he could muster the courage to brush those bangs aside, would they feel as soft as they looked?

He shook his head. "So, two or three hours in the OR. You are sure?"

"If everything goes well, yes."

There it was again . . . *if.* The biggest little word in the English language.

Emily turned the notebook slightly, so that she could read aloud some of the notes she'd scribbled in the printouts' margins: After the operation, Williams would likely prescribe quinidine, to control the beats of Gabe's heart, a drug that, in some cases, causes nausea or cramps, vomiting, loss of appetite, dizziness.

"Why not some other medication, one that will not cause so many side effects?"

"There are one or two. Which I'm sure

Alex, I mean Dr. Williams, will order if the quinidine proves problematic."

Problematic. Interesting way to avoid saying *dangerous.* "If I could, I would trade places with Gabe."

"I believe you. You're a wonderful, loving father."

"Not always. Just ask my mother."

Emily's brow furrowed. "Mothers can be tough on their kids, sometimes unnecessarily so."

Spoken like a woman taught by experience. And yet, she'd never said anything to lead him to believe that. Phillip drank the last of his lemonade. "What I mean is, my choices of late have not brought my mother much peace of mind. Or a feeling of pride."

"Because you don't speak or dress like, well, like other Amish?"

He let silence answer her question.

"You own a thriving business, a home, and care for a sickly son and an aging mother. Sorry if this sounds harsh, but I'd think she'd be *beyond* proud of you!"

God willing, she wouldn't repeat the "why did you go back to the old ways?" question. Because in his current frame of mind, Phillip didn't trust himself to keep the reasons to himself. Besides, if he didn't fully understand what was going on in his muddled mind, how did he hope to explain it to Emily?

"That," he answered, "and I can't recall the last time I attended a church service."

"Oh?"

Talk like this — quiet and caring and clearly personal — would only make it harder to quash the affection he felt toward her. And yet he heard himself say, "The whole 'Trust God, always do His will' stuff . . . There are too many Bakers in the graveyard because people relied solely on Him. Not me. I refuse to bow down to a being so heartless." Once the words were out, he wished he could take them back. He believed in God and wanted to trust that He would bring Gabe through this calamity. Would that miracle revive what had died with his father, his brother, his wife?

"Oh," she said again; this time, her voice barely registered as a whisper. Then the clinical doctor tone returned as she began listing further details pertaining to Gabe's post-op care.

Her quick prayer earlier should have told him that Emily was a believer. Had his irreverent words given her reason to mistrust him?

Phillip hoped so . . .

. . . and hoped anything *but.*

CHAPTER SEVEN

"I am *not* leaving this boy's side."

Sarah wouldn't have needed to jab the air with the long, silvery knitting needle to get her point across. When her voice took on that no-nonsense tone and she glared over her wire-rimmed glasses, people tended to take her seriously. And Phillip was no exception.

He said a silent thank-you to the nurse who'd dragged the extra recliner into Gabe's room. This one, like Sarah's, boasted wide arms and a pop-up footrest. Phillip settled into it, the notebook open on his lap, and tried to make sense of what Emily had penned into every white space. The words blurred, making it impossible to decipher her tidy, feminine script.

Phillip scrubbed a hand over his face, rubbed his eyes, massaged his temples, and prayed for peace of mind. He wanted to believe God would guide the surgical team's hands, so that afterward, Gabe could run and play like his cousins. One question blocked total trust: If the Almighty was truly in charge, would Gabe be sick in the first place? And if he continued allowing such thoughts into his head, would the Almighty even listen?

"What is wrong with you?"

His mother's voice startled him, and he nearly dropped the notebook.

"Perhaps it is *you* who should go home. A good night's sleep in your own bed. That is what you need." Her frown deepened. "Not reading the drivel in that big heavy book."

Drivel perfectly described Sarah's opinions about hospitals, doctors, and everything related to them. Ignoring the cutting remark, Phillip turned his attention back to the notebook, and hoped she'd finished complaining.

Moments later, her soft snoring told him that she'd dozed off. He got up, thinking to relieve her of the yarn and needles resting in her ample lap. But Gabe stirred and sighed softly, and he stepped up to the bed instead. Odd, he thought, that the boy's cheeks looked flushed when the only thing covering him was a thin sheet. Gently, so as not to wake him, he bent at the waist and pressed his lips to Gabe's forehead. Straightening, he summoned self-control and made his way to his mother's chair. Gently, he shook her shoulder.

"What's wrong?" came her whisper.

"Gabe has spiked a fever. I need to —"

"How do you know?"

"I used your tried-and-true, never-fails method, a kiss to the forehead."

She started to get up, as if to do it herself, and prove him wrong. But Phillip stood between her and Gabe's hospital bed. "I'm going to the nurses' station to ask them to call Dr. White and see about getting him some medication to bring the temperature down."

"Nonsense," she huffed. "What he needs is an ice bath. That is the only thing guaranteed to —"

Phillip hung his head and held up one hand, silencing her. "You know that I respect your opinions, *Maemm,* that I love you more than life itself and appreciate everything you've sacrificed for Gabe and me." He paused, partly for effect, partly to gather the courage to say what must be said. "But Gabe is *my* son and I will always do what I believe is in his best interest, no matter who disagrees."

She shoved the glasses higher on her nose, and as he approached the door, he heard her disapproving snort. She'd likely give him the silent treatment for speaking to her that way, but Phillip didn't care. Yes, she'd been good to him and Gabe, and although he appreciated everything she'd done to help out since Rebecca's death, Phillip had meant it when he'd said that as Gabe's father, he'd do anything in his power to protect and care for his child, and no one had better try to stop him.

Two nurses stood side by side at the desktop computer, quietly discussing a patient chart. The youngest looked up and smiled. "Mr. Baker . . ."

She must have read concern on his face, for her smile vanished.

"Is everything all right?"

"I'm afraid not. Gabe has a fever. I need to get in touch with Dr. White."

The other nurse rushed toward Gabe's room. "I'll get his vitals, Barbara," she told her partner, "so you can report them once you reach Dr. White."

"Oh great," Barbara said. "Time alone with *her.*" She quickly gathered her self-control. "Relax, Mr. Baker. I'll call her, right now. Knowing Dr. White, she's probably somewhere in the hospital, and unless she's involved in some sort of emergency, she'll be here in a matter of minutes."

Hearing that, Phillip relaxed. A little. Still, there was something in the woman's voice . . . resentment?

"Can I get you anything? Coffee? Soda? Bottled water?"

It had only been a few hours since leaving the café with Emily. "No, no, but thanks. I'm fine. I'll just wait for Dr. White in Gabe's room."

He'd no sooner settled into the big vinyl recliner than Gabe rolled onto one side, facing him.

"What time is it, Dad?"

With no pockets in his Amish trousers, he'd been forced to leave his watch at home. The clock above the nurses' station had read 9:22. "Nearly nine thirty. Time for four-year-old boys to sleep."

"But Dad, my head hurts. My neck, too."

On his feet again, Phillip picked up the pink plastic cup beside the boy's supper tray. He held the bendable straw to Gabe's lips.

"Don't want any," Gabe said, turning his head.

"That's okay. Drink anyway."

He helped Gabe sit up and waited patiently as he swallowed a few sips.

"I don't like warm water."

"That's okay," Phillip repeated. "Water is

good for you. It'll flush out the germs that are making your head and neck hurt."

The boy didn't seem convinced but took another sip anyway.

And then, as if in answer to an unasked plea to God, Emily entered the room. She met his eyes, but only briefly, as she walked up to the bed.

"He says his head hurts," Phillip informed her. "His neck, too."

For a nanosecond, her eyes darkened with concern, but she masked it by opening her medical bag to retrieve her stethoscope. Nodding as she listened to her young patient's heart and lungs, it seemed she was deliberately avoiding his gaze.

Both nurses hurried into the room. One powered up the computer in the corner while the other wrapped Gabe's upper arm in a blood pressure cuff and slid an oximeter onto his forefinger. "My goodness," she said, looking at Emily, "his li'l hands are *cold*!" Eyes on Gabe again, she added, "Soon as I'm finished here, I'll get you a warm blanket."

If Gabe heard her, he showed no sign of it. "Can we turn out the lights, Dad? They hurt my eyes."

The nurse hit the button above his bed, and the room dimmed considerably.

The boy glanced around the room. "Dad? *Dad?*"

Phillip left his post near the windows and clasped his son's hand. The nurse had been right. His fingers were cold. "I'm right here, Son."

"My legs hurt. When can I go home and sleep in my own bed? This one makes crunchy noises. And it's *hard.*"

From the other side of the bed, Emily grasped his free hand. "We're all working hard to get you home again soon. I know you've heard that before, but it's true, Gabe."

She patted his hand and instructed the nurses to administer four hundred milligrams of Caldolor. "A fifteen-minute drip," she said, "then check his vitals again."

"Yes, *Doctor.*"

And there it was again . . . that resentful tone in the nurse's voice. His own interactions with Dr. White had been positive, but then, he didn't have to work with her, day in and day out.

"Caldolor," Phillip repeated. "What is it?"

"Basically, it's ibuprofen. It'll bring down his fever and reduce his discomfort."

Sarah grunted. "Ice bath," she muttered. "*That* is what he needs."

Emily faced the grandmother. "If the IV

115

meds don't work quickly, that's exactly what we'll do. But only as a last resort. Because no one likes being submerged in ice water. Especially children Gabe's age, and in his condition."

Phillip noted her all-business stance and tone, and hoped it would stifle any objections his mother might make. He was far more interested in hearing what Dr. White believed was causing Gabe's fever, aches, and pains.

"May I have a word with you, Dr. White? Alone?"

Another grunt from Sarah, who followed up with, "You just returned from two hours alone with her. What more can she tell you?"

Gabe, who'd been quiet to this point, started to sit up.

Phillip bent at the waist and said, "Close your eyes, Son, and rest. I know it won't be easy with all the noise and activity around here, but try. Do it for me, all right?"

Reluctance flickered in the boy's eyes, but he nodded.

"That's my good boy. Dr. White and I will be right outside, and I promise to be back in just a few minutes."

Gabe replied with another nod, then squeezed his eyes shut.

Now Phillip faced his mother. "*Maemm,*

you and I will talk later." He hoped she'd hear his silent plea: *Please be quiet and stop making comments that will upset the boy.*

Emily was on her cell phone when he joined her near the elevators.

"I can't be sure until we run some tests," he heard her say, "but if I had to guess, I'd say it's meningitis."

The breath caught in Phillip's throat. Meningitis had killed his former boss's only son. The bacteria had spread quickly through the boy's college dorm, putting half a dozen formerly healthy youngsters — some who were powerful athletes — into the hospital. Was Emily talking about Gabe, or one of her other patients?

"When I send down the blood tests, let's put a rush on them. Because if it *is* meningitis, we'll need a CT scan, a lumbar puncture."

Head down and one palm lifting the bangs from her forehead, Emily began to pace the width of the hall.

"Oh, and would you do me a huge favor, and call the pharmacy," she continued, "to make sure they have plenty of cefotaxime, ceftriaxone, and gentamicin on hand? We can't be sure until we review the labs which will be most effective. This patient . . . he's only four, Brugada syndrome. Yes, yes, the drugs will likely put a slight strain on his heart, but since we know about the Brugada going in, we can take precautions, monitor him closely. *If* this is meningitis — and I hope and pray it isn't — we'll need to run tests on his father and grandmother. All the nurses who've worked with him. Even the dietary staff that has been delivering his meals."

Turning slightly, she noticed him. The look of dread on her face was all the evidence Phillip needed to know that even without tests, Emily felt fairly certain Gabe was in trouble. Serious trouble.

"Call me when you know more, will you? And thanks, Carl. I owe you one."

She walked right up to him, grabbed his hand, and led him into the family lounge, across from the elevators.

"You're white as a bedsheet. Sit down before you fall down."

"I'm fine." He wasn't, but Phillip needed to stay ready to hit the ground running if need be, get to Gabe's side as fast as possible, after she delivered the rest of the news.

"How long were you standing there?"

He didn't like her tone. Didn't like the way she stood, one hand on her hip, eyes narrowed, brow furrowed. Maybe this attitude was responsible for the nurse's odd behavior.

"Don't talk to me as if you're a teacher and I'm some misbehaving schoolboy. If you wanted privacy, you should have placed that call behind closed doors. Besides, let's not forget it's *my son* you were talking about!"

Apparently, she didn't like his tone, either. "Exactly how much did you overhear?"

He considered repeating what he'd already said, adding that she had no right to speak to him that way. Gathering his self-control, Phillip said, "Enough to know you believe Gabe has meningitis."

"We're not sure yet. It could be something relatively insignificant. A minor bacterial infection that we can control with antibiotics. But in either case, we're lucky he was here, in the hospital, when the symptoms began. Catching it early like this gives us an edge."

He could almost hear his mother and Bishop Fisher insisting that luck had nothing to do with it. *God led him here,* they'd say. *And maybe they're right . . .*

"The drugs . . . you're afraid they could do further damage to his heart?"

"Not damage, exactly. Just an added strain, like he'd get climbing the stairs, or running with his cousins."

Her eyes told another story. "Don't lie to

me, Emily. I've dealt with bad news before. If you can't give it to me straight, I'll request a new doctor for Gabe. One who won't sugarcoat things."

Emily marched toward him, stopping mere inches from where he stood. "I have *never* lied to a patient, nor have I lied to a patient's family. I've done everything humanly possible to keep you informed about Gabe's disorder, about our plans to help him." She drilled a forefinger into his chest. "If that isn't good enough for you, then yes, you *should* look into finding another —"

He didn't know what came over him, but Phillip wrapped his hand around hers and pulled her close. So close that he could feel her heart, beating hard against his chest.

"Emily . . . I-I'm sorry," he ground out.

And then he kissed her.

CHAPTER EIGHT

Hours later, in the hall outside Gabe's hospital room, Emily heard voices, and paused to pull herself together.

"How long have I been here, *Grossmammi*?"

"This is your third full day in the hospital."

Only three days? It didn't seem possible that in so short a time, she'd come to think of him as more than a patient. So much more. And his father . . .

Emily pressed fingertips to her lips. Lips that, hours ago, Gabe's father had kissed.

Not only had she allowed the kiss, she'd fully participated in it. Enjoyed it so much, in fact, that when it ended, disappointment shrouded her. That, and embarrassment, because in the nanosecond beforehand, worry, helpless frustration, and fear had lined his face. Afterward, in the seconds before he turned and those long, lean legs

121

carried him out of sight, she'd read guilt. Or regret. Maybe even both.

What had she been thinking, meeting him toe to toe, jabbing at his chest like an adversary — especially knowing his state of mind! A *good* doctor would have found a better, more professional way to help him understand that everything she'd done to that point had been in Gabe's best interests. In *Phillip's* best interests, too.

It would be easy to blame lack of sleep. Her heavy patient load. Skipped meals. Too much time bent over medical journal articles related to Gabe's condition. But in truth, her personal attachment to the boy — and his father — had been responsible for the commotion in her head, in her heart. It was an easy explanation. But *easy* wouldn't salve her conscience. Emily felt that she owed Phillip an apology. And assurances that, from here on out, professionalism would dictate her words and actions . . . and reactions. The good Lord knew that lack of professionalism had cost her dearly in the past, when she and Alex —

"Emily?"

The soft baritone startled her, and when she whirled around to face him, she nearly lost her balance. In one deft moment, both powerful hands shot out, gripped her shoulders, and steadied her.

If only he could steady her heartbeat, too.

She looked up into the stunning face so near her own and took note of his unemotional expression. Sadness overwhelmed her, because it could mean only one thing: He wished he could erase that almost-perfect moment in time.

Emily stepped back, away from his protective embrace.

"I was just on my way into Gabe's room. To check his vitals. See what the nurses and lab techs recorded in his file." She was rambling and knew it, and yet she continued. "He's had a busy night, what with all the blood draws. Scans. Other tests."

"He made me proud. Only time he complained was during the spinal tap."

Emily winced, knowing how painful it could be. "I should have been here with him."

His left brow lifted, as if to say, *Yes, you should.*

"I know he isn't your only patient. Besides, Chrissy — one of the nurses — let me stay to hold his hand."

"Chrissy. Yes. She's a real pro."

"Uh-huh. Yes. A pro." Phillip pointed at her medical bag. "You brought the results of Gabe's tests? Or are they in the computer?"

"Of course."

Now, he gestured toward the chairs that lined the wall across from the elevators. "Let's sit, so you can fill me in."

"Of course," she repeated as he led the way.

Was this how it would be between them now? Emily had consciously prayed for help in controlling her ever-growing affection for him; she hoped his coolly businesslike demeanor wasn't the answer from above.

Or did she?

Emily sat, intentionally leaving an empty chair between them. "As you know," she said, placing her bag on the blue vinyl seat, "I was concerned about Gabe's aches and fever. He does have a low-grade infection, but it isn't meningitis."

In the middle of the night, her eyes had filled with grateful tears, reading the results. When lab tech Teri asked what had caused them, Emily forced a laugh. "Forgot to take my allergy pill today." She'd never had a knack for half-truths and hid a telltale blush behind the computer monitor. Better that than have Teri and the other lab techs suspect the truth: She'd started to fall for Phillip Baker.

Leaning forward, he clasped and unclasped his hands in the space between his knees. "If not meningitis, then what?"

"A minor infection, one that's easily controlled with medication."

On his feet now, he began to pace. "But the operation . . . does this mean Gabe will lose his place on Dr. Williams's surgery schedule?"

"Dr. Williams couldn't have performed the operation until the end of the week, anyway. By then, the antibiotics should have the infection well under control."

The pacing stopped. "Should?"

To the casual observer, he might seem composed and in control of his emotions. But Emily knew better. Dark circles shadowed his beautiful eyes, and he didn't move with the same sure-footed gait as before.

Her dad liked to say that lies, even the little white ones told to make others feel better, had a tendency to multiply. Phillip had already accused her of being less than honest with him. He probably wouldn't believe her if she said, "It'll be all right, Phillip."

But she said it anyway.

He slapped a hand to the back of his neck, then dropped heavily onto the chair once more.

"Ah, Emily, if only I could believe that."

"You can. And you should. It'll be good for Gabe to see you feeling confident. It'll be good for you, too."

He sat back, leaned his head on the wall, and closed his eyes. And on the heels of a ragged sigh, said, "Guess I owe you an apology."

Why ask *for what?* when she already knew. In her opinion, Phillip had nothing to be sorry for. She'd been at least as much to blame for that instant of intimacy. To spare them both having to relive the moment, Emily stood and gathered her things.

"I'm going in to check on Gabe. And make sure Mike has updated his file."

His brow furrowed with confusion. "Mike?"

"Gabe's new day nurse. I've worked with him before. He's great with kids and old people."

"In other words, he'll have no trouble getting along with my mother."

It wasn't much of a smile . . . just enough to give her hope that he'd forgiven her for her earlier lapse.

"She is clever — I will give her that."

"What do you mean?" By his definition, the word meant shrewd. While Sarah hadn't been blatantly rude when dealing with Emily, she hadn't exactly kept her feelings hidden, either.

"The things she knows, and the things she says are proof of her book smarts. But that is a worldly thing. Where is the proof of her spirituality?" Sarah clucked her tongue. "Do you worry for the state of her soul, as I do?"

Hours spent here in his son's room, studying to understand Gabe's condition and treatment, and keeping up with customer needs had eaten up every spare moment. He'd barely managed to fit in sleep and meals. When would he have had time to question Emily's religious beliefs?

Now, with the subject at the forefront in his mind, Phillip said, "The things she knows and says are proof that she cares more about others than herself. And she has never said a bad word about anyone, at least in my presence." *Besides, I saw her praying at the café.*

"This world is filled with nice people who do the right things for the wrong reasons."

Gabe, who'd been napping, opened his eyes. "I love Dr. White."

"You are a good boy," Sarah said. "But you are *four*. What you know about love would fit in my thimble."

"I know how to love Dad, and you, and

Aunt Hannah, and Onkle Eli, and my cousins John and Paul . . ."

Phillip's heart swelled with pride. Leave it to Gabe to put his judgmental grandmother in her place without being hurtful or disrespectful.

". . . and though I am mad at God, I know how to love Him, too."

If asked, Phillip would say he'd done a good job of hiding his personal feelings toward the Almighty. Evidently, not good enough, since Gabe had sensed his anger and decided to emulate it. A boy his age ought to believe in the power, protection, and forgiveness of a loving God. And just as soon as Gabe was home and healthy, Phillip would sit him down and make things right.

"Loving God is as it should be," Sarah said. "You do not have meningitis, thanks be to God's answer to prayer."

"You prayed for me, *Grossmammi*?"

Sarah held up her knitting project. "With every stitch of this sweater, I whispered, 'If it is Your Will, dear Lord, deliver Gabriel from his sickness.' "

Gabe bowed his head and smoothed the blanket Emily had draped over his legs earlier. "And what if it isn't His will?"

Phillip heard the steady, high-pitched beeps of Gabe's heart monitor; the din of voices — nurses, doctors, other patients and their family members — drifting in from the hall; his own heart, drumming hard in response to the simple, straightforward question. He heard the apprehension in his boy's voice, too. As part of his own schooling, Phillip had memorized dozens of Bible verses that referenced God's love for children. But not one promised to shelter them from pain, illness, or death.

Gabe sat up straighter and repeated his question.

Phillip hadn't prayed in a long time, but he prayed now: *Lord, give me the words that will ease his mind — and his heart.*

"I believe that God wants you to get well as much as we do."

All three Bakers turned toward the strong, convincing voice.

"God wants me to get well?"

Emily walked up to the bed and pressed fingertips against his wrist. "Of course He does. You're going to be fine, just fine. You have to have faith. You'll see!"

The boy didn't look convinced. Emily must have seen it, too, because she said, "Nurse Jody tells me that you slept well last night."

"I suppose."

"And that you ate all of your supper."

"Yes. Well, except for the green Jell-O."

Emily smiled and leaned in to say, "I know about three people who like green Jell-O, so that doesn't count."

"Then why do they make it?"

For a second there, Emily looked confused. "Well, I suppose because the manufacturer thinks they have as much a right to *green* Jell-O as we have to . . . What's your favorite flavor?"

"Red." He smacked his lips.

"What if only three people like red Jell-O and they stopped making it?"

"Oh," Gabe said in a thoughtful, whispery voice, "I get it now. Yes. They should make all of the flavors so that all of the Jell-O eaters will be happy."

Emily ruffled his hair. Then, unpocketing her stethoscope, she hung it from her ears. "Your fever is gone. How 'bout those aches and pains? Are they gone, too?"

He nodded.

"Well then," she said, pressing the tool's diaphragm to his chest, "I think it's time to prepare for our trip to Baltimore."

Phillip stood across from her. "How soon?"

"I spoke with Al— Dr. Williams, and he promised to make time to speak with us — with you, to explain everything, tomorrow evening. If we leave first thing in the morning, we'll be able to get Gabe registered in plenty of time for the meeting."

His mother's knitting needles hit the floor with a metallic *click* as she jumped up, eyes shimmering with unshed tears. She turned toward the wall to hide them, but not soon enough.

"Please do not cry, *Grossmammi.* The operation will fix my heart. And anyways, Dr. White says I'm going to be fine."

Gabe might only be four, as Sarah had so sharply pointed out, but he was bright, intuitive, and empathetic. Even if she managed not to voice her opinions aloud — highly unlikely — Gabe would pick up on her attitude. Phillip couldn't risk that. *Wouldn't* risk that, not even for his beloved mother. He knew she'd never intentionally hurt her youngest grandson, but reaction and result, in this case, were one and the same.

"I have a few loose ends to tie up," Emily said, draping the stethoscope around her neck. "Can we meet later tonight, to work out the details of our trip?"

Our trip? He'd rest easier, knowing she'd be in the operating room, but surely she didn't expect them to travel together.

"I am going to the chapel," Sarah said,

"to pray, to seek God's guidance. Everything is happening too hastily. A sign that things are not happening according to His will, if you ask me."

She hadn't asked him. Rarely asked him anything. But in Phillip's estimation, things were happening too *slowly.* They'd been here at Garrett Regional for going on four days now, while Gabe endured test after test, and Phillip struggled to decipher all the test results.

"Come with me, Phillip," Sarah said from the doorway. "Humble yourself before the Lord. Set aside your disrespect. Beg His forgiveness. Maybe then He will guide us, tell us the right thing to do."

"We're already doing the right thing, *Maemm.*"

Sarah grumbled something under her breath and left them.

Emily picked up her medical bag. One hand resting on his forearm, she whispered, "Don't be angry with her, Phillip. She's of a generation that did things differently. It's only natural that she's afraid of what she doesn't understand. And I believe that would be true even if she wasn't Amish."

"I appreciate your attempt to smooth things over," he whispered back, "but I've been dealing with my mother for every one

132

of my thirty-four years. I can handle this."

She gave his arm a slight squeeze, then turned him loose and walked toward the door. "I'm sure you can. But . . . *should* you?"

"You're a believer in the old 'choose your battles well' adage, I see."

Emily's shoulders lifted in a tiny shrug.

"I'll be back by five," he told her. "We can talk anytime after that. If you still have time, that is."

"For this, I'll *make* time."

To her credit, she didn't ask *Back from where?* because he hadn't yet figured out how to tell Gabe that he was taking Sarah home, and that she wouldn't travel with them to Baltimore.

"Eat something," Emily said. "And try to get some rest. You look exhausted."

Phillip watched her disappear around the corner, remembering how earlier that day, he'd caught a glimpse of himself while washing up in the tiny hospital bathroom. "You look as tired as you feel," he'd told his reflection.

But he wouldn't rest. *Couldn't* rest. Not until the surgeon assured him that Gabe's operation had been a success.

Chapter Nine

"What do you mean, I cannot go with you?"

Eyes on the road, he said, "You've already done so much, with very little sleep and not much to eat."

"That is a poor excuse if ever I heard one. You know as well as I that I have never been one who needs much sleep."

His little speech had come as close to the truth as he cared to get. He tried a different tack.

"Gabe will need you more than ever after he's released from the hospital, so it's important that you take care of yourself."

What were the chances that her silence meant she understood . . . and agreed?

"You can fool yourself, but you cannot fool me. You cannot fool *God,* either. Admit it. You are looking for ways to spend time alone with the doctor, and Gabe has nothing to do with it."

He gripped the steering wheel so tightly,

his knuckles ached. *"Maemm . . ."*

"I prayed about it. In the chapel. I think I understand why you are drawn to her."

Oh, this oughta be good, he thought.

"You changed after losing Rebecca."

The changes in him predated his wife's death, by *years.*

"Dr. White is good at what she does. Her findings have brought you some comfort, some hope that because of her involvement, Gabe can be cured."

True, on both counts.

"Even I can admit that she is easy on the eyes, that her voice borders on mesmerizing. And the way she looks at you?" Again, Sarah clucked her tongue. "But Phillip, these are not reasons to draw closer to her. She is *not* a suitable replacement for Rebecca."

He'd never given a thought to replacing his wife, not even with a born and bred Pleasant Valley woman.

"Maemm, how many times do I have to say it? Gabe is the only connection between Dr. White and me."

"No one wants to see you happy again more than me. But no good can come of lying to yourself, Son. It's true that you have strayed from our ways of late, but you are still Amish. You will *always* be Amish. Many changes have taken place in Pleasant Valley during the past few decades." She counted on her fingers. "Electricity. Telephones. Plumbing. Gasoline-powered vehicles. Some in the community have televisions. Radios. Computers and the Internet! But we are *still Plain,* far too Plain for the likes of Dr. White."

"I hate to sound trite, but aren't you putting the cart before the horse? Dr. White has never shown any personal interest in me."

Memory of that magnificent moment in the hospital hallway proved otherwise. He recalled the way she'd leaned into him, soft sighs drifting into his ears, big caring heart drumming against his chest. Phillip had kissed just two other women in his lifetime. Martha King, and Rebecca. Secret interactions with Martha, while pleasant enough, had never roused feelings of love. Her impatience to become a wife and mother had led her to marry Jonah Lamb. Rebecca, on the other hand, never truly warmed to Phillip's touch, not even after becoming Mrs. Baker. Her stiff response to physical contact of any kind always left him feeling like some sort of degenerate. Had he responded so differently to Emily because he was older and wiser now? Were his reactions rooted in gratitude for all she was doing for

Gabe? Or proof that he'd strayed so far from God that worldly urges had taken control of him?

"We should stop at Hannah's," he said, mostly to get his mind off Emily and that perfect kiss.

"Why? So she can babysit me while you are in Baltimore?"

"I could be gone for weeks. You shouldn't be alone that long — even though you *can* get by on no sleep and skipped meals."

"Weeks? But Dr. White said the operation would only last a few hours, and that the surgeon would only keep Gabe in the hospital for several days."

"She also told us that, should complications arise, it could take two, even three times longer."

"Oh. Yes. I do remember that."

From the corner of his eye, he saw her lower her head.

"Pray with me, Phillip."

His mother was fighting tears. He could tell by her gruff, gravelly voice.

"Stop this truck and pray with me, right now."

He found a suitable place to pull over. Once he'd shifted to park, she struggled to unbuckle her seat belt.

"Stupid, maddening contraptions!" she

complained. "If more people just trusted the Lord to keep them safe, we would not need laws that force us to use them!" With the buckle in her lap, Sarah added, "Yet another reason it was wrong to leave the old ways behind. We did not need seat belts in our buggies."

Phillip snorted. "As usual, you've conveniently forgotten how many children suffered when frightened horses reared up, spilling them onto the road. Those that survived impact with the asphalt often suffered permanent head injury. And what about those who were run over by cars that didn't have time to stop?"

"As usual? Why, listening to you, one would get the idea that I habitually stretch the truth." She faced forward. "Now, let us pray."

Phillip rested both hands on the steering wheel as she began:

"O Lord, we ask You to comfort us during this time of distress. Forgive our doubts, and the anger that separates us from You. We faithfully ask You, O Father, to help us set a good example for Gabriel, so that he will grow into a man who honors You with his words and with his actions. Watch over him, heal him, bring him home to us, soon. We ask these things, believing You have heard and will answer according to Your will. Amen."

She fell silent, and Phillip sensed that his mother expected him to fill that silence with a prayer of his own. Instead, he said, "Easy to see why the bishop discourages women from praying aloud during services."

"Oh?"

"Your words would put him and all the elders to shame."

Her quiet laughter didn't last long. Fiddling with the seat belt again, she shook her fist. "Stupid, maddening contraptions!" Sarah repeated.

Phillip put the truck into drive and eased into traffic on Route 219. His plan was simple: Stop at his sister's house and bring her up to date, then take his mother home where, hopefully, she'd pack enough clothing to stay a few nights with Hannah, Eli, and the boys. He'd pack, too, and once he'd safely delivered her back to Hannah's, he'd make his way to the hospital to hear Emily's thoughts about the trip to Baltimore.

Something his mother had said earlier came to mind . . . that he was leaving her home to spend time alone with Emily. She hadn't been right about that, but then, she hadn't been wrong, either. Almost without exception, Gabe dozed off within the first ten minutes of a drive. After days of nurses and lab techs waking him every few hours, he'd probably fall asleep in two minutes, and sleep all the way to Johns Hopkins.

"Where will you sleep in Baltimore, Son?"

"In Gabe's room, of course."

"What about meals?"

"I'm sure the hospital has a cafeteria. And I can probably order meals from the kitchen, just like at Garrett Regional, that'll be delivered with Gabe's trays. When he's allowed a regular diet."

"What do you mean, a regular diet?"

"Emily . . . Dr. White explained that his meals may be somewhat restricted at first."

"Oh fine. Just when he will need healthy food the most, they will deprive him of it?"

"Only for a day or two."

"Well, since you've made up your mind, I will have to accept it."

The insinuation wasn't lost on Phillip. His mother had made it clear that she opposed the operation, and he'd decided to go ahead with it anyway. This wasn't the time or place to revisit the subject, so he said, "The food won't be anywhere near as good as your cooking, but I'll accept it."

She ignored his feeble attempt at a joke. "And Dr. White? Where will she sleep?"

And there it was, the real reason she'd

begun this line of questioning.

"She said something about making use of intern and resident quarters at the hospital."

"Still," Sarah said, "I will pray that you will not be tempted to sin."

Memory of that kiss resurfaced. Phillip shifted in his seat and ground his molars together. It wasn't likely they'd be alone long enough for a repeat, but if the opportunity presented itself, would he —

Suddenly, the road sign for the lane leading to Hannah's came into view, and Phillip jerked the steering wheel, spewing grit and gravel as he swerved into the drive.

"Phillip!" Sarah shouted, gripping the dash. "Where is your mind!" A brief pause, and then, "As if I didn't know . . ."

"Sorry, *Maemm.*"

"Fix your eyes on *God,*" she said, repositioning herself in the passenger seat. "He will release you from this hold Dr. White has on you."

His mother had made several good points, there was no denying it, and until he figured out a few things, it might be best to keep his mind off Emily.

He parked the truck as Hannah turned from the clothesline.

"What are you doing here!" she called, waving as Phillip helped their mother exit the vehicle.

The instant Sarah's feet hit the gravel driveway, she wriggled free of Phillip's grasp.

"Gabe and Phillip are leaving for Baltimore in the morning. Your brother does not want me there, and because he thinks I am too old and feeble to be left on my own, he hopes to palm me off on you. *That,*" she said, "is why we are here."

"*Maemm,* that isn't true, and you know it."

Hannah wrapped Sarah in a welcoming hug. "We would love to have you," she said, "but if you would rather not, we are happy to look in on you at your own home from time to time."

In either case, his spirited mother would be fine on her own. And a few days free from her pessimism sounded good, real good to Phillip. He tensed and waited for the cutting remark that would surely follow his sister's offer.

"I have no home. I gave up my home when Rebecca died, remember?"

She'd directed her glare and cutting remark his way, but even if she hadn't, Phillip couldn't deny the truth of it. He started to tell her that his home was hers, and always would be, when his sister loosed a squeal of disapproval.

This time, it was Hannah who said, "*Maemm!* That isn't true, and you know it! Phillip and Gabe have always considered it your home, too."

She ignored their mother's reproachful sniff.

"When you said you might like to raise chickens, Phillip built you a chicken coop, and bought you fat hens, did he not?"

Sarah fiddled with the fraying straps of the hand-stitched tote that held her knitting gear.

"And when you wanted to grow vegetables, he plowed up half the backyard, bought every plant you asked for, helped you put them in the ground, then built a fence to protect the plants from rabbits and deer, right?"

She didn't wait for their mother to respond but continued with, "He made sure you had jars and lids and a canning kettle, dug a root cellar so you could store what you grew, too, because he knew how you longed to put up the things you grew. Rearranged the parlor so that your favorite rocker would fit better beside the woodstove and replaced the mattress that once caused your backaches with something brand-new. *And* to make room for your favorite tables and chairs, he got rid of his own — things he had built and bought for Rebecca! So if you do not feel it is your home, too" — Hannah's arms lifted, and she let them slap against her sides — "then I do not know what to say!"

A blush crept into their mother's cheeks, and Phillip felt bad for her. Gabe's health-related issues hadn't been easy on her, either, particularly given her feelings about doctors, hospitals, and modern medicine.

"We should probably get back on the road," he told her. "I need to go to the bank and withdraw some money for the trip, make a few calls to customers, and throw a spare shirt and trousers into a bag." After all his sister had just said, he didn't have the heart to ask if his mother preferred to stay at the house or come with him to pack a few things to bring to Hannah's.

"Go," Hannah said, giving him a gentle shove. "She will be fine, right here. The boys will love having her, and she can come with me to the shop. *Maemm* and I are the same size, so she is welcome to wear my clothes."

"No," Sarah said, "I will go home."

Was it his imagination? Or had she put a little extra emphasis on the last word?

"And that," she added, "is where I will stay."

Phillip had expected her to pick up the

interrogation right where she'd left off.

He'd been wrong. Instead, she talked about the weather, and how dry it had been these past weeks. It made her even more grateful, she added, that he'd installed a spigot on the well and attached a long hose to it, because watering her garden was faster and easier now.

Once in the house, Sarah rushed around opening curtains and windows to let in the fresh air, then set about brewing a pot of coffee.

"When did you last eat?" she asked.

Realizing she was looking for things to occupy her hands — and probably her mind — he admitted that he wasn't hungry.

"I will make sandwiches," she said, "some for now, some that you can eat on the road tomorrow."

Phillip stood beside her and pressed a kiss to her temple. "Thank you, *Maemm*. I'll be in the workshop, making calls to customers. I won't be long. I promise."

"They will understand. Once you explain your reasons for delivering their engines late."

During recent conversations, his customers had all wished Gabe well, and said things like "Family comes first," and "Try to forget about work."

Now, one by one, they repeated their well wishes, and he left the shop feeling confident that the business would survive, despite time missed.

When he returned to the kitchen, he found Sarah bent over the table, weeping softly.

He went to her, and squatting beside her chair, took her hands in his. "*Maemm,* what is it?"

"I didn't say a proper good-bye to Gabe," she said around a sob. "What if . . . what if . . ."

What if the worst happened, he finished mentally, and she never saw the boy again.

"As I recall, you covered him with his favorite quilt before we left. The one you made for his first birthday." He squeezed her hands. "I've lost count of the times he fell asleep, hugging it, as if it could hug him back. Besides, you asked for God's blessing on him. He will do well."

She wriggled free of his grasp, used one corner of her apron to dry her eyes. "I will ask Hannah to take me to the hospital again tomorrow.

"Now, eat," she said, pointing at the sandwich and soup she'd set out for him, "before the bread grows hard."

Rising, he crossed the room, and standing

at the sink to wash up, said, "Thanks, *Maemm.*"

When he sat across from her, she said, "May I ask a question?"

He tensed slightly. "Of course. Anything."

"For a little while lately, you dressed and talked Amish. But you have gone back to behaving like an Englisher. It pains me, Phillip."

Dressing and talking Amish, to paraphrase her words, had required concentration, and with Gabe's health occupying so much of his mind, it hadn't taken long for Phillip to abandon the effort. To date, he'd failed to help her understand why he'd rejected the Amish ways in the first place. What made him think he'd succeed now?

Still, his mother of all people deserved a response. He chose his words carefully. "When Gabe and I return from Baltimore, things will change."

Thankfully, she didn't press him for specifics, and for that, Phillip was thankful. Because if, God forbid, things didn't go well, Phillip couldn't see himself returning to Pleasant Valley. At least, not to live.

If things went better than expected, well, he wasn't sure he'd stay then, either.

CHAPTER TEN

"Good morning, Mr. Baker."

As usual, she smiled and, as usual, there was music in her womanly voice. She'd piled her hair atop her head, and the tendrils that had escaped her bun curled beside her appealing face. Phillip resisted the urge to tuck them behind her ears. He could almost see her reaction, and it made him angry — with himself, for not having the backbone to maintain a professional distance — with Emily, for being so alluring.

And yet he said, "I thought we decided not to stand on formality, *Dr. White.*"

She laughed, a soft, delightful sound. "Oh. Right." Dainty fingertips tapped the side of her head. "Duh. Old habits and all that."

"I didn't realize we knew each other well enough to have formed habits."

Until then, she'd seemed a bit preoccupied, glancing from her cell phone to the numbers above the elevator doors to

Phillip, but the question commanded her full attention. As Emily studied his face, faint worry lines formed between her brows.

"When was the last time you got a full night's sleep?"

In all honesty, he couldn't remember. "I've never needed much sleep."

The elevator arrived, and once the car emptied, they stepped inside.

"Let me prescribe something," she said, pressing the number three. "Just a few tablets. It's an arduous drive to Baltimore, and once we reach Johns Hopkins, you'll be inundated with things."

"Such as?"

"Like a tour of the pediatric cardiology ward. There will be forms to sign. And Dr. Williams will want to meet with us. You know, *things*?"

Yes, he knew, because she'd already outlined it all. Phillip didn't respond, though, because his mind had locked on one word: *Us.*

"You'll be there? When Gabe and I meet with the surgeon?"

She looked shocked that he'd even asked. "As his doctor of record, and since I'll assist in the OR, yes. I'll be there for you, for everything." Emily bit her lower lip, looking apprehensive and disappointed. "Would you rather I wasn't?"

Phillip shook his head as the elevator stopped on the third floor, and as she prepared to exit, Emily placed a hand on his forearm.

"As soon as I've finished my rounds, I'll come to Gabe's room. We can finalize travel arrangements and . . ." She stood in the doorway, preventing the doors from closing. ". . . and I want you to know if there's something you need to get off your chest, I'll listen." Her fingers tightened on his sleeve. "And that I'll help, any way I can. With *anything*."

Did she realize that by standing there, looking up at him with those huge, long-lashed eyes, talking like someone who genuinely cared — not just about Gabe, but about *him* — she made him want to pull her close and hold on tight, and forget the promise that would protect him from falling in love with her?

Obviously, she *didn't* realize, because if anything, her concern for him — for *him* — intensified. If he continued standing there . . .

Difficult as it was to do, he turned, made his way to the end of the hall, and opened the door he'd been avoiding since Emily's brother and his partner rushed Gabe to

Garrett's ER.

The room was small. Quiet. Dimly lit. Phillip walked between rows of identical pews and knelt at the rail.

Perhaps, surrounded by flickering candle-light and in the shadow of the big wooden cross, God would assure him that Gabe would be all right. That *he'd* be all right once he and his son were no longer part of Emily's daily routine.

Seated in the chapel's front pew, Phillip focused so intensely on the cross that the candles' glow blurred. It had been so long since he'd prayed. Did he even remember *how*?

He searched his memory for something, learned as a boy, that might jump-start things, and could almost hear Bishop Fisher's croaky voice: *"We pray to give praise and thanks, and to ask God to bless a loved one with protection. . . ."*

Head bowed and eyes shut tight, he whispered, "Lord, don't hold my stubborn nature against Gabe, who believes in You with all his heart. Heal him, because life without him would be . . ." Phillip couldn't complete the thought, because such a thing was inconceivable.

And then Emily came to mind. Emily,

whose diagnosis had finally given him an explanation for his son's frail health. Emily, whose connections with Johns Hopkins and a top-notch surgeon gave him hope — gave the entire family hope — that soon, Gabe might run and play and laugh without growing faint . . . or worse. "You're a fool," he muttered, "if you think she's interested in you as anything more than Gabe's father."

"Oh, but you are wrong, Brother."

The quiet, husky voice startled him. Phillip turned to face his sister. Had he really been so lost in thought that he hadn't heard the door open? Hadn't heard her footsteps? Hadn't heard her sit directly behind him?

"Hannah. How long have you been there?"

"Exactly long enough. I brought *Maemm* to the hospital this morning." She got up, then sat beside him. "It is good that you are talking with God."

"Yeah, well, we'll just have to wait and see if He heard me."

"He listens, always. You know this." Hannah turned sideways, so that she could look directly into his eyes. "Your life has been hard. Too many losses in too short a time. No one understands better than God why you are angry, why you have trouble believing. He has heard, and He will answer."

But would He answer in Gabe's favor? "From your lips to His ear."

"What you said about Dr. White, that she has no interest in you as anything but Gabe's father? You are wrong."

A dry chuckle escaped his lips. "Oh, I am, huh?"

"Always the pessimist."

Funny, that's what Eli, what he and his mother had always called *her*.

"I have eyes, Phillip. During my few visits here, I have tried to stay in the background and keep my opinions and questions to myself. But I have seen the way she looks at you. I have ears, too, and I have heard the way her voice changes when she speaks to you. Everything about her changes, as a matter of fact, from her smile to the way she stands. You have not noticed this?"

"No. But if you're even slightly right, about these changes, I mean, it's only because Emily — Dr. White — is a good person. A good person and a good doctor who cares deeply about her patients. I'm sure if we had an opportunity to watch her interact with other patients, we'd see the same things."

"Always the pessimist," she said again. "I know that many men have no respect for the things women think and feel. But you have always been better than those few. You must put your blindness aside, brother of mine, and listen to me." She grabbed his hand, held on tight, and gave it a good shake. "I can tell you which ladies of the community are in love with their husbands, and which are going through the motions because they believe it is God's will for them to do their duty without complaint."

"*How* can you tell?"

"You could tell, too . . . if you chose to *see*. Love shines in a wife's eyes when she looks at her husband. It softens her voice and gentles her touch. I feel these things with Eli and know that I am blessed. And all of these things tell me that Emily — Dr. White — is falling in love with you. If she is not *already* in love with you."

What did it matter if Hannah's assessment was correct? He'd lived all his years in Pleasant Valley, an Amishman, despite his refusal to speak or dress as the other members of the community did. Emily, on the other hand, had been raised English. The gap between the two seemed deep, and too wide for any bridge to connect them. Not even if that bridge was called *love*.

"I know what you are thinking. . . ."

Phillip fixed his gaze on the cross again. "That I want God to heal Gabe? That I

154

expect Him to make sure the operation is successful, that my boy's recovery will be swift and complete. . . ."

That I can find a way to pay the hospital bills, here and in Baltimore. That I can decide whether or not I want to raise Gabe in a community where seeking continued medical attention could be frowned upon.

"I am a mother, so I understand your worries."

But she didn't understand. How could she?

"If John or Paul were going through all of this, and I was expected to rely completely on God's will alone . . ."

Her eyes dampened, but to her credit, Hannah quickly regained control of herself.

"I am first and foremost a believer, and I have put my faith in God. That is why I say Gabe *will* have a healthy future."

"And if you're wrong?"

She squeezed his hand again. "You must forbid such thoughts. Your son needs to see that you believe, so that *he* will believe. That is what will make him strong of faith as he meets this, the greatest challenge of his young life."

Challenge. What a strange way to look at it.

"You owe it to him to at least try."

Now, Phillip squeezed *her* hand. "Thank you, Hannah. You're a good sister."

"I will leave you in peace now, to converse with the Father. But first . . . I have not lost a spouse, as you have, and cannot imagine such pain. But Phillip, we *both* lost grandparents, a brother and a father, and like you, I often wonder if they might still be with us if we had depended less on God's will alone, and more on modern medicine."

She got to her feet and bent at the waist to press a kiss to his forehead. "This is the mystery of faith, is it not?"

Eyes on the cross once more, Phillip nodded.

"I will pray that God answers your prayers, so that you will have reason to believe. There is comfort in that — in believing — you know."

No, he didn't know. But Phillip was willing to try. Because Hannah was right. He owed it to Gabe to at least put in the effort.

All through rounds, Emily pictured Phillip's face, lined by misery and uneasiness. She'd seriously considered wrapping her arms around him, offering words of solace, words to assure him that his little boy would be fine, just fine.

But since she wasn't one hundred percent

sure Gabe would pull through the operation, let alone recover enough to live a normal life, Emily leaned on her father's go-to adage: "Discretion is the better part of valor."

Under normal circumstances, she'd never voluntarily travel to another hospital, particularly with a patient and his family, even if someone like Alex had the power to ease the transition. But these were hardly normal circumstances.

The instant she entered Gabe's room, Phillip's mother pointed at Gabe's bed and shushed her.

"He fell asleep just minutes ago. The child has not slept well. Who *can* sleep in this place, filled as it is with inconsiderate people, always poking and prodding."

"They are only doing their job," her daughter said. "How else can they know if Gabe is doing well or poorly?"

Sarah glared at Hannah. "They might use the *eyes* given them by the good Lord."

Hannah looked at Emily and shrugged helplessly.

"Where is my son?" Sarah asked.

She must be imagining things, because surely the woman hadn't meant to imply Emily kept track of her son's whereabouts.

"I can't say for certain, but last I saw him,

it appeared he was on his way to the chapel."

"He is there, still," Hannah said.

"I find it difficult to believe," Sarah said.

That it had been hours since she'd seen him? Or that he might have been heading for the chapel?

"Phillip has lost his faith. The chapel," Sarah said, "is the last place he would go."

Hannah patted her mother's hand. "*Maemm,* we cannot be certain his faith is gone. Phillip has been under great stress since Gabe was brought here. Perhaps he is seeking solace, or answers from the Almighty. I have just come from the chapel, where he was praying with all his heart. It gave me hope, *Maemm,* that he will come around."

Sarah pooh-poohed the idea. "I am surprised that he would spend time in an Englisher chapel with his only child here, afraid, possibly dying, and —"

"*Maemm!* Gabe might hear!"

"He is young, but not so young he does not realize that his father's attentions have been . . . sidetracked."

And he sees you, Emily thought, *as the side-tracker.*

"He should be here, with Gabe."

"I will go back," Hannah offered. She looked at Emily again, pleadingly this time.

"I will bring him with me when I return." On the way out, she grasped Emily's hands, and leaning close, whispered, "I apologize. My mother has cared for Gabe since his own mother's death. This is hard for her, too."

"I understand. No apology necessary."

"You *are* kind, just as Phillip described."

Sarah waited until her daughter had left the room to say, "I hope you have no intention of waking my poor grandson. He needs his sleep."

This might be the perfect opportunity to let the woman know that Gabe's well-being was foremost in her mind, and perhaps assure Mrs. Baker that although things looked bleak, there was good reason to believe the boy would fare well.

She sat in the straight-backed chair beside Sarah's recliner. "I've finished my rounds for the day, so there's no rush on checking Gabe's vitals." Hands clasped on her knees, Emily added, "I'm happy to answer as many of your questions as I can . . . while he sleeps."

"As many as you can?"

"I'm bound by hospital protocols and state law," she began, then did her best to explain HIPAA regulations that barred her from revealing details of the case, and how, as part of their Hippocratic oath, doctors vowed to protect their patients in every way possible . . . including their privacy.

"But Hannah is right. Since *die mudder* died, I have been far more to him than *die grossmammi.* Besides, Phillip is not your patient, and you've given *him* all the details."

In other words, as blood kin, she should be privy to the particulars, too. "True. But as Gabe's father, Phillip is obligated to make decisions on behalf of his son. And he can't act in the boy's best interests unless he knows everything. *Everything.*" Emily paused. "But, as Gabe's father, *Phillip* is free to share as much with you as he chooses."

Sarah sat quietly for a few minutes, alternately nodding and sighing.

"Why is a woman your age not married?"

The question stunned her. Somehow, she found the presence of mind to say, "I dedicated countless hours over the years to becoming a doctor. Hours that wives normally spend with their husbands. Had I married, that wouldn't have been fair to anyone, least of all my family."

"Then why not become a nurse? Or a teacher? I have met Englishers who do those jobs, Englishers who are married, who have children."

The answer was simple: "While teaching

and nursing are noble callings, neither called to *me*. I've wanted to become a doctor since I was a little girl, when my mother struggled with a lifelong illness, and medications and following doctors' orders bolstered her health."

"You give no credit to God, none at all?"

"Of course. I have complete faith in the Almighty. But I also believe that it was God, Himself, who created men and women who enter the medical field, and blessed them with the gifts required to diagnose and heal their patients."

Again, Sarah sat in silence, nodding.

"What are your feelings toward my son?"

If she'd known Sarah might ask *that* . . . Emily admitted that even with some warning, she wouldn't have known how to answer!

"Well?"

The truth, experience had taught her, was always the best course of action.

"I have great respect for Phillip. He's an easy man to admire — hard-working, dedicated to you, his sister and her family, and his love for Gabe is written on his face, and recognizable in everything he does."

"Let me be clear, Dr. White. What I want to know is, are you in love with him?"

If Sarah had asked, "Can you see yourself

in a personal relationship with him?" or "Are you attracted to him?" Emily would have had to say yes. But *love*?

"As you know, Phillip and I only met a short while ago."

"That, Dr. White, is not an answer."

"It's the only truthful answer I can give you, Mrs. Baker."

"Answer to what?"

Emily and Sarah looked toward the door, where Phillip stood, looking tired and worried . . . and annoyed.

Embarrassment colored Sarah's cheeks, and Emily, sensing the woman's apprehension, said, "I was just explaining the HIPAA laws to your mother. I stressed that while I'm not at liberty to provide her with details about Gabe's case, you're completely within your rights to share any information about the surgery and subsequent treatment with her."

His face relaxed, but only slightly. Unless she was mistaken, he realized that her answer had one purpose: to cover for Sarah. Would he appreciate her effort, or think less of her because of it?

"I spoke with Dr. Williams a few minutes ago." She continued with, "He's cleared his schedule for the next two days so that he can concentrate on Gabe."

"I look forward to our meeting, so I can thank him in person."

"Speaking of which, will four o'clock tomorrow afternoon work for you?"

"Yes, I think you're right. If we leave here early enough in the morning, we should get there with time to spare."

Faint lines on his forehead told her that, with things coming to a head, Phillip's tension had escalated, and Emily understood better than most why: Would his aging pickup truck survive the drive? How would he pay for the operation, for Gabe's stay at Hopkins, follow-up treatments and medications, and the boy's care here at Garrett Regional? Could he come up with a suitable excuse for leaving his mother behind?

"I think it's best if I drive," she said. "My car is a sedan, easier for Gabe to get into and out of, with space in the trunk for our luggage."

He started to protest, but she stopped him with, "Plus, it gets great gas mileage."

Gabe tried to sit up. "How long does it take?" he asked, knuckling his eyes. "To get to Baltimore, I mean."

Emily sat on the edge of his bed and, pressing her stethoscope's diaphragm to his chest, said, "Four hours, give or take a few minutes." The weak *lub-dub-dub* of his heartbeat concerned her, but she hid her worry behind a smile. "It'll depend on how much construction traffic we encounter." Knowing he wouldn't be allowed to eat or drink anything after midnight tomorrow, she added, "We'll stop in Hagerstown — that's the halfway point — for a bite to eat."

He brightened a bit. "A real sit-down restaurant?"

"Sure. Why not?"

"Hamburger and fries? And ice cream?"

He probably wouldn't have much of an appetite for a few days following surgery, so she patted his knee. "You bet."

He leaned right a bit, to get a better look at his father. "I can, Dad?"

Phillip's expression relaxed and a loving smile crinkled the corners of his eyes. "Of course."

The man loved his boy, that much was clear. Emily had a feeling his answer would have been the same, even if Gabe had asked him to tether the sun.

"I should be getting home," Hannah said. "Eli and the boys will think I've become an Englisher."

Sarah chuckled. "Ach. They know better than that!"

"I'll drive you. And you, too, *Maemm.*" He'd let her talk him into one more visit, and seeing how relieved it made her to see Gabe again, Phillip knew he'd made the right decision. "This extra little visit was unexpected, so please don't fight me on this. I'll take you home now."

"I can hire a taxi," his sister said, "to take both of us home. You should stay with Gabe."

Phillip met Emily's eyes. "He's in good hands here." Looking from his sister to his mother, he added, "I got sidetracked when I was at home earlier and forgot to pack a few things for Gabe and me. And I need to make a withdrawal from the bank."

"Several birds with one stone?" Hannah asked.

Sarah grunted. "I expect that is true. Making things easy on himself — while calming his guilty conscience — with one trip to Pleasant Valley."

His demeanor changed, instantly, from somewhat relaxed to tense. Phillip did his best to hide it.

"Gather your things," he told both women. "The sooner we leave, the sooner I can get back to Gabe."

"Yes. We know *that* is the most important thing on your mind."

Hannah gasped quietly. *"Maemm!"*

"It's all right," he said.

But it wasn't. Emily saw the hurt and disappointment on Phillip's face, in his fatigued stance. She'd seen this far too often in the behavior of relatives who, unable to express their worries, let fear and frustration guide their words. She wished Sarah could manage to demonstrate proof of her faith in God's will, for her own well-being as well as for Gabe and Phillip.

He checked his watch, gave the winder a few turns. "I should be back in a couple of hours," he told Emily, repocketing it. "Can I bring you a sandwich or something?"

"No, but thanks. I'll grab something at the café." She winked at Gabe. "I might even bring back a couple slices of Hobe's famous apple pie."

It made her feel good, seeing the smile on the boy's face. On his father's face, too. They deserved to be happy *and* healthy.

"We are ready," Sarah announced, hanging her sewing bag over one arm. Adjusting her bonnet, she stood beside Phillip at Gabe's bedside. "How long will you be in Baltimore, Son?"

"I can't say for sure. Three days? A week?"

"God willing, no longer!" Sarah quickly added, "I only ask so I am sure to pack enough clean clothing for the two of you."

Sarah and Hannah took turns hugging

Gabe. "We love you, little one, and you will be in our prayers," Hannah said. "Do everything the doctors tell you to do so you can come home to us soon. John and Paul will want to play many games with you!"

"Well," Sarah interrupted, "are we leaving or are we not?"

He wrapped Gabe in a long, protective hug. "I know it won't be easy," he said, pressing a kiss to the boy's temple, "but try and take a nap while I'm gone, all right?"

"Yes, Dad. I will try."

Phillip followed his mother and sister to the door, and as they stepped into the hall, he mouthed, "Sorry," and pointed toward Sarah.

"Drive safely," she said, and grinning, mouthed back, "Good luck."

If she got any sleep at all tonight, Emily knew she'd see that handsome smile in her dreams.

CHAPTER ELEVEN

Hannah insisted on sitting in the middle of the pickup's bench seat. "It is easier for me to slide over," she explained.

Phillip helped Sarah into the truck and hoped his sister could read the gratitude in his eyes, because their mother had made it clear that she had no intention of easing up on him.

"In case I forget," he told his sister, "be sure to thank John and Paul for sending Gabe the toy trucks Eli made. I'm sure he'll appreciate having things nearby that remind him of home."

"You should have seen all the other things they wanted to send. Why, it would have taken a wagon to hold them all!"

"They're good boys. No surprise there. You and Eli are good parents."

She gave him a playful elbow jab. "Why, thank you, little Brother!"

Perhaps hearing about her other grandsons would get his mother's mind off his transgressions.

They'd barely reached the highway when Sarah said, "You behave as if you are the only person to suffer loss, Phillip."

"*Maemm,* please, not now. He already has enough on his mind."

"I do not recall asking for your opinion, Daughter. He needs to admit that his burden is no heavier than anyone else's."

He patted his sister's knee. "Thanks, kiddo, but it's okay. I'm getting used to it."

Sarah continued by reminding them of the many life events she'd trusted to God: her parents, killed in a buggy accident during her teens; her sister, succumbing to pneumonia shortly before her first child was born; her own husband, dying of infection after the barbed wire he'd been stretching snapped.

"I endured it all without complaint or anger," she told her children, "even when your brother Samuel died three months after his fall from the barn loft."

And the Baker family wasn't alone, Sarah pointed out. Many in the community had suffered similar horrors. "The sorrow brought all of us to our knees, but we accepted God's will without question. Anything less was . . . is . . . *un*acceptable!"

They rode in silence for the better part of a mile. And then Hannah turned slightly.

"I feel I must say something."

Sarah clucked her tongue, but Hannah ignored it.

"I do not agree with Bishop Fisher, that all suffering is God's will. In your shoes, Phillip, I would feel exactly as you do. And I believe that many who have loved and lost do, too."

Sarah leaned forward and looked around her daughter. "See there, Phillip? Your defiance is like a contagious disease. I hope you are happy, leading your sister into temptation."

He didn't bother pointing out that Hannah, nearly two years older, had led him on many late-night escapades, like sneaking into town for ice cream, paid for with coins she'd found after church services. She'd shown him how to tamp tobacco into their grandfather's pipe, and how to light and smoke it. It had been Hannah who'd led the way as they pounded on neighbors' doors, then hid in the shrubbery to snicker at the exasperated reactions. Remembering the fun, adventuresome girl she'd been made him grin a bit.

"Phillip is not to blame for the way I feel, *Maemm*. My *heart* is! Eli and the boys are my life, my *world.* If anything happened to them . . ." She shook her head so hard that her bonnet fell off. "Which would you have us believe, that bad things, like sickness, accidents, *death* are God's will? Because if you do, how can we believe that all good things are His gifts to us?" She jerked the hat back onto her head. "As for me, I do not believe the Father deliberately sends heartache to His children in order to teach them to trust, to have faith! I believe that bad things just . . . *are.*"

Although Phillip agreed with everything Hannah had said, he felt obligated to put an end to this discussion. For as long as he could remember, his mother and sister had behaved more like friends than mother and daughter, laughing, sharing secrets and shortcuts as they sewed and baked things for Hannah's shop. His situation was directly responsible for the hard feelings between them now, and he felt bad about that. *Give me the words,* he prayed, *to bring them together again. . . .*

"*Maemm,* Hannah," he began, "it breaks my heart that my problems have made you doubt each other. Please forgive me?"

Neither woman spoke for a long moment, and then Sarah said, "There is nothing to forgive, Son. You are a grown man with a mind of your own. God will work in your life as He sees fit. Only He can change your heart. I pray it happens soon, though, so that Gabe will —"

"Maemm," Hannah interrupted, "if you are about to say that if Phillip does not come around before the operation, God will use Gabe to punish him, I cannot be responsible for what I might say."

"Your *vodder* and I raised you to believe you need not fear such things . . . when you live the Amish way."

Hannah squeezed his knee again. "I give up," she said.

His mother had sacrificed much to help out after Rebecca died. She performed every chore — laundry, cooking, cleaning, tending Gabe and himself, too — often anticipating their needs, all without grumbling. And all she asked in return was that he live, as she'd put it, the Amish way.

But the Amish way had cost him the brother who'd been friend, confidant, advisor, instructor. Cost him the father whose patient tutelage had fortified Phillip with the confidence to open his own business. A handful of others in the community might have disagreed with her, had Sarah decided to seek medical attention for her husband and son instead of relying on faith alone, but they wouldn't have stood in her way. If she hadn't weighed him down with doubt and guilt after his first mention of bringing Rebecca to a doctor, would he have acted sooner?

To acknowledge it, even in the privacy of his mind, was to admit his anger should be directed toward his mother, not God the Father. The thought that came next did nothing to ease his anxiety:

You are a full-grown man; it was your *duty to do right by your wife, not your mother's.*

He couldn't blame his mother. Or God. The responsibility fell squarely on his shoulders, and his alone.

If only he'd been man enough to do the right thing, to admit that he shared Hannah's conviction: God did not calculatedly send heartache to His children in order to test and teach them about trust and faith. He'd been taught that God absolved all sin, even the sin of misplaced anger.

He pulled the truck into Hannah and Eli's long, winding drive, stopping near the big covered porch. Phillip jumped down from the cab and hurried around to the passenger side, intent on helping his mother and sister onto the gravel.

Sarah stood aside as Hannah joined them. "Come in," Hannah said. "I'll fix you both some lemonade. And if there are any left, I'll put out a plate of sugar cookies, too."

"Thanks, but I need to get home, throw a few things into a bag, and get back to Gabe." He gave her a hug. "Can we put off the gathering until he's home from Baltimore?"

"Of course. The boys will be disappointed, Eli, too, but you did promise not to be away too long."

By the time he turned around, Sarah had already climbed into the truck.

"*Maemm,* you should stay with us, save Phillip having to come back to drop you off after he packs."

Staring straight ahead, their mother shook her head. "I am not coming back. I will be perfectly fine on my own, at . . . at home."

Brother and sister exchanged a glance before Hannah added, "But will you not get lonely, over there all by yourself?"

"I will use the time to pray." She turned just long enough to glare at Phillip. "The good Lord knows I have much to pray *about.*"

So much for her "there's nothing to forgive" line, he thought.

Hannah exhaled an audible sigh. "Can you at least come in long enough for me to make you a sandwich, Phillip?"

"Thanks, you're a sweetheart, but I'll grab something from the cafeteria."

"It will be closed by the time you get back."

How long would this stalling last? he wondered. "There are plenty of vending machines."

"Ah, now your pockets are lined with money, and your stomach is lined with steel," Sarah put in.

For decades now, she'd been in full command of her own life and the lives of her children and grandchildren. Gabe's condition, however, was out of her control, and it seemed to Phillip that not even leaning on faith and God's will had helped her cope. That, he believed, explained his mother's cantankerous attitude. She'd always been there for him. Supporting *her* now was the right thing to do, no matter how difficult or, to use Hannah's word, challenging.

Drawing her into a light hug, Phillip smiled. "Hannah's right, there is a lot on my mind right now. But I'm fine, and spoiled as I am by your fine cooking, I'll still be fine, even if my meals come from a machine for a couple of days."

Seconds before she walked away, he felt her stiffen. His mother didn't get into a mood like this often, but when she did, he'd learned to let it take its course. As she climbed into the pickup's cab, he walked around to the driver's side. "I'll call your shop when I can, to give you updates," he told Hannah. "Hug the boys for me, okay?"

"You know I will."

He slid the gearshift to reverse and turned the truck around. Would his mother give him the silent treatment during the drive between Hannah's house and his?

Not if he had anything to say about it.

"I'll take care of Gabe," he said. "I'll take care of myself, too."

"Your bodily health does not concern me. The state of your soul does."

"I'm right with God, *Maemm,* so please stop worrying."

"Easy for you to say. *Your* son has no plans to leave the community."

He hadn't told a soul of his dreams of opening a shop in town, where he could double his income and pay the bills already stacked on his desk as well as those not yet delivered from the hospital. It would mean staying in Pleasant Valley longer than he'd hoped, and that wouldn't be easy. But then, what in life *was*?

Staying in the community held another advantage: He'd have time to figure out how he'd explain the move to Gabe . . .

. . . and how he'd live with the shame and pain his potential shunning would cause his mother.

Chapter Twelve

Pete dipped a French fry into ketchup, then used it as a pointer.

"Let me get this straight. You want me to drive you, and the Baker guy, and his sick kid, all the way to Hopkins. In an ambo. Tomorrow. For *free.*"

"I volunteered to take them in my car, but the more I think about it, the more I realize what a bad idea it is."

He bit off the tip of the fry. "Yeah. Good point. The kid would be miserable in that boxy li'l four cylinder." He finished the fry. "Besides," he said around it, "no medical equipment — not that he'll need it — but still. And no power doors. No power seats. Getting him in and out? Sheesh. Talk about uncomfortable."

He never passed up a chance to tease her about her inexpensive but serviceable car. Grinning, Emily rolled her eyes.

"And how will you keep him entertained

for three hours?"

In past discussions, she'd defended her choice to omit a multifaceted entertainment system from the options package. Instead of taking the bait this time, Emily said, "Takes me *four* to get to Baltimore."

"Because you drive like an old lady."

She pretended to scowl. "If the speed limit signs say sixty-five —"

"Last I heard, it's seventy." Pete squirted more ketchup onto his plate.

"Would you like some fries to go with your ketchup?"

Now it was Pete's turn to roll his eyes. "It won't be easy, since you waited until the last minute to spring this on me, but I'll reach out to a couple of pals. Maybe I can call in a favor." He picked up his burger. "But you know what that means, right?"

"That now, I'll owe *you* a favor."

"You betcha. A big one. A *really* big one."

Despite his tendency to play the tough guy role to the hilt, Emily trusted Pete. With good reason. She predicted he'd claim payback in the form of a meal, much like this one, and knew without a doubt that she'd guessed correctly. His training made it easy for him to understand the importance of Gabe's traveling in a vehicle equipped with all the drugs and instruments required for airway management, oxygenation, ventilation, hemodynamic monitoring, and resuscitation. Equally important, at least one skilled EMT on board, capable of tracking Gabe's physical *and* emotional stability during the trip, since something as seemingly innocuous as vibration could cause nausea, headaches, and more.

"Even if an ambo is available, it might cost a good bit," Pete said. "How will Baker pay for it?"

She was well aware that Phillip had no insurance, and that he'd probably already drained whatever savings he might have had. "You can assure your friend that he'll be paid, in full."

"A thousand bucks. Maybe more?"

Emily shrugged. A healthy rainy-day fund was one of the perks of being single and living frugally . . . and alone.

"Baker doesn't strike me as the type who'll accept monetary help. What'll you do when he refuses to let you pick up the tab?"

"I'm not going to tell him there *is* a tab." It was her turn to use a French fry as a pointer. "And neither will you."

Pete's eyebrows rose. "So you're gonna lie to him? And expect me to do the same? *And* you think he'll accept our stories?"

"I'll find a way to explain things so that

180

we won't have to lie, not outright anyway, so he won't feel beholden. Because Phillip *would* see it as charity. He's honest as the day is long. And despite being Amish, he's proud. Too proud to let me help, even if I pretend it's a loan."

"Pretend?" Pete shook his head. "Aw, I *knew* it."

There were two reasons she didn't need to ask *what* he knew. One, he'd always been able to read her like the proverbial book. She knew him pretty well, too, so two, he'd tell her, even if she didn't ask him to.

"Em. Sis. C'mon now. Really? Are you *crazy*? Yeah, sure, he's a nice enough guy. But he's Amish. You're not. No way you two could have a future together. *No way*."

"You're misreading the situation, just like his mother. I told her, and I'll tell you, *Gabe* is the only connection between Phillip and me."

Pete snorted. "At the risk of sounding crude, that's hooey."

Emily laughed. "Hooey?"

"Garbage. Baloney. Hogwash. Call it what you will, it's still nonsense."

She felt the heat of a blush rush into her face. "I ought to know how I feel, Pete."

"Yeah, well, you know what Abe Lincoln said . . ."

"Yeah, well, as I've said before, many experts believe that his 'fool me' quote is" — she smirked — *"hooey."*

In place of the rebuttal she'd anticipated, Pete scrolled through the contacts list on his cell phone. Emily heard the unmistakable sound of ringing on the other end, and then Pete said, "George. Pete White here. Got a favor to ask ya. Kinda big one. You sittin' down?"

Please, Lord, let this George *guy say yes. And while you're answering prayers, help me find an above-board way to tell Phillip about this. . . .*

"Dr. White!"

Gabe was sitting up, smiling and pink-cheeked, and looked genuinely pleased to see her. If she didn't know better, Emily would have said he was recovering from a tonsillectomy, instead of awaiting major heart surgery.

"Wow. You're one happy boy, aren't you! Did they give you chocolate cake for dessert again?"

"No. Chocolate *pudding.*"

She pinched his big toe. "Now I'm sorry I didn't order dessert after my supper. You're making me hungry for sweets!"

"Did you eat with my dad?"

"No, I expect he's home, packing for the two of you."

"So you ate, all by yourself?"

"No, with my brother."

"The one who brought me here?"

"Yes, Pete."

"Oh, I like him. A lot. He is a very nice man."

It was easy to agree with the boy. "And I like you. A lot. You're a very nice boy!"

Giggling, Gabe drew his knees to his chest. Then suddenly, his smile dimmed.

And Emily thought she knew why: In a few hours, they'd load him into the ambulance, and he'd start out on the road to health and well-being. A good thing, if all went as planned, but scary to a four-year-old boy whose days, to this point, had been filled with ailments and physical weakness that barred him from enjoying life like every other child his age.

She sat on the bed, facing him. "Getting a little nervous, are you?"

He nodded, hugged his knees tighter, and rested his chin there.

"I'd feel the same way if I were you." As an Amish boy, he hadn't yet attended school, but Emily believed that Phillip and his mother deserved much praise for encouraging Gabe's outgoing personality, extensive vocabulary, and comfort in conversing with adults. She'd explained his condition in words he could understand and described what he could expect upon arriving at Johns Hopkins, too. And while he seemed to understand at the time, experience taught her that children retained and comprehended such information quite differently from her adult patients.

"I'll bet you still have a lot of questions, don't you?"

He lifted one shoulder. And Emily understood it to mean that yes, he had questions, but because of his age, he didn't know how to put them into words.

"Are you wondering about Dr. Williams, who'll perform your operation?"

"Yes. A little," he said quietly.

Emily held his hand and described Alex's medical background. "He is an excellent doctor who has performed this operation many, many times. So you can be sure he's very good at what he does."

Seeing that Gabe understood, she continued. "You'll have a chance to meet him, tomorrow, not long after we arrive in Baltimore. I've spoken with a few of the nurses who work with him regularly, and they promised to give us a tour of the hospital, so you'll feel more at ease when we're moving you from your room to the OR, and from the recovery room back to your room."

He maintained full eye contact, a signal that he had heard and grasped what she'd said.

"The operation will take a few hours, but you won't even notice, because you'll be sound asleep, thanks to some medicine."

"Will the medicine get into me through a needle?"

She gave his hand a tender squeeze. "Yes, but you probably won't even feel the prick, because everyone at Hopkins is very good at what they do."

"What if I *do* feel it?"

"If you do — and I don't think you will — you're allowed to holler."

That, at least, inspired a tiny grin. "Really? I can yell?"

"Yup. At the top of your lungs if you want to!"

"Wow." The smile grew slightly.

"After the operation, you'll sleep a lot, for a day, maybe even two."

"Why?"

Emily lifted his hand and counted on his fingers. "For one thing, it'll take a while for the medicine to work itself out of your system. Plus, because your heart isn't working as hard as it should, you've been feeling tired for a long, long time. The operation itself will make you feel even more tired. At least until you begin to heal. So it's a good thing, a very good thing, that you'll sleep a lot."

"Because my body will need rest, so that I can start healing and leave the hospital as soon as I am feeling better."

"Yes, Gabe! That's it, exactly!"

"When I go home again, can I play with my cousins?"

"You mean games like hide-and-seek, and tag?" Her heart throbbed at the sight of his full-blown smile. "For a few weeks, you won't feel like running around. But little by little, you'll gain strength, and you'll be able to keep up with them. What are their names?"

"John and Paul. They are older than me, but they are fun!"

"That's wonderful. I had cousins like that, and I'm sure you'll remember all that fun when you're a father with children of your own."

Gabe looked disgusted. "Oh, I am not getting married."

"Why not?"

"Because my wife would be a girl, and I'd have to *kiss* her." He grimaced. "I do not want to kiss a girl!"

Laughing, Emily drew him close in a hug. "Oh Gabe, you're such a joy." She held him at arm's length to add, "I could be wrong, but I don't think so: Someday, when you're all grown up, you'll meet a very special young woman, and when you do, you'll feel very differently about everything. Even kissing."

He shrugged again. "Maybe. But I don't think so."

Gabe leaned into his pillows, a serious expression replacing the kiss-induced revulsion on his face.

"Dr. White, can I ask you a question?"

"Of course. Anything."

"And you will tell me the real truth?"

"Yes . . ."

"Do you think I am going to die?"

"You're going to be fine, just fine."

A half-truth was better than an outright lie, Emily thought, remembering what Alex had said: *I've seen the X-rays and scans. The boy has a fifty-fifty chance of pulling through the surgery. Even if he makes it through the first week, a cold, the flu, too much activity that causes a bleed could put him at death's door.*

"You're going to be fine," she repeated. *Because you have to be!*

"Promise?"

Emily raised her right hand. "I believe that. Promise." She always wanted long-lasting, positive results for her patients, but never more than now.

"Whew," he responded. "My dad will be glad to hear that. So will my *grossmammi.*" He paused, then said, "Where is your mother and father?"

She pictured the man who'd supported her every decision, who'd sometimes given unwanted advice that had been difficult to hear, but never wrong. What would he say about her ever-growing feelings for Phillip? Emily thought of her mother, too, who'd done everything possible to protect her family from the ravages of diabetes. "She's in heaven."

Eyes narrowed, Gabe said, "You do not really believe in such a place, do you?"

"Oh yes, I certainly do. It makes me feel good, picturing her up there, smiling and happy and pain-free, surrounded by angels and —" His wary, "too old for his age" expression silenced her. "You don't?"

"No, because . . ." He met her eyes. "Dr. White, do you think I have a soul?"

"*Everyone* has a soul." She tweaked his nose. "It's the part of us that's most special to God."

"God." He hesitated. "So you think there

is a God?"

She hadn't thought it possible for a child his age to sound so skeptical. "Absolutely, positively, one hundred percent."

"And you think He loves us?"

"Yes, Gabe. He loves us. All of us. All of the time."

"I want to believe, but . . ." He laid a hand over his heart. "I have watched a lot of TV here in the hospital, and on the news there are forest fires. Floods. Tornadoes. People getting shot. Children dying of sicknesses. Would a *good* God do these things? Would He take my mother — and yours — and give me a heart that doesn't work right?"

He looked defeated, and every bit as miserable as he sounded. Emily wanted to ease his mind, to bolster his faith. But she'd never been one who'd spouted her spiritual beliefs. Not in college when fellow students pooh-poohed those who believed in Him. Not in med school, when professors and peers cited scientific studies, conducted solely to disprove His existence. And while she *did* believe, wholeheartedly, Emily had never argued with them, because she didn't know *how.* She had to figure it out, right here, right now, because this sweet, sickly little boy was afraid — though no one had said it straight out — about what would become of him if he didn't survive the operation. And he needed to go into that surgical suite feeling as upbeat and confident as possible!

"I can tell you what *I* think, Gabe, but it might not answer your questions. First of all, I totally agree with your community's beliefs . . . that maybe God allows us to suffer, just a little, sometimes, to make us stronger."

Gabe exhaled a long sigh. "Oh, so it *is* about faith, then."

His bored tone told her that he'd heard the word ad nauseam. "Yes, I suppose you could put it that way." Emily scooted closer, placed her hands on his shoulders, and looked into his wide-eyed, innocent face. "It isn't easy, believing in things you can't see, like heaven and God." She fingercombed his bangs. "Do you believe your dad loves you?"

"Yes!"

"Even though you can't *see* that love?"

"I see it in his eyes. I hear it in his voice."

"God loves you, too. And when you believe that, even when it's hard and scary and confusing, *that* is faith."

Gabe leaned forward, wrapped his arms around her, and snuggled close. "Will you be my friend even after the operation, Dr.

White?"

She'd cared for many people, children included, whose conditions were at least as precarious as Gabe's. What was it about this boy that made her wish he was more, so much more, than a patient?

Emily hugged him tighter. "I'd love that." And she meant it.

"I heard my dad talking to the bishop one time. They did not know I was in the shop because I was hiding under the workbench. I heard Dad say he does not believe in God."

Emily and Phillip had never discussed religion in any meaningful way, but hearing that his convictions had been shaken to that degree came as no surprise. He'd suffered the loss of several close relatives, and now his only son faced an uncertain future. That had to be challenging, even for someone raised in an Amish community, surrounded by devout believers.

Anyone facing major surgery would look worried, but Gabe's conduct gave new meaning to the word. Smarter than a child three times his age, he'd figured out that the pending operation could kill him, and that every medical decision made on his behalf had widened the gap between his father and grandmother.

191

"Will you do me a favor, Gabe?"

"Oh yes, Dr. White. I would like that!"

"I've overstayed my welcome, and tired you out. So try to get some rest, okay? Do it for me?"

He gave the request a moment's thought. "If I try, will you do a favor for *me*?"

"Sure, if I can."

"I was afraid, but you helped my afraid to go away. Will you do it for my dad? Help him believe in God so he will not be afraid about my heart anymore?"

Emily blinked away the sting of tears. "Aw, sweetie," she began, "I'll —"

"I'm not afraid, Son."

"Good grief, Phillip, you startled me! How long have you been standing there?"

A slow, tantalizing smile lit his eyes. "Long enough," he said. "Exactly long enough."

CHAPTER THIRTEEN

Emily, seated at the foot of Gabe's bed, faced Phillip. The Gabe-induced fear that had coiled in his gut relaxed a bit. She'd handled his boy's questions with genuine warmth, not clinical professionalism. In her place, Phillip didn't think he could have done anywhere near as well. He was about to thank her when she said, "Phillip . . ."

She usually wore her hair up. He'd never seen her without the starched white lab coat and had no idea what style or color of clothing hid under it. Put a bonnet and apron on her, he'd thought more than once, and she could almost pass for an Amish woman. Tonight, she'd worn her hair down, and it draped over her shoulders like a mahogany cape. Her pink blouse reflected in her cheeks, made her freckles stand out. And the skirt that stopped just above her knees —

". . . we need to talk about the trip to

Baltimore."

Pull yourself together, Baker, or she'll think you've gone mad. "Your friend didn't cancel the operation, I hope."

"No. Of course not. Wait. My *friend*?"

"Yeah. You know . . ." The doctor whose name had the power to dim the light in her eyes. The thought of her staring adoringly into *Williams's* eyes had the power to make Phillip clench his jaw. "The doctor who's gonna fix Gabe's heart? You're, ah, old pals, right?"

Her cheeks reddened, and she was blinking so fast, he could almost feel the breeze from her long lashes. Phillip felt bad about having caused her discomfort. "So about the trip. You need me to drive, after all?"

"No. In fact, my brother volunteered to drive us. In an ambulance. Because its suspension system will keep Gabe more comfortable. And it's fully equipped. Medications. Monitoring devices. Not that I think he'll need them, but, as the sages say, it's best to err on the side of caution, you know?"

What he knew was, she'd never talked that fast. Why did she sound so nervous? Was she keeping something from him? Something associated with the operation?

Phillip looked at his son. "Will you look at

that? He took your advice, about trying to sleep, and he's deep in dreamland now. So, no need to tiptoe around the truth . . . *Emily.*"

"Tiptoe . . . ? What!"

"The real reason our travel plans changed."

She stared him down. "Your mother should have named you Thomas."

It took a few seconds to get the joke — doubting Thomas — but Phillip wasn't amused. "You have to admit, this ambulance story came from out of nowhere."

Emily lifted her chin slightly and pursed her lips. "It isn't a *story,* Phillip. I made the decision in Gabe's best interests. He would have been miserable, riding so many hours in my car. And Pete agrees." She spent a moment smoothing the pleats of her black skirt. "I'm a little surprised that after all this time, you don't trust me."

All *what* time? he wondered. They hadn't known each other a full week!

He stopped himself from saying *I* do *trust you . . . where Gabe is concerned* because, by her own admission, she'd made a judgment call about the emergency vehicle, one that directly impacted his son, without running it past him. Reality hit him like a hard slap: By *his* own admission, they'd met a week ago. Five days, to be precise. Only a crazy man would allow himself to become emotionally attached to a near stranger in such a short time. Phillip had already told himself — more times than he cared to admit — to get control of his emotions. He hadn't been thinking straight, and the indecision made him feel stupid. Ridiculous. As immature as his neighbors' giggling girls, who destroyed daisies while playing "he loves me, he loves me not" to decide which boy to marry.

Phillip groaned under his breath. "So when do we leave?"

"Pete says we'll hit some traffic in Frederick and Hagerstown, but leaving at seven o'clock should get us through the worst of it without any major delays."

After dropping his mother off at home, Phillip had gone to his shop. His regular customers must have heard about Gabe's situation, because he found no new messages on the answering machine. New bills had arrived, though, for electricity. Grocery deliveries from Browning's. His heartbeat quickened just thinking about the short stack of windowed envelopes.

"Did Pete happen to mention what it's going to cost?"

"He . . . well, he volunteered."

"Yes, so you said. Really nice of him. But the *vehicle* isn't free, right?"

"It's . . . I . . . Pete called in a few favors." Emily picked at a nub in the fabric of her skirt. "It won't cost you anything."

What a peculiar way to answer the question. "It won't cost *me* anything?"

Her cheeks flushed, not much, but enough to tell him he'd made her nervous again. He wasn't happy about that, but if she thought he intended to accept charity . . .

"Dad —" Gabe interrupted sleepily as he woke, levering himself onto one elbow. "Is *Grossmammi* coming back?"

"No, Son. She will stay at home while we go to Johns Hopkins."

"Did you pack us some clothes?"

The question, Phillip believed, was Gabe's little-boy way of asking for reassurances: If he died on the operating table, he wouldn't need clean shirts and trousers, now would he?

Phillip chuckled. "I packed so many things that your grandmother scolded me!"

Gabe grinned. "She is probably worried about having to wash it all when we get home."

It was good, *so* good to hear that Gabe expected to return to Pleasant Valley. And he had Emily to thank for the boy's confidence.

"Dr. White?"

Emily faced Gabe. "Hmm?"

"I am not allowed to eat tonight, right?"

"The cutoff hour is midnight."

"I will be asleep by then. Probably." A silly smile lit up his ashy face.

"Ah," Emily said, winking, "you have a special request, do you?"

"I liked the buttered noodles and mashed potatoes with gravy. But I would really like more ice cream. And chocolate cake . . ."

"But sweetie, where will you put it all!"

Phillip liked the way his laughter and hers blended in perfect harmony. Three steps, that's all it would take to sit between them, and initiate a family hug. Oh, to have a cup of coffee, bottled water, *some* thing to hold, and sip, to distract him from what couldn't — shouldn't — happen.

"Did *Grossmammi* find my list?"

The question shattered the image. "What list?"

"I tore pictures from a magazine," Gabe said, pointing to the stack on his bedside table. "Pies. Cakes. Muffins. Bread. All my favorite things. So she would know what to *bakka* for my . . . for when . . ." Unable to find the right word, Gabe groaned. "For the

198

day I go back to *der haus.*"

"Your homecoming?" Phillip offered.

"Yes! That's it! My homecoming! It will be a very special, happy day. Like the Fourth of July. And Christmas. And my birthday that is *on* the Fourth of July!" Hands clapping, Gabe added, "*Der gschwisderkinds* John and Paul and *Ant* Hannah and *Onkle* Eli will merry with us, yah?"

Interesting, Phillip thought, how in his excitement, Gabe only remembered the *Deutsch* words for *house, bake, aunt, uncle,* and *cousins.* Should he answer with the truth, or something more optimistic?

Emily replied in his stead. "No partying for you, little man, at least not at first. We talked about this, remember? How your body will be very tired, and you can easily catch cold. After you've had time to heal and rest, then you can celebrate to your heart's content."

"How long will I rest?"

Phillip had memorized nearly every word in the pages Emily had printed for him and knew that Gabe's recovery could take months.

Yet again, Emily answered for him. "Everyone is different. Some children are ready to run and play in a few weeks. Others take longer."

Gabe frowned. "How much longer?"

She reminded him of a rabbit, caught in a trap. This time, Phillip came to her rescue.

"It will take as long as it takes, Son, and we will be grateful for every healthy day."

"I cannot wait to be healthy. I want to climb a tree. Go fishing. And beat *der gschwisderkinds* in a footrace!"

Gabe expected things to go well, and God willing, they would. A glance at Emily's face told him she hoped so, too, and from the tender, motherly expression, her hopes went beyond adding another success story to her case files.

Phillip sat back and pretended to listen as she and Gabe listed things he could do while recuperating. Board and card games, coloring books, identifying birds that perched in the trees near his window. Pretended, because her exchange with Gabe added yet another item to his already too-long Reasons to Like Emily list.

One of Gabe's nurses came in, and after checking his vitals, entered the numbers into the computer. Emily, standing beside her, scanned the monitor. The women pointed, nodded, even shared a smile or two, behaving more like friends than co-workers. It eased the slight concern that had arisen when one of the nurses seemed to have hard feelings toward Emily. Months ago, he'd read an article that attempted to prove the nurses-resent-doctors theory. One particular quote stood out among others: "There's definitely a pecking order, at least in some doctors' minds. They treat us like peons, barking orders, rushing through exams, and leaving us to correct their mistakes and deal with frightened, in-pain patients." He'd witnessed numerous interactions between Emily and nurses, between Emily and orderlies, between Emily and other doctors, and except for that single occasion, one thing stood out: her talent for putting people at ease.

And the list grew.

How was he supposed to rein in his feelings if she continued giving him reasons not to!

A young man carrying a gray plastic tray joined them. "Got most of your special requests, Gabie," he said, sliding it onto the food cart. "Even chocolate cake!"

Gabe clapped his hands. "Yay! Thank you, Benny!"

Benny scribbled something on a napkin, adding it to the tray. "That's my cell number. You want anything else, you call, and I'll do whatever I can to get it for you, okay?" On his way to the door, he paused in front of Phillip. "That's some kid you've got there, sir. Everybody loves him."

"I know exactly how they feel," he said as the nurse removed stainless steel coverings from plates and bowls.

"Wow," she said. "Just . . . wow! There's enough here to feed a family of six." She propped a fist on a hip. "Why didn't *I* get an invitation to this party you're throwing!"

"You are funny, Nurse Amy. You know there is no party." Laughing, Gabe flexed his bicep. "Eating makes us strong, is that not what you said?"

"You bet I said it, 'cause it's true." She mussed his bangs. "Well, off I go to check on my other patients!"

"I should go, too." Emily followed the nurse to the door. "I need to check on a few patients, make sure my shifts are covered for the next few days. Run home and pack a bag. You know, *stuff.*"

"You should not run," Gabe said. "I saw a lady fall yesterday. These floors are slippery!"

"You did? I hope she wasn't hurt!"

"Oh, she got right up again." Gabe paused. "But she probably has a bruise on her knee now!"

"Thank you for the advice. I promise to walk."

"I like your smile."

"I like yours, too."

"And I think you're very pretty."

"Why, thank you, Gabe. And I think you're a handsome boy."

"Dr. White? Will your husband come to Baltimore with us?"

Did she look as though someone had smacked her — hard — because once upon a time, she'd hoped to become a doctor's wife? *Mrs. Alex Williams,* to be precise?

"I'm not . . . I don't have a husband."

While Phillip stood, silently wondering when she'd tell Gabe about the ambulance ride to Hopkins, the boy said, "What about children? Do you have any of those?"

"Nope, 'fraid not."

Gabe shook his head. "That is too bad. I think you would be a very good mother." He looked at Phillip. "Do you think so, Dad?"

He replied without hesitation. "I do."

The words echoed in his head, reminding him of the day he'd stood toe to toe with Rebecca in the church at the foot of Backbone Mountain. In the Amish community, arranged marriages like theirs were as routine as the "we've fallen in love" kind, so when the bishop asked, "Do you have confidence, brother, that the Lord provided

our sister as a marriage partner for you?"
he'd quickly said, "I do." Fisher continued
with, "Do you promise that if she should
need your help, you will care for her as is
fitting a Christian husband?" And again,
he'd said, "I do." That final question,
though, haunted him, still: "Do you both
promise to treat one another with forbear-
ance and patience, and not part from each
other until God separates you by death?"
Haunted him because, as he and Rebecca
chorused "I do," dismay, not a new bride's
joy, registered on her face . . . a countenance
she donned each time they came together
as husband and wife.

Gabe's voice broke into his thoughts. "Dr.
White is leaving, Dad. You should hug her
good-bye."

A myriad of expressions skittered across
her face: Shock. Embarrassment. Confusion. Anxiety.

"I . . . ah . . . I'm a mess," she said, grab-
bing her bag. "I'll see both of you tomorrow, bright and early." And then she was
gone.

Gabe shook silverware from its white
paper envelope, and it landed on the For-
mica tabletop with a metallic clatter.

"Why didn't you hug her?"

How could he explain what he didn't

understand himself?

Gabe speared half a dozen elbow noodles. "*I* hugged her." He drew the back of his hand over his mouth, then licked off the golden cheese sauce. "Do you ever get lonely, Dad?"

"Not often," he said, smirking, "thanks to you and the rest of our rowdy family."

"Yeah, we make lots of noise when we are together."

Hopefully, the boy's curiosity had been sated. Finally.

"Dad?"

Phillip tensed. "Your second supper is getting cold, Gabe."

He shoveled a scoop of mashed potatoes into his mouth. "Do you like her?" he asked around it.

"Don't talk with your mouth full, Son."

After impaling a forkful of meat loaf he said, "I think she is pretty."

Phillip thought so, too, from the top of her curly-haired head to the soles of her tiny feet.

"Do you think she is as pretty as Mama?"

Tall and frail with pale blue eyes, wispy blond hair, and a solemn nature, Rebecca had been Emily's opposite in just about every way.

"A different kind of pretty."

It hit him suddenly that Gabe's brave talk was exactly that: talk. Perhaps he wasn't entirely convinced he'd survive the operation. Was he worried that if he didn't, Phillip would be . . . lonesome?

Using his fork, Gabe pointed at the notebook on the seat of the straight-backed chair. "Uh-oh."

Phillip picked it up. "I'll see if I can catch up with her." Pausing in the doorway, he said, "Finish your supper while I'm gone. If you can find room for it in that already-full belly of yours!"

And there she stood, facing the windows at the end of the hall, waiting for the elevator. Phillip jogged toward her. At the sound of his footsteps, she turned, and even at this distance, he could see the *Oh no, not him* expression on her face.

"You forgot your notebook," he said, holding it out to her.

Emily reached for it, then jerked back her hand. "Thanks, but that isn't mine. It probably belongs to one of the nurses. Or a resident who's studying something related to . . . hearts."

"Yes, many have visited Gabe. And your patience with them was admirable." Now, things began to make sense. Gabe hadn't said it was Emily's. *You heard what you*

206

wanted to hear, he told himself.

"These elevators," he said, staring at the numbers above the doors. "Slow, aren't they?"

"Oh, they're not so bad." She smiled. "I stopped in a couple of patients' rooms first or I'd be on my way home by now."

She took a step forward and grabbed his hand.

"I know you're worried about Gabe, but you needn't be. I could say it a hundred times more, and you might still be worried, but Alex really *is* a very skilled surgeon. I don't like to give false hope, but I have a good feeling about this. I know it's easier said than done under the circumstances, and in a place like this, but I hope you and Gabe will get a good night's sleep."

Backlit by the evening sun that slanted through the windows, she all but glowed. She cared, and not just about Gabe. Emily cared about him, too. Phillip saw it in her eyes, felt it in her touch.

He'd never been the type who did anything without first giving it a lot of thought.

Until now.

He drew her close and kissed her.

And she let him.

CHAPTER FOURTEEN

The four-hour drive from Oakland to Baltimore went smoothly, and so had their arrival and check-in at Johns Hopkins.

Pete rested a hand on Phillip's shoulder. "I gotta say, that kid of yours is as smart as they come. Tell him something once, he remembers it." He laughed. "And those questions! I had a hard time answering them all. I think I might need a refresher course."

Grinning, Phillip watched two nurses help Gabe into bed.

"He's light as a feather," said one.

The other agreed. "Yeah, but six months from now, he'll weigh twice as much!"

"All comfy, sweetie?" the first asked.

"Yes. Thank you."

"Smart," she said, winking, "cute as a button, and polite, too." She gave his knee a playful slap. "Think maybe you can squeeze in a nap?"

Gabe nodded, and the nurses left the

room with a promise to return within the hour. He looked older than his years. Looked exhausted, too, thanks to a restless night of tossing and turning, whimpering and moaning. Once, while tidying his covers, Phillip noticed that tears had dampened the pillowcase, and almost lost it himself. He'd steeled himself, though, because if Gabe woke up and saw his father blubbering like a frightened child —

"Guess what, Dad! I know what a jump bag is, *and* what's in it. It's different from a medicine bag, you know." He settled back into the pillows. "And a valve mask. And a spine board. There are monitors in the ambo, too. That's what Pete calls it. An ambo. Oh, and blankets, and flashlights, and batteries, and bandages . . ." He inhaled a deep breath. "When I grow up, I want to be a paramedic, just like Pete!"

Not an impossible dream, Phillip thought . . . if the operation was successful.

"You're makin' me blush, kiddo," Pete said from the hall. "And when you're ready to sign up, I'll help any way I can."

He waved for Phillip to join him. "Didn't want to say anything in front of Gabe, since he can't eat, but I'm going to the cafeteria, grab a burger or something. What can I bring you?"

"Nothing, but thanks." Food was the last thing on Phillip's mind. "Any idea where your sister is?"

"Hunting down sleeping quarters for herself and me. Not that I expect either of us will make use of 'em." He glanced at his watch. "I expect she's firming up your meeting with Williams, too."

Pete's look of disapproval made Phillip say, "Not your favorite person, huh?"

"Oh, he's good at what he does. Excellent, actually. But he's an arrogant gasbag. A know-it-all. And he broke Emily's heart, so no, he isn't my favorite person."

It broke *his* heart to hear that she'd been so deeply hurt.

"What happened to end things?"

"She turned down his proposal. And like any self-respecting narcissist, he had a hard time believing any woman would reject him."

Phillip had looked into Williams's background. It was hard not to be impressed by the list of academic, athletic, and medical accolades that ran onto a second page, where the list of the surgical procedures he'd developed appeared. Good-looking, wealthy, successful, respected by his peers . . .

"Why did she say no?"

"For starters, he's a serial cheater. Bad enough he stepped out on her half a dozen times, but he seemed to enjoy flaunting it, too."

"Then . . . if he didn't want to settle down, why propose in the first place?"

"My best guess, she would've been good for his image. Smart, respected, well liked, and easy on the eyes."

Phillip agreed with every point.

"Just between you and me," Pete continued, "I think Em said no because she didn't believe anything would change him. Not even marriage. Plus, he had this nasty habit of embarrassing her every chance he got."

"Embarrass her? But *how*? She seems almost perfect to me."

"Yeah, well, she's no threat to *you*."

Phillip didn't get it and said so.

"She barely had to study, and still aced every test in school. Everybody liked her. Professors, patients and their families, staff, coworkers . . ." Pete shrugged. "He called her an underachiever because she wasn't interested in taking additional courses that would guarantee name recognition in the hoity-toity medical journals. And said no one of worth is ever satisfied with" — he drew quote marks in the air — "*enough.* Called her lazy. Didn't care who was listening — family, friends, peers — or how she reacted to his insults." He slammed a fist into an open palm. "I can't tell you how often I wanted to shut that jerk up . . . with a left hook to the throat. But . . ." He finished with a shrug.

"Let me guess . . . You held your temper because Emily asked you to."

"She hates conflict. Hates hurting people's feelings. Said if I called Williams out, it might embarrass the jerk, believe it or not." He shook his head.

Yes, Phillip could believe it. "Sounds like it all worked out for the best, though. She deserves better than that."

Pete searched Phillip's face for a long moment. "What she *deserves* is a guy who'll treat her like a lady, even if it isn't considered politically correct in some circles. Someone who'll recognize her finer qualities and appreciate what a prize she is." He paused, nodded once, and added, "A guy like *you.*"

Phillip didn't know how to reply.

Pete's stomach rumbled. Loudly. The men shared a moment of companionable laughter.

"Better grab that burger," Phillip said, "before one of the nurses writes you up for disturbing the peace."

"I know, right?" He patted his belly. "Say, while I'm down there, I'll call Em, see if she managed to lock Dr. Jerkface into a time for your meeting. My guess? He'll keep y'all waiting until an hour or so before the surgery. Just because he can."

"I hope you're wrong. We're all on edge, and a last-minute meeting won't be good for any of us."

"What time is surgery?" Pete asked, back-pedaling toward the elevators.

"Three o'clock."

Again, Pete glanced at his watch. "Wow." Then, "You might want to consider eating *some*thing, too, even if you aren't hungry. Way I hear it, this operation can take hours."

Six, maybe eight, according to everything he'd read. He'd kept as many details as possible to himself, mostly to quell Sarah's worries.

Pete's stomach grumbled again as he stepped into the car. "Don't think too long, or *you'll* get written up for disturbing the peace!"

Minutes after Phillip returned to Gabe's side, an orderly rolled a folding cot into the room. "Dr. White said you'd be needin' this," the young man said. He patted the stack of linens on top. "Need any help, makin' up the bed?"

"No, thanks. I can do it."

"Think you'll want an extra pillow or anything?"

"Thanks," he repeated, "but I doubt I'd use it anyway."

When the man left, Gabe said, "That looks better than the squeaky ol' chair in my other room, huh, Dad."

"Sure does."

"I am thirsty," Gabe said.

"When I meet with Dr. Williams, I'll ask if you can have a sip or two of water."

"Will you see him soon?"

He remembered what Pete had said, about the possibility of Williams postponing the get-together until the last possible minute.

"In an hour or two, I hope."

"But Dad, I am thirsty *now.*"

It wasn't like Gabe to whine or complain. Phillip wanted nothing more than to ease the boy's discomfort.

"Remember what Dr. White said, about keeping your stomach empty so you won't get queasy during the operation."

Gabe sighed. "Yes. I remember."

"Ice chips are allowed," Emily said as she came into the room. She dropped her medical bag and a small duffel near the door. "Not too many, though, because your dad is right — you don't want a queasy stomach

214

going into surgery."

Gabe held out his arms, and Emily filled them. Her sweet smile reminded him of the white-robed angel he'd seen in a Baltimore storefront years ago, its ceramic face radiating peace and love and all the sentiments associated with Christmas.

"I am so happy to see you," Gabe said. "I thought you would never get here!"

"I had to check in with a few patients back in Oakland," she said, releasing him. She faced the computer in the corner, fingers flying over the keyboard as she called up Gabe's chart. Numbers, codes, and symbols appeared on a pale blue background, each posted in columns and rows and outlined by rectangular black boxes. After giving the document an approving nod, she hit a key that turned the screen black again.

"Think you'll be okay for a half hour or so?" she asked Gabe.

"Yes. I suppose." His voice echoed his uncertainty. "Why?"

"Dr. Williams wants your dad to fill out some forms, and I thought I'd help him find the right office."

"When will I meet Dr. Williams?"

"Soon." She aimed a quick glance in Phillip's direction before turning her attention back to Gabe. "So you'll be all right then? While I help your dad?"

Gabe picked up his call button. "Oh yes, I will be fine. All I have to do is push this red key," he said, pointing, "and a nurse will come, because it will send an infrared signal to the nurses' station."

"Infrared?" Phillip repeated. "Where did you learn such a big word?"

Gabe's face glowed with admiration as he looked at Emily. "Dr. White told me about it. She is the smartest girl I know." Eyes on Phillip once more, he added, "Do you think so, too, Dad?"

"Yes, I think so, too." He could have listed a dozen reasons, but this was neither the time nor the place.

Emily stepped into the hallway and waved him closer.

"We won't be long," she said over her shoulder. "On the way to Dr. Williams's office, I'll stop at the nurses' station, ask one of them to bring you some ice chips."

The boy's smile seemed all the thanks she needed. As promised, she paused to ask one of the nurses to make sure Gabe got his cup of ice, and after thanking her, crossed the hall and knuckled the elevator's Down button. "I hope I remember how to get to his office. This place is enormous, and I haven't been here in a while."

Her hands were shaking. Nervous about assisting in the operation? Or apprehensive about spending so many hours under the watchful eye of the great Dr. Alex Williams?

"How long since you've seen him?"

Eyes fixed on the numbers panel above the doors, her voice wavered slightly. "I haven't exactly kept track."

Phillip wasn't buying it. But the doors opened, and half a dozen people exited the car. She didn't have any trouble recalling which floor his office was on, he noticed as she pressed the four.

"Think he'll make time for us now, or keep us waiting?"

She lifted one shoulder as an aide joined them. "Good," the blue-garbed woman said, "you've already chosen the fourth floor."

No one spoke as the elevator lurched upward, and when the doors opened this time, an orderly stood, patiently waiting beside a gurney. His patient, a blanketed man wearing an oxygen mask, lifted his head. "Hey, Dr. White," he said. "What're you doin' here?"

She and Phillip exited. "Assisting in an operation on one of my patients. And you?"

"This ol' ticker again. Thanks for recommending Dr. Williams. Probably saved my life."

"I'm glad you're on the mend."

She patted his hand, hidden under the blanket. And as the orderly backed the gurney into the elevator, he added, "You're not in Baltimore to stay, I hope."

"No, only until it's safe to take the li'l guy back to Oakland."

"That's good to hear. Soon as I'm on my feet, I want to start seeing you. You know, for follow-ups. Wife needs a GP, too."

Phillip wondered why Emily didn't point out that she was a diagnostician, not a general practitioner.

"Good seeing you."

And as the doors whooshed shut, she said, "You too."

And then she rubbed her temples. Sighed heavily. Shook her head.

"Emily? What's wrong?"

"Oh, nothing."

He wasn't buying that, either.

Down the hall, an office door jerked open and a tall black-haired man leaned into the hall. Spotting her, he said, "Emily. *There* you are."

Her footsteps slowed. "As usual, you refused to let us make a specific appointment, so we can't be late."

Dark brows rose on his high forehead. "The more things change, the more they stay the same," he quoted as she approached, finishing up with, "I see you're still always on the defensive."

Already, Phillip understood what Pete had said about the man's tendency to put her on the spot, every chance he got.

"This is Phillip Baker," Emily said, "the father of the little boy we'll operate on later today."

Williams stepped aside, waved them into his waiting room. "Good to meet you," he said. "Forms all filled out?"

"We only just *got* here, Alex." She made eye contact with the middle-aged woman behind the reception counter. "Are you the person we need to see about new patient forms?"

She answered with a quiet "Yes," and slid a clipboard toward Alex. "Be sure to return the pen, please?"

Williams's brow furrowed slightly. "Pearl, really. That tone isn't necessary."

She removed her wire-rimmed glasses. "But Dr. Williams," she said, fidgeting with her own pen, "I thought you said —"

He pointed at a small round table in the corner. "Have a seat while you fill out the paperwork. Pearl, get Mr. Baker a bottle of water." He looked at Phillip. "Unless you'd rather have coffee."

Phillip aimed his reply in Pearl's direction. "Thanks, but I'm fine." Then he pulled out a chair and clicked the pen into the on position as Williams opened another door. Gold-leafed letters on the opaque glass spelled out DR. ALEXANDER J. WILLIAMS, MD, FACC.

"Emily? May I have a word?" Williams said.

Phillip detected dread in her posture, in her expression. Pete hadn't exaggerated when he'd said the breakup had been less than amicable. It made him wonder why she had recommended — and volunteered to assist — a surgeon who stirred up bad memories. In an instant, he knew: She'd put Gabe's well-being ahead of her own discomfort. He made another mental entry on his Reasons to Like Emily list. Later, he'd thank her for that. And ask what the final four initials on Williams's door stood for.

After completing the form, he delivered it to Pearl.

"Ready for that coffee now?" she asked.

"I'm good, thanks." He nodded toward Williams's office door. "Any idea how long they might be in there?"

"Depends." She smirked. "I have a feeling it's not a work-related meeting, so your guess is as good as mine."

What had Williams said or done to give Pearl such an impression? He did his best not to show disapproval and took a seat on one of two caramel-colored brown sofas, then grabbed a magazine. While pretending to leaf through it, Phillip decided to give them five minutes in there. Then he'd rap on the door, let her know he'd been away from his son long enough. It was up to her after that: She could use the announcement as an excuse to call a halt to the meeting or wish him luck finding his way back to Gabe's room.

Six minutes later, he got up and walked toward the office.

Pearl stopped typing. "Oh, you can't go in there, Mr. Baker. Dr. Williams hates unannounced interruptions."

He knocked on the glass. "We'll consider this my announcement, then."

A few seconds passed before the door opened. Emily looked angry. Agitated. Exasperated. What had Williams done to cause it? Would she tell him? If not, would asking upset her even more?

Phillip wished he'd listened to Pearl. "I, ah, I'm sorry to disturb you. Just wanted to let you know . . . I'm on my way back to Gabe's room."

"You aren't disturbing us. We're through here." After a quick glance toward Williams, Emily added, *"Right?"*

Now, the *surgeon* looked uncomfortable. One forefinger held back the gold cufflinked sleeve of his starched white shirt. "See you in two hours." He walked quickly toward her and, one hand on the bronze-toned doorknob, said, "I trust you'll be on time?" Then he shut the door.

Emily, fists balled up at her sides, growled under her breath. "That man," she said through clenched teeth, "can be so . . . so —"

"If I had a dollar for every time I heard that," Pearl injected. An empathetic smile softened her expression. "I'll say a prayer for your little boy. And one for you, too, Dr. White. You're going to need it."

CHAPTER FIFTEEN

"Will you sit *down*? You're gonna wear a groove in that tile."

Phillip stopped pacing long enough to say, "I can't sit. I keep wondering how things are going in there."

"I know Em. She'll be out shortly to update you. Now park it, will ya?"

He chose the chair across from Pete's. "It's good of you to stay. But you don't need to. I'll be fine."

"I want to be here, for you *and* Emily." He paused, then said, "So what's on your mind? Besides Gabe and the operation, I mean."

He'd feel ridiculous, admitting jealousy of an old beau. When he'd asked what Williams said to put her in such a foul mood, she'd waved the question away. The notion that she still cared enough about the man to let him upset her that much . . .

"Tell me, Pete, what's going on between

Emily and that nurse back at Garrett Regional?"

"Who, Barbara?" Pete shook his head. "That woman needs to get a grip."

Phillip waited, and hoped Pete's explanation might help him better understand Emily's attachment to Williams.

"There's this male nurse, see. Mike Shaffer. Nice guy. Does a good job, far as I can tell. And well, Barbara was *all* wrapped up in him. Followed him around like a well-trained pup. Bu-u-t . . ."

"But Mike was interested in Emily," Phillip finished.

"Yup."

It seemed he'd opened the proverbial can of worms: Had Emily been interested in Mike, too?

"Easy, pal," Pete teased. "Em was nice to him, but that was it. No surprise there. She's nice to everyone, y'know? Mike made some half-baked attempts to ask her out, and when she said no a coupla times, he got the message. Moved on to some nurse who left the hospital to work for some pediatrician in McHenry. Barbara . . . Barbara did *not* take it well. You want my opinion? She convinced herself that Emily is the reason they're not . . ." He crossed index finger over forefinger.

"Wow."

"Yeah, wow," Pete agreed. "Are Amish women bitter like that?"

"You're askin' the wrong guy. What I know about women wouldn't fill a thimble."

"Aw, gimme a break. You have a mother and a sister. You were married. You seriously expect me to believe there aren't a couple young beauties in Pleasant Valley with their bonnets set for good-lookin', eligible you?"

Phillip joined Pete's quiet laughter. "Trust me, no one in the community has shown any interest in me."

"No kiddin'?"

"No kiddin'."

"Mind if I ask you a question?"

"You can ask. . . ."

"Yeah, yeah, we've been down that road before. But be honest now. How hard has it been to swap the Pennsylvania Dutch–style talk for, what do you guys call it?"

"English."

"Yeah, right. You guys call us *Englishers*." He rested an ankle on a knee. "Feel free to tell me to butt out."

"Okay . . ."

"Your family isn't all over you, nagging you to *stop* speaking 'English' and go back to the German? And they aren't making you nuts, asking where your suspenders and straw hat are, and why you don't wear a beard?"

Phillip thought he'd answered these questions, days ago, but apparently, not well enough to satisfy Pete's curiosity. What harm could come from going over it, again?

"At first, the bishop and a few of the elders had a problem with it. But I keep my head down. Work hard. Help out when I see a need. Take care of my mother and Gabe. I suppose they decided to take the 'leave well enough alone' mindset."

"So then, no talk of shunning you."

The word hit like a punch. *If* he left the community, Phillip wanted to do it on his own terms, with no hard feelings between him and family and friends. He was even less prepared for the second punch: He didn't want to leave the Plain life, especially not by way of shunning.

"Not yet."

Pete chuckled. "Whew, right?"

"Yeah, whew." Should he confess the thoughts that had been tumbling in his head since long before Gabe's diagnosis? That he'd wanted *out*? That if he wasn't worried about breaking his mother's heart, if he could find someone trustworthy to care for Gabe, he might have packed up and left months ago?

"So answer me something, Phil. Let's say you meet some nice Englisher gal, and the two of you hit it off. What happens then? I mean, does she move to Pleasant Valley with you and your mom and Gabe? Or do you and Gabe set up house with her in . . . in whatever town she lives in?"

Phillip didn't have to be a genius to figure out who Pete was talking about. But being a genius might have helped him come up with honest answers to the tough questions.

"I only ask because, well, I've seen the way you and Emily look at each other."

"You're making too much of that." *Everyone* was making too much of it! "She's just trying to picture me with the Amish beard."

"Oh, you're hilarious. I can see it now . . ." He swiped at the air, as if painting a marquee: "Phillip Baker, the country's first Amish comic." Pete quickly grew serious as he said, "Phil. I mean this: You can be honest with me." He lifted a hand, as if taking an oath. "I won't tell a soul. Not even Emily. Admit it. You're sweet on her, aren't you?"

"Sweet on her? Were you born in the last century?"

"Okay. All right. Fine. If cracking jokes makes it easier to avoid the truth . . ."

"Here's the truth, Pete. My only son is in

the OR, fighting for his life. Your sister is his doctor. Her decisions have been good for him, from ordering all those tests to find out what's wrong with him to introducing us to Williams. Convincing you that I'm not sweet on your sister . . . Suffice it to say that isn't first and foremost in my mind right now."

"I hear ya, Phil. My apologies. Sometimes the stuff that comes outta my mouth —"

"I'm not sure if my feelings for Emily are rooted in gratitude, or if there's more to it. But like I said, this isn't the time or place to talk about it."

Her brother nodded. "I think you're wrong. It's eating at you. Anyone can see that. So why not 'fess up? Get it out in the open — at least with me — so you can start figuring things out." He met Phillip's eyes. "I know things would be challenging, what with you being Amish and her being English and all, but just so you know, I haven't changed my mind: I still think you'd be good for each other. Real good. *And* Gabe thinks the world of her. She's crazy about him, too." He held up a hand to forestall any retort Phillip might make. "I'm sure your mom does a bang-up job, taking care of the kid. But she isn't getting any younger, y'know. Maybe she'd *like* a break."

"Sounds like you've given the matter a great deal of thought."

"Sounds like *you've* been reading legal journals."

The moment of companionable laughter ended when Phillip got up, started pacing again. He paused near the doors to the surgical suite. "How long has it been?"

"Two hours. Two and a half, maybe."

He drove a hand through his hair. "Feels like twice that."

Pete stood, stretched, and said around a yawn, "How 'bout I see if I can scare us up some coffee. Maybe a bagel, or a Danish or something."

Phillip didn't need a drink. Didn't need something to eat. All he needed was to hear that his boy was all right, that between them, Williams and Emily were giving Gabe a chance at a good, long future.

Williams and Emily. He didn't like the sound of that. Liked the way it felt even less.

And there you go, thinking only of yourself again! When had he become such a self-centered, selfish man? Pete had been here for more than an hour, hadn't taken a sip or a bite in all that time. Maybe his offer was a hint that *he* wanted something to eat and drink but didn't want to do it in front of Phillip.

"That'd be great. Thanks, Pete."

Phillip decided that while Pete was gone, he'd spend some time in the chapel. God was probably less pleased with him than he was with himself, but he had to believe the Almighty wouldn't hold the sins of the father against an innocent, sickly little boy.

Phillip wandered the halls for what seemed like half an hour, stopping when he reached the administration building. There, under a great glass dome, stood a statue of Jesus, arms spread as if welcoming all who entered. Phillip stared up at the kindly face, mesmerized by the compassion in the Savior's eyes.

"You know who this is?" said the elderly woman beside him.

"Why, it's Jesus of course."

"Oh, He's not just Jesus. This here," she said, "is a duplicate of the *Christus Consolator*. He's made of one hundred percent Carrara marble, don't you know. Yessir, He surely is."

She grabbed Phillip's arm, urged him to look back up into the kindly face.

"This Jesus, He's been here since, well, I can't remember when He got here, exactly. But I remember this: They brought Him here from the wharf. Pulled Him over on a wooden sled, yessir, and it was drawn by four horses. And that wagon rolled all the way up Broadway. Didn't stop until it got to the north entrance, there." She jerked a thumb over her shoulder, then patted the statue's right foot. "See how His toes are all worn down?"

"I do."

"You know how they got that way?" She didn't wait for a reply. "It happened bit by bit, year by year, because hundreds of people, maybe even thousands of people, have rubbed His feet as they go by. They ask Him to watch over things. Doctors and nurses ask Him to bless the work of their hands. Patients beg for healing. Mothers and fathers, sisters and brothers, all want the same thing — healing for their loved ones."

She heaved a great sigh. "I believe the original plan was, beautiful as He is, He'd be some kinda fine decoration. But He's so much more. Why, this statue became a symbol of hope." She nodded. "Yessir, hope. That's what He is, all right."

Now, the woman looked up into Phillip's face. "Tell me, son, what brings *you* here, to the feet of Jesus?"

"My, ah, my little boy. He's in surgery right now. His heart is —"

"No need to go into the details," she interrupted. "*He* knows your need. And He will answer your prayers."

Phillip's experience with prayer hadn't left him much reason to feel optimistic. And yet, looking into her dark eyes, hope flickered in his heart.

"I see that you're wearing those peculiar work shoes. Talk a bit funny, too." She narrowed one eye. "You one of those Amish fellas?"

Chuckling, he said, "Yes, I'm Amish."

"Pennsylvania?"

"Maryland's Allegheny Mountains."

"Well, shoo-eee, you're a long way from home, ain't you?"

"A few hours . . ."

She squinted the other eye. "Now, wait just a li'l minute here. I thought you Amish didn't believe in medicine. Or doctors. Or hospitals."

"That's true for some communities."

"But not yours?"

"My community is New Order Amish, so on occasion, modern medicine is allowed." It felt strange, calling it *his* community, because he hadn't felt part of Pleasant Valley for a long time. If they'd loosened the rules for his father, his brother, Rebecca . . .

Phillip glanced around, wondering about the woman's family members. "What brings you here?"

"My husband. He had a heart attack. Big one. 'Widow-maker,' they called it. Doctor by the name of Duke gave him a four-way bypass. He's up in the CICU right now, sleepin' off the drugs."

"My son is being operated on right now."

"You taking him home soon?"

"That'll depend on how things go during the next few hours."

"Oh, he'll be fine. Just fine. I feel it in my bones."

"And your husband? How long will he be here?"

"Oh, the doctor says a week, maybe more. Lord but I'm glad I called nine-one-one when I did. Right after I made him eat four aspirins, dry, like they were M&Ms. I said, 'No water for you, mister! You just set there with your La-Z-Boy's footrest down, and cough. Cough hard. Cough a lot,' I said. The doctor said I saved his life." She snickered behind one withered hand. "First time that man sasses me, don't you know I'm gonna remind him of that!"

"Your husband is a lucky man."

"Blessed, not lucky. What about you, son? Where's your wife?"

"I, ah, she died. A few years ago."

She shook her head. "Mmm-mmm-mmm.

Now ain't that a sorry shame. Young handsome man like you, all alone here with a sick child. How old is the boy?"

"Four. Soon to be five."

"Mmm-mmm-mmm. Poor li'l thing." She touched the statue's toes again. "So in all this time since your wife passed, why didn't you remarry? Can't be easy, raising a young'un all by yourself."

"My mother helps out."

"Well bless her old soul." The woman cackled. "You got somebody in mind, though, I can tell."

"Oh?"

"Can't say why, exactly, but . . . you got a *look* about you. Like the love bug bit you good and hard." She snickered again but sobered quickly. "Now, stop frettin', son. I'm a good judge of character. Everybody says so. You're a good man. A decent man. I can see it in your eyes. You've got no reason to feel guilty about lovin' someone new. Why, I expect even your wife would tell you the same. It's what I'd tell my husband, if the good Lord saw fit to call me home!"

He didn't feel guilty . . . exactly. Confused. Frustrated. Annoyed by the community's inflexible rules —

"Ah, I get it. She isn't Amish, is she?"

How she'd guessed such a thing, Phillip

couldn't say. Would she still think he was good and decent if he admitted that he'd broken another inflexible rule by falling for Gabe's doctor?

"Quit your worrying now, hear? It's like that old song says. Y'gotta have hope. And remember, *He's* watching your boy. Watching as closely as if the little one was His own." She winked. "Because the truth is, that boy of yours *is* His own."

She hitched her purse strap higher on her shoulder. "Guess I best be getting back to my man. I want to be there when he wakes up. Just needed a minute here with *Him,* to put my mind right. But you get that, don't you?"

Phillip nodded, and she said, "I'll say a prayer for you and your boy, Mr. Amish."

"Thank you. I'll do the same."

"Never doubted it for a minute. Like I said, you're a good and decent man. I can see it in your eyes. Take a little advice from somebody who's run around the block a time or two: Whatever's eatin' at your soul, let it go. Holding on to things like that, well, they'll fester, make you even more miserable than you already are."

"Thanks," he said again, and when she rounded the corner, Phillip touched the statue's toes. Eyes closed, he whispered,

"I'm asking for Gabe, not myself: Watch over him. Heal him, so I can bring him home to live a long, happy, healthy life."

"Mister?"

He looked down at the small girl standing near his elbow. She couldn't have been more than six. What sort of parent would allow a young child to wander, alone, in a hospital so large people called it a small city?

"Where's your mother?"

"Over there." She pointed across the way, where a man and woman stood, each clutching the hands of twin boys. "Mama said you looked sad, because maybe someone you love died."

Several someones, to be precise. But she didn't need to hear that. "My little boy is upstairs, in the operating room."

Nodding, she held up a wrinkled tissue. "Mama said you might need this, to wipe away your teardrops."

Until that moment, Phillip hadn't realized his eyes were damp. Blinking, he returned the woman's smile. "Thank you," he said, accepting the tissue. "And thank your mama, too."

The girl grinned, exposing four missing front teeth. Before long, Gabe would have a smile like that.

He hoped. . . .

"She said to tell you we're praying for you!" And then she dashed off without another word or a backward glance, leaving Phillip to accept that since finding the statue, two people had promised to pray for him and Gabe.

The elderly woman had been right: The statue was a conduit to hope. Perhaps his indecision about leaving Pleasant Valley had been orchestrated by the Almighty: If he'd gone away when the idea first struck, he wouldn't have been near Garrett Regional when Gabe collapsed. Wouldn't have been near Emily, who'd led them here, to the best hospital and surgeon on the East Coast. *Definitely something to seriously consider . . .*

He made his way to the long, curved staircase, followed it to the elevators. When at last he reached Gabe's room, it didn't surprise him to find Pete fast asleep in a stiff-backed chair. Smiling, Phillip shook his head. How like Emily's brother to return from the cafeteria with doughnuts, muffins, candy bars, and cheese-filled crackers. For a reason he couldn't explain, the strange assortment of snacks lifted his sagging spirits, and he felt more optimistic about Gabe's future than he had since before Emily's diagnosis.

He pictured her, hunched over the operating table, doing everything in her power to help Dr. Williams save Gabe. Pete was probably right. It wouldn't be easy, merging their Amish and Englisher worlds.

Yesterday at this time, an admission like that would have left him feeling anything *but* hopeful.

Stretching, Pete said around a yawn, "So, you're finally back. Where've you been? The chapel?"

"Thought about it. Couldn't find it. Ended up at the big Jesus statue instead."

"It shows."

Phillip didn't have to ask what Pete meant; calm, he decided, must be a by-product of hope.

"Hey, what do you know about the initials doctors pile up behind their names?"

Pete's face wrinkled with confusion. "Huh?"

"FACC. What's it stand for?"

" 'Fellow of the American College of Cardiology.' It's quite an honor. Doctors have to work hard to earn membership in that exclusive club. It's one of the things Williams used to nag Emily about."

"You have my word."

Pete looked confused again. "About?"

"If something develops between your sister and me, I promise never to nag her."

"Better not." He shook a fist in the air. "I'd hate for either of us to find out the hard way that you have a glass jaw."

During their months apart, Emily had changed in so many ways. She hadn't defended herself against his "you're late" accusation. Held her own as he outlined his step-by-step plans for the boy's surgery. Hadn't given up an iota of information when he pressed her for details about the child's father. It incensed him that she'd fallen for the big, oafish Amishman. And she had fallen for him. Alex could tell, because once upon a time, she'd directed that caring, eyes-for-you-only look at *him.*

Even gowned and masked and hair hidden under a snug skullcap, she looked stunning. Her hands were sure and steady, her gaze serious and straightforward, and within minutes, she'd commanded the respect and cooperation of the surgical team. *His* surgical team. Alex had never wanted her more.

Dr. Rubens had already administered fentanyl-midazolam and monitored the boy's vitals while an OR nurse — Jennings? Mason? — painted his narrow, newly shaved pale chest with Betadine. They were ready.

Alex adjusted his mask, thinking about the two minutes he'd spent with Baker, who'd looked alert and sounded fully informed during the explanation of the ICD insertion. "You know what that is?" Alex had asked. And without hesitation, Baker said, "Implantable cardioverter-defibrillator, the device that will monitor Gabe's heart rhythm and deliver electrical shocks if it starts beating abnormally." He'd continued with a textbook description of the flexible, insulated wire leads that Alex would insert just under the boy's collarbone and secure to the ventricles. He also understood that his son would remain in the hospital for a few days, and that in the coming weeks the ICD could send unnecessary shocks, even if the heartbeat wasn't life-threatening. And he knew which medication to administer if that should happen. Emily, Alex knew, was responsible for the guy's calm, on-target recitation of facts.

He'd been a fool to let her go. With a woman like that by his side —

"Doctor," she said, "should we wrap things up?"

Hands elevated, he said, "Yes. Of course." He avoided her eyes. Her big, long-lashed, sometimes-green-sometimes-brown eyes. Eyes that had once beamed with love, for *him*.

"Doctor?" Jennings-or-Mason said. "Okay

to bandage him up and get him to recovery?"

"Yes," he repeated. "Of course." Alex cleared his throat. "Good work, team."

Now, he looked at Emily. "You want to deliver the good news to the, ah, the father?"

That look on her face . . . he didn't recognize it. But if he had to guess, Alex would have called it indifferent. He'd rather see loathing. At least that would mean she felt *some*thing for him.

"No," she said — and he didn't recognize that tone of voice, either — "you should do it."

He removed his gloves and tossed them onto the tray. If he had any hope of reviving what he'd nearly smothered, he had to tread carefully. And slowly. Trouble was, he didn't have much time. In a day, maybe three, she'd return to Oakland. With her little-boy patient and his anything-but-little Amish daddy. And more likely than not, she'd spend every possible moment with them between now and then.

Feeling helpless, and more than a little hopeless, Alex blasted through the doors between the surgical suite and the waiting area.

"Mr. Baker?"

The man was on his feet in an instant.

"How's Gabe?"

"Things went well, very well. No reason to expect anything but a full recovery."

Pete stepped up beside the father. "That's great news, man." He dropped a brotherly hand onto Baker's shoulder. "Great news."

Alex's mouth went dry. If Pete was here, offering moral support at a time like this, well, what did *that* say about the relationship between Baker and Emily?

Her brother held out a hand. "How're things, Doc?"

He willed himself to grasp it. "Fine. Good. You?"

"Fine. Good," Pete echoed.

"When can I see Gabe?" Baker wanted to know.

At his last physical, Alex had measured six foot one. Yet he had to look up slightly to meet Baker's eyes. Emily had never been the "wowed by broad shoulders" type. A good thing, since he'd never exactly been a heavyweight. And unlike other women he'd dated, she wasn't captivated by his Beneteau Oceanis sailboat. The 1960 Porsche Spyder or plush Harbor East condo. If it impressed her that maître d's at the city's most elegant restaurants knew him by name, or that his friends list included politicians, entertainers, and business moguls, it didn't show. If he'd been as poor and plain as this Amishman, she would have accepted him, as is. Why hadn't he appreciated that about her when they were a couple?

Alex collected himself. "He'll be in recovery for another hour, maybe two."

"Then back to his room?"

"Yes."

Baker leaned slightly left to peer over Alex's shoulder. "Where's Emily?"

What he wouldn't give to tell Baker *She's on her way back to Oakland* or *At my condo, starting dinner for me.* It killed him to say, "Scrubbing up, I imagine."

"Can we wait for her in the recovery room?" Pete asked.

Alex wanted to shout, *No!* Instead, he reminded himself to speak cautiously. "I guess it can't hurt to bend the rules." He stepped aside. "Just follow the green stripe on the floor. You can't miss it."

Just as the men plowed through the doors, Alex saw her, making her way down the hall. The skullcap had mussed her thick curls, and without the bulky surgical gown, she looked tinier, younger than he remembered. Her smile said what words needn't: She was happy to see them. *Both* of them. He watched as she stepped between them, linked her arms with theirs, and walked toward the recovery room. When they told her that he'd bent the rules for them, would it help put him back in her good graces?

A guy can hope, he thought. *A guy can hope. . . .*

CHAPTER SIXTEEN

"It's wrong, I tell you. Just plain wrong. A doctor should never, *ever* get romantically involved with a patient," Barbara announced.

Mike stood, hands on hips and shaking his head. "First of all, Gabe's dad isn't a patient. And secondly, you have no proof that there's anything romantic between him and Dr. White."

"I don't care. It's wrong. *She's* wrong. And it isn't the first time. You know that better than anyone."

"Nothing happened between Dr. White and me. How many times do I have to say it!"

"Fine. Defend her. It's only fair that she has *some*one in her corner."

"Barbara, you need to drop this complaint. You're going to make a fool of yourself."

Arms folded across her chest, she said, "We'll see who looks like the fool."

"Have you even read the manual?"

If that stubborn pout was any indicator, she had not.

"I know romance between doctor and patient is frowned upon," he said. "Once the medical connection ends, though, things change, and there are no hard and fast rules against it." Mike rested his hands on her shoulders, gave her a gentle shake. "In any case, I don't remember reading anything that says it's against the rules for a doctor to associate with the *relative* of a patient."

Barbara slapped his hands away. "Oh, but you're wrong." She slid an iPad from her purse, scrolled through a few pages, and paraphrased: "What matters is how involved the third party is with the medical decision-making process. They cite an example here; if you're a pediatrician working with a three-year-old, dating that child's mom might cross the line." She met his eyes. "Do you get it now? It's wrong, just as I said it was."

"Maybe, but it's still on you to prove there's something going on between them. And to prove Dr. White is exploiting Mr. Baker's trust, or using the relationship to influence his decisions about Gabe."

"Yeah? Really?" She scrolled to another page. "The AMA has dealt with this before. In fact, they published an article about sexual or romantic relations between physicians and" — she drew quote marks in the air — " 'key third parties.' You want proof? Take a look at the AMA's Code of Medical Ethics, Opinion 8.145."

"You're reaching, Barbara. Reaching *way* out there."

"I saw them, Mike. Plain as day, in the middle of a well-lit hospital hallway. She planted one on him. And it lasted a good minute. Two, maybe. I wasn't the only one who saw them. Sheila, Marsha, Libby . . . others, too. We were all shocked. Disgusted. And we're going to do something about it."

Would she have stirred up this hornet's nest if he'd responded to Barbara's flirtations? Mike didn't think so. Dr. White had been polite about it, as was her way, but she'd rejected him, flat out. If anyone had a right to be this angry with her, it was he, not Barbara!

"So they kissed. What's the big deal?"

"What's the . . ." She expelled a groan of frustration. "Mr. Baker is Amish, for starters. Those people are like babes in the woods. They're not used to dealing with predators like Dr. White. He's an innocent, probably has no idea what she did . . . what she's still doing. And as if that isn't bad enough, he's vulnerable, too. Raising that

247

little boy alone and scared to death that he might lose him. Enter the great protector, to arrange an operation at Hopkins, performed by a friend who *just so happens* to be the best in the field. So that now, in addition to being innocent and vulnerable, he's beholden to her too! She's using him, Mike. Can't you see that?"

"What I see," he said, "is that you've painted a dark, ugly picture, and somehow talked a few of your cronies into seeing the same thing. But so far, everything you've said is based on your opinion. And that isn't enough, not nearly enough, to drag Dr. White before the ethics board."

"Not just my opinion. Half a dozen of us are in agreement."

"Does that mean you've already filed a complaint?"

"We're working on the, ah, the *wording.*"

"And when the complaint is free of run-on sentences and dangling modifiers, when all your t's are crossed and your i's are dotted, are you planning to give her a copy?"

"Nope."

Oh, how he wanted to wipe that smug, self-assured smirk from her face!

"Y'know, I never realized just how lucky I am."

"Lucky?"

Her haughty look dimmed, and in its place appeared complete bewilderment.

"I came this close" — he held the pads of his forefinger and thumb nearly together — "to getting involved with you." Mike grimaced. "I feel sorry for Dr. White."

Eyes wide, she said, "You're not going to tell her, are you?"

Yeah, he probably would.

"I thought we were friends."

An old catchphrase came to mind: *"With friends like you . . ."*

She stood close enough that he felt her breath on his cheek when she said, "If you warn her, you'll be sorry."

Maybe, he thought, walking away from her, but not as sorry as he'd feel if he *didn't* warn Dr. White.

"You're sure you don't want more coffee cake, Dad?"

Dutton White Jr. patted his round belly. "Miranda, darlin', if I take one more bite, I'll explode!"

Last time Emily had seen her dad looking this contented had been last Christmas morning, when he'd sat cross-legged on the floor near the tree, passing out packages her sister had wrapped and labeled for her own kids and Joe's.

Now, Dutton pushed back from the big round table. "Does my heart good to see all three of you together."

"You two really should move back to Baltimore," Miranda said. "Just think of all the hours you'd save, driving back and forth on those dangerous, eighteen-wheeler-clogged highways."

"Aw, truck traffic doesn't bother me," Pete said. "But find me a job, and you've got yourself a deal. I've always felt right at home up there in your guest room. Why not make it permanent?"

Miranda's youngest fist-pumped the air. "Do it, Uncle Pete!" His older sister chimed in with, "Yeah! And every Saturday night, we could watch those black-and-white TV shows you like so much, just like when you're here for Thanksgiving and Christmas!"

On the occasions when they'd made the Baltimore-bound trip together, the constant ruckus and lack of privacy had been Joe's main complaint during the drive back to Oakland. Once, she'd teased him, blaming his need for quiet and solitude for his confirmed bachelor status, and he'd countered with, "It'd be different if the noisy busybodies were *mine*."

"That isn't a half-bad idea," Dutton said.

"I won't be around forever, you know."

Joe, grinning like the Cheshire cat, said, "Hmpf. You know what they say . . . 'Only the good die young.' "

It was good, Emily thought, being surrounded by her loving family. All those hours in the OR proved she could spend time with Alex, and not want to wallow in "what could have been" thoughts. It proved something else: Everyone on the team had made it clear that she'd fit right in . . . if a move to Baltimore was in her plans . . .

"Wipe that 'if only' look off your face, Em. You can't leave Garrett Regional, and we both know why."

Dutton, Joe, and Miranda watched her, and so did her nieces and nephews. *Please, Pete.* Please *don't mention* —

"She's too invested in the little boy she brought to Hopkins."

"Why? He doesn't have parents?" Joe asked.

Pete winked, then sent a *don't worry* look her way. "He's Amish, see, and big-hearted Emily is worried — at least this is what *I* think — that he won't get the proper ongoing care now that his operation is over."

Dutton asked, "What's wrong with him?"

"His heart wasn't beating properly," she began, "so we implanted a device that will

251

regulate it."

Everyone seemed suitably impressed, and then Joe said, "Hate to be a party pooper, but I need to get back to the office."

"Tiffany will be here any minute," Miranda added, "to pick me up for the PTA meeting."

"I told Andy I'd meet him at the park." Dutton rubbed his palms together. "Today, I'm gonna wipe up that chessboard with him!"

"Think Mrs. Collins would mind dropping me off at the mall? Caitlin and Penny are meeting me there," Miranda's daughter said. Her son piped up with, "Yeah, and can you take me to Jimmy's? It's right on the way."

"So much for 'you guys oughta uproot your lives, move back to Baltimore for more' " — Pete expelled an exaggerated cough — " 'family closeness.' "

Amid grins and giggles, they grabbed purses, briefcases, keys, and jackets and made their way to the door.

"Make yourselves at home," Miranda said. "Be sure to lock up on your way out."

As soon as the door clicked shut behind her, Emily began gathering paper plates and napkins while Pete stacked the brunch dishes.

"Thanks, Pete, for not blowing the whistle on me."

He'd just bitten the point off a wide slice of apple crumb coffee cake. "Hey. I've always had your back," he said around it. "No reason to shake things up now."

"Still, I appreciate it. Things would have gotten real uncomfortable, real fast, if they found out about Phillip."

Pete snickered. "That's the closest you've come to admitting I was right." Then, "But why would things get prickly? You're single, he's single . . . no harm, no foul." He grabbed a clean paper plate from the cabinet above the sink, carried it toward the family room. "Let's put our feet up, watch some mindless TV sitcoms. No telling when we'll get another chance to relax, surrounded by the comforts of somebody else's home."

Laughing, Emily dropped onto the love seat. "If that's your way of hinting for info on Gabe's condition, I can tell you this: I anticipate a full recovery. With a little luck, he'll be sleeping in his own little bed this time next week."

"I never doubted it for a minute. What I'm wondering is . . . how are things between you and Dr. Dread?"

He'd never liked her ex, and when the relationship ended, Pete never missed a chance to insult Alex.

"He behaved like a consummate pro and a perfect gentleman."

"Hmpf."

"It was a pleasant surprise, believe me."

"So the field is clear, then."

"For . . . ?"

"For you to move forward with the Phillip thing."

"The . . . *what*?"

"C'mon, Em. 'Fess up. You've got a major crush on the guy. There isn't a thing wrong with that." He scrolled through the TV's guide, stopped on a movie set on an Amish farm.

"I've seen that one before. Twice."

"Yeah, me too." He turned down the volume. "But if a big-city FBI agent and an Amish woman could make it work — with the mob pokin' round — why not you and Phillip?"

"It's fiction, for one thing. And the way things ended, we don't know whether or not the characters ended up together."

"Funny, I figured he went back, and the community welcomed him."

Emily had always hoped the same thing. "But still, it's fiction," she repeated.

"Yeah, well, think about this for a minute. Phil's mom could probably use a break. And

Gabe could definitely use a medical professional nearby, to oversee his recovery."

Emily exhaled a heavy sigh. "Pete . . ."

"What? It could work. GPS the distance between your house and Phil's. You'll see for yourself. It's a five-mile drive. Ten minutes, tops. Even a super-busy, über-popular doc like yourself can squeeze that into her schedule. All treelined back roads, I might add, so, tranquility, to boot!"

It did sound lovely. But she couldn't see herself settling into his Amish community. And although Phillip had expressed discontent with the Plain life, she couldn't see him giving it up for the city, either. Emily shook her head.

"Where there's a will," Pete quoted, "there's a way."

"Yeah, and if it ain't broke, don't fix it."

"Dance like nobody's watching."

Laughing, Emily said, "Now you're reaching for straws."

"Oooh, good one. Wish I'd-a thought of it." He sobered slightly. "But you know I'm right. You want a life with him? Go for it. I'm with you, all the way."

She wasn't ready to get into this right now. Didn't know if she'd ever be ready. "I should get back to the hospital. Think Miranda will mind if we borrow her SUV?"

"She told us where the keys are, in case we want to pick up a few things. But I'll take you."

He'd parked the emergency vehicle in their sister's driveway. "Your boss was more than generous, giving you permission to use the ambulance to transport Gabe to Hopkins and back again. We shouldn't take advantage."

"Jake won't see it that way. He knows we have family in town. And I said I'd owe him one. Anyway, it's just a short drive."

He turned off the TV, placed the pizza box on the kitchen table and, jangling his keys, said, "Let's skedaddle, 'cause you-know-who is wondering where you are."

She'd invited Phillip to join them at Miranda's, and he'd wisely declined. She could almost read his mind, churning with reasons why a meeting like that could prove awkward for everyone. "Thanks," he'd said, "but I think I'll stay here, in case Gabe needs me." Right now, he was probably pacing the small space at the foot of Gabe's hospital bed, his gaze flicking from the door to the clock, wondering how much longer before Gabe could sit up. Talk. *Smile.* Was he also wondering how soon she'd return to his side?

"You know I'm right," Pete had said. *"You*

want a life with him? Go for it. I'm with you, all the way."

In the coming weeks, as she monitored Gabe's recovery, Emily would have plenty of time to think and pray, and consider whether to discuss the subject of *them* with Phillip . . .

. . . or not.

According to the clock, she'd been gone for three hours. Why then, did it seem more like three days?

Because, you fool, you're in love with her.

"Dad?"

Phillip stood at Gabe's side. "What is it, Son?"

"Did you call *Grossmammi?*"

"I did. Called your aunt Hannah, too. They're both real happy that you're doing so well. Said to tell you they miss you and can't wait to see you. John and Paul said the same."

"When can I go home?"

"Well, Dr. Williams needs to have a look at your incision, at your chart, and if everything is fine — and I expect it will be — he'll want to keep an eye on you for a few days before signing your release papers."

"What about Dr. White?"

"Oh, I'm sure she'll weigh in, too."

"Where is she?"

"She and Pete are spending a little time with family. Living four hours away makes gatherings a little tough, so they decided to make good use of their time in Baltimore."

"I would not like it if we lived far from family."

Phillip's grip on the bed's guardrail tightened. He wouldn't like it, either. Yes, he still had unresolved issues with the community's rules, but even so, he couldn't imagine living far from his family.

The right side of his boy's mouth lifted slightly. "Your stomach is rumbling again. Did you skip breakfast?"

"I grabbed a muffin from the doughnut cart," Phillip told him.

"*Grossmammi* would scold you for that."

"You're right. So let's not tell her, okay?"

"Only if she asks."

"Thanks, li'l buddy." He mussed Gabe's hair. "Do you hurt anywhere?"

"No. It itches under the bandage, though."

"You know better than to scratch it, right?"

"Yes. Dr. White told me that scratching could break the stitches." Eyes wide, he added, "I do not want my insides falling outside!"

"That wouldn't happen, even if you

popped a stitch or two. But she's right. It's best to leave the incision alone."

"Soon, they will bring my lunch. If you talk to the nurses, they can order a tray for you. Then we could eat together. Almost as good as being home again."

"Great idea. Stay put while I get in an order."

"Da-a-ad . . ."

"Yeah?"

"Where would I *go*?" He thumped the right bed guard, then the left.

"I see your point." He tweaked Gabe's nose, then hurried toward the nurses' station.

"Sorry I waited until the last minute to do this," he said, "but is it too late to order a lunch tray? Nothing special. Whatever they're bringing for Gabe is fine."

"Happy to do it for you, Mr. Baker." The nurse picked up the phone, pecked the keys that connected her to the dietary department, and asked that a second tray be delivered to Gabe's room. She looked over his shoulder and, smiling, said, "Dr. White! Have you been back long?"

"Only a few minutes."

Emily was wearing jeans and a pale pink shirt that matched her tiny sneakers. Phillip thought she looked gorgeous with her hair pulled back in a girlish ponytail. But who was he kidding? He thought she looked gorgeous when her hair fell across her slender shoulders, when she braided it, when she twisted it into a bun atop her head. If she wore a long, plain dress and apron and a cap on her head . . .

Phillip shook his head. "We can get you a tray," he told her, "and you can join us for lunch."

When she smiled up at him that way, it was all Phillip could do not to kiss her.

"The family got together for brunch, but I wasn't all that hungry. I need to check on Gabe, anyway, so . . ."

"Couple of questions I'd like to ask you first, in private, if that's okay."

"Sure. Of course. Let's see if the family waiting area is available."

"If it isn't," the nurse said with a wink, "feel free to use the nurses' lounge."

They thanked her and hurried to the end of the hall.

"Empty," he said, "thank God."

"You wanted to ask —"

"How was the visit with your family?"

Phillip wrapped his arms around her, pulled her close. And she didn't fight it. In a minute, he intended to kiss her, but first things first. "Everyone healthy? Happy to see you?"

"Too happy, you might say. They're all on a mission to get Pete and me to transfer back to Baltimore."

Fear thudded in his heart. "Wait. Permanently? But . . . but you can't!"

Emily blinked up at him, as if to say, *Why can't I?*

"Your patients would miss you. Gabe, for one." *And so would I!*

"A move like that would take months of planning. I'd need to find a job. A place to live. Get the utilities turned off here, and turned on there. Fill out change of address forms for magazine subscriptions. Packing everything up. Arranging for a moving van. Stuff like that takes time."

"Then I advise against it. With your work schedule, time is one thing you don't have. At least, not in excess."

She tidied his collar, then smoothed his shirt's button flap with a wifely pat-pat-pat. "I'll definitely give your opinion serious consideration."

"What I think means that much to you, does it?"

Emily pursed her lips, fully prepared to answer his question. He silenced her with a kiss. A long, delicious, pulse-pounding kiss. And when it ended, he said, "Sorry to just spring that on you. I couldn't help myself. I realize we have a lot to talk about before . . ."

"Yes, yes we do."

Smiling prettily, she lifted her shoulders in a dainty shrug. When Emily blushed, she woke his desire to kiss her again.

And so he did.

"Keep that up," she said breathily, "and people will think you like me or something!"

Like you? Phillip almost laughed out loud. *Emily White, I* love *you!*

"So that's it? You just called me in here to" — she licked her lips — "to let me know that you missed me?"

"How's Gabe?" He already knew the answer to that, thanks to the nurse who'd explained every lab test result.

"I haven't checked his latest vitals, but I'm sure he's doing fine. Because . . ."

Because *Alex* is good at what he does?

". . . because he's a little fighter. And fighters almost always do well."

Almost? Phillip didn't think he wanted her to clarify that.

She grasped his hand, gave it a quick squeeze, then turned him loose.

"Let's go see for ourselves." She led the way to Gabe's room.

"Get everything, ah, worked out?" the

nurse asked as she and Phillip passed by.

"For the most part, yes," Emily said. "Has lunch been delivered yet?"

"Yep, and Gabe's thrilled. They brought him sweet potato fries and crispy chicken, air-fried, of course, and chocolate cake."

They found Gabe sitting up, happily munching his meal. With one hand over his mouth, he said, "Your food is over there, Dad, on the windowsill."

Phillip wasn't hungry but, knowing he needed to keep up his strength, he placed his tray on the wheeled food cart and rolled it up to the chair in the corner. Emily stood in the opposite corner, reading the computer screen, then moved to Gabe's bedside.

"You can keep eating," she said, fingertips pressed to his inner wrist. "I just want to check your pulse and stuff like that."

Phillip half listened as she asked if Gabe felt tired, about aches and pains, dizziness. The other half of his brain recalled how, after spending time at the feet of the Jesus statue, he'd thought about whether or not things could work out between an Amishman and an Englisher. It hadn't been easy, admitting that their differences outweighed the similarities: Her educational accomplishments were as long as his forearm, while his reading materials consisted of manuals that explained how to operate power tools. Her work had earned the respect of administrators and peers alike, and even his regular customers knew they could replace him in no time. Her family ties were strong; except for Gabe, he preferred to spend time alone. Despite all that, Pete insisted that things could work out . . . if they were willing to make the effort.

Was he willing? Was *she*?

"Headache?"

Phillip had been so lost in thought that he hadn't even noticed her approach. Startled, he dropped his fork, and it hit the tray with a clatter.

"No."

She pressed a palm to his forehead. "It's been a stressful couple of days. It wouldn't surprise me if your immune system took a hit."

"Really, I'm fine."

Emily bent at the waist and, lips a mere inch from his earlobe, whispered, "Oh, I agree, Mr. Baker. You're fine, all right."

He'd never seen her this way before . . . playful and flirty as a young girl. Phillip liked it. Liked it a lot. He might have said so . . .

. . . if Alex Williams hadn't chosen that moment to walk into the room.

Emily stood up straight and, smiling, said, "Alex. Hello."

The surgeon made no effort to mask his disapproval of what he'd witnessed. Made no attempt to reply, either. After placing his medical bag and suit coat at the foot of Gabe's bed, he inspected the food tray.

"Not bad, li'l guy, not bad at all. A good appetite is a good sign."

Gabe put down his fork. "Does that mean I get to go home today?"

Laughing, Alex found his stethoscope and pressed its diaphragm to Gabe's chest. Eyes on the red and yellow emergency and electrical receptacles above the headboard, he said, "If things continue as they have been, day after tomorrow. Maybe."

When Gabe's smile disappeared, Alex tacked on, "I'll be back, every day, to check on you, make sure everything is shipshape." Straightening, he retrieved his jacket, slung it over his shoulder. "Any questions?"

"I only had one, and you already answered it."

"Sorry, li'l guy. But if we send you home before you're ready, you'll just end up right back here."

"I understand. I am not happy about it, but as my dad always says, 'A man is not a man until he learns to cope with things he

265

cannot control.' "

Alex met Phillip's eyes, a look of grudging admiration on his face. Turning his attention to Gabe again, he said, "Your father is a very wise man." His gaze flicked to Emily. "He has excellent taste, too."

"Oh," Gabe said, "he did not eat breakfast here with me." He sent a loving glance toward Phillip. "Most days, he does not eat breakfast at all."

Alex tucked the stethoscope back into his bag. "Well then, here's something you can teach *him:* 'Breakfast is the most important meal of the day.' "

"Oh, he knows that one." Gabe giggled. "My *grossmammi* says it *all* the time, right, Dad?"

Phillip stiffened, wondering how the surgeon might respond.

"Seems your dad and I have more than one thing in common." Alex sent a caring smile in Emily's direction. "I don't usually eat breakfast, either."

Alex shrugged into his jacket and, as he gripped the handle of his bag, said, "I'll be back first thing in the morning. Keep up the good work, and you might just get to sleep in your own bed in a few nights."

Emily positioned herself directly across from Alex. "Isn't that great news, Gabe? I'll have to call Pete, make sure he'll be ready to roll at a moment's notice."

Alex frowned, then met Phillip's eyes. "Any questions, Mr. Baker?"

Standing beside Emily, he shook his head. "No, no questions. But I'd like to say that I'm grateful." Reaching across Gabe to shake the doctor's hand, he said, "Thank you seems a paltry thing to say under the circumstances." As Williams clasped his hand, Phillip said, "But thank you."

"Just doin' my job." Halfway to the door, he faced Emily. "A word, Dr. White?"

She hesitated, but only for an instant. Phillip had to give it to her. There were no former girlfriends in his past, but he doubted he'd handle work-related *or* social interactions anywhere near as well as she did.

His stomach tightened when, as they entered the hall, Williams's palm rested on her lower back, tightened still more when she didn't reject the possessive gesture. Memory of the way her warm little body melded to his when she'd received his kiss — when she'd *returned* it with equal ardor — sparked in his mind. Had she responded that way to Williams? Had the two of them shared *more* than kisses?

"Dad? *Dad?*"

The boy's worried voice broke into his thoughts.

"What's wrong, li'l buddy?"

"You told Dr. White that your head does not hurt. But *does* it?"

"No, I'm fine, Son."

"Then . . . why is your face all crinkled up like the time you hit your thumb with a hammer?"

He could explain with, *I'm thinking about the bills that have piled up while we were away* or *It's going to take me months to catch up.* But Gabe, big-hearted and too smart for his own good, would blame himself, and right now, healing should be the only thing on his mind.

He stretched out on the bed, draped an arm over Gabe's shoulders. "Guess sleeping in our own beds is gonna be good for both of us, huh?"

It had been the right thing to say, because immediately, Gabe relaxed. "I can hardly wait to get home. It feels like we have been away for a whole long year instead of a little short week!" Then, using the pad of his forefinger, he plugged the hole in his drinking straw, trapping apple juice. Uncovering it, he watched the golden liquid dribble back into the cup. "Look, Dad, a siphon."

"Right you are, Son. Right you are."

A month or so ago, Gabe had joined him in the shop, tiny booted feet firmly planted on the *mummy schtool* that helped him to reach the workbench. Always eager to learn, Gabe watched closely as Phillip suctioned gasoline from a broken chain saw, using a thin black tube. With no prompting from Phillip, he'd recalled an earlier lesson, about how pressure and gravity worked together to draw a liquid from an enclosed space . . . in that case, a combine. That a boy his age could so easily pull the lessons together amazed Phillip, but then, Gabe had been amazing him from day one: walking by nine months, forming sentences before he was two, teaching himself to read — one pudgy finger following every line in his grand-mother's cookbook — and how to multiply and divide by listening as she doubled or halved recipes. In a couple of months, he'd turn five, but Phillip still hadn't found a suitable description for how he felt when others commented on his boy's wit and intelligence. It came to him just then: *blessed*. And thanks to Emily . . .

The mere thought of how close he'd come to losing his precious son put a lump in his throat. And he hadn't forgotten the list of warnings Emily and Williams had recited, either: The ICD might malfunction; the anti-arrhythmic drugs might cause bronchial spasms and put Gabe into cardiac arrest . . . Better to concentrate on what should go right, he decided, instead of the many frightening things that could go wrong. With Emily at their side, overseeing tests to make sure the defibrillator was doing its job, tracking Gabe's overall health and well-being, he saw no reason to believe anything would change.

Not even if she and Williams picked up where they'd left off?

Eyes clenched tight, he ground his molars together. *You're being ridiculous.* Because what grown man would feel this way about a woman he'd known for — how had Gabe put it — a little short week?

Emily feels something for you, too, his heart said.

She's just doing her job, said his brain.

No, his heart insisted, *one person doesn't kiss another person that way unless —*

She probably still has feelings for what's-his-name. You saw the way he touched her . . . the way she let *him touch her . . .*

They're colleagues, nothing more. She's all I'll ever need.

Oh, grow up. In a day or two, you're going home. Home to your Amish community and your Amish mother and your Amish job. Keep-

ing Gabe safe and healthy, that's what you should be thinking about, not a romance that you cooked up because you were lonely and afraid of losing Gabe.

Speaking of Gabe, he'd have a full-time medical person nearby at all times if —

If, countered his brain, *biggest li'l word in the English language. And speaking of* English . . . *Emily is a city girl with a city girl's tastes, a career woman with a busy, productive, very* English *life. She's a good woman with a big heart. Those hugs? Those kisses? Just her 'good doctor' way of consoling a sick little boy's worried father.*

Yeah, well, what about the way she whispered in my ear a little while ago, all girlish and flirty and saying I'm fine. *Was she consoling me* then?

Yeah, well, ask yourself this: What woman in her right mind would trade her career, her busy life and all its movies and plays and restaurants for an undereducated Amish mechanic, with a sickly little boy and more bills than hairs on his head . . . who still lives with his mother?

It hurt to admit it, but his brain was right. Emily would never give up everything for someone with so little to offer.

Tears stung his eyes, and to hide them, he

buried his face in Gabe's hair.

Gabe snuggled closer. "Love you, Dad."

It wasn't easy, but somehow, Phillip managed to say, "Love you more."

And it was true. So true that the lump in his throat began to throb.

"Well now, isn't this a pretty picture."

"Emily." He sat up straighter. Was she actually upset, or had his disquieting thoughts only made it seem that way? "Are you . . . is everything all right?"

"Why wouldn't it be?"

"You and Dr. Williams . . . you two talked for quite a long time. I thought maybe . . ." He glanced down at Gabe, to indicate they might have discussed the boy's condition.

She waved the comment away, a good thing, because Gabe was listening. Closely.

"It was . . ." Frowning slightly, Emily said, "Alex barely mentioned Gabe."

Her lips — lips that had tenderly brushed his ear such a short time ago — drew down at the corners. And a blush colored her cheeks. Had Williams hurt her, yet again?

"I told him what a wonderful caretaker your mother is and assured him Gabe will be in good hands." Zeroing in on her young patient, she smiled like a doting mother. "Vitals have a tendency to change as the day goes on, but if your numbers remain in

272

the safe zone, he'll let you go home, first thing in the morning."

During the ride to Hopkins, she and Phillip had shared the narrow bench in the back of the ambulance, laughing and joking to ease Gabe's fears. But thanks to his recent mind ramblings, he believed, the trip home wouldn't feel anywhere near as warm. With any luck, during the hours-long ride, she'd lecture him about Gabe's care. Doze off . . . and snore. Sing off-key. It didn't matter *what,* as long as she armed him with reasons to like her a little less.

"When was the last time you ate something?"

Good, he thought. The nagging had begun, already. "Found a muffin in the family lounge. And there's a whole tray of food over there."

"Mmm-hmm." One fist resting on a curvy hip, she said, "And how much of it did you actually eat?"

It was the sort of concerned, caring question a wife might ask. *A wife? Knock it off, Baker. You're supposed to be looking for her* flaws, *not her strengths.*

Emily slid a brand-new coloring book and an unopened box of crayons from her bag. "Here's a little something to keep you busy while I make sure your dad has a proper meal." Aiming the remote at the TV, she tuned in to the cartoon channel. "We won't be long." She winked, then grabbed a handful of Phillip's shirt. "Promise."

Part of him wanted to plant his feet and refuse to follow. But only a small part.

"Where are we going?"

"To the cafeteria. Heard through the grapevine that they're serving lasagna for lunch."

Hands pocketed, he fell into step beside her. "It was good to see Gabe enjoying his breakfast."

"It sure was."

Small talk. Again. But this time, it didn't annoy Phillip. This time, it felt *right.*

"Does it seem to you that we spend a lot of time in elevators?" he asked.

"And waiting for elevators."

"Getting on and off of elevators."

Their laughter echoed in the car. But it was short-lived, because Phillip was trying *not* to enjoy her company.

Before he knew it, they were sharing a table near the windows, poking their fork tines into their lasagna.

"You're going to make yourself sick," she said. "Gabe came through surgery really well, and he's getting better with every passing minute. So relax, will you?"

Tell me it's over between you and Williams, he thought, *and that you* could *live on a forty-acre parcel of farmland in Amish-land. That you'll let them baptize you.* Then *I'll relax.*

Her cell phone buzzed, and as she read the screen, a furrow formed between her brows.

"What? Bad news about a patient?"

"I'm . . . I'm not sure." She turned the device so that he could read the message:

Hope the little boy is doing well. Call me ASAP. Something really important to tell you.

Mike

"Any idea what he's talking about?"

"Only one way to find out." She hit the Return Call button and sat back, fingertips drumming the tabletop, the toe of one tiny, pink-sneakered foot tapping the green-flecked floor. "Rats," she muttered, "it's connecting to voice mail." Several seconds later, she perked up, smiling as if the male nurse was seated with them. "Mike. Hi. It's Emily. Emily White? Sorry I missed your call. Get back to me as soon as you can. Thanks." Pressing the End Call icon, she looked from his bowl of fruit to his eyes.

275

"Do I need to spoon-feed you?"

"Look, Emily, I appreciate your looking out for me, but —"

Now, her phone rang, startling them both. "Mike. Hi. What's up?"

She listened for a moment. Scowled. Got to her feet so fast that she nearly overturned her chair. Phillip considered following her, but if she had wanted him to hear her side of the conversation, would she have stormed off that way?

Emily returned a minute or two later, red-faced and breathing heavily.

"Bad news?"

"No. Yes. Well, it could be. I guess. But I hope not."

Chuckling, Phillip pushed his tray to the center of the table. "All right. I admit it. I have no idea what you're talking about."

She sat down, dropping the phone into her pocket. "Someone saw us," she said from behind her hand, "and she's bringing me before the AMA's ethics board."

"You're the most ethical person I know. So, who's doing that? Better question is, why?"

"Barbara Evans. One of the nurses. She saw us, Phillip."

Not just one of the nurses, Phillip remembered, but the nurse who'd convinced herself Emily had caused Mike's lack of interest in her.

"Wait a minute here. Did you just say she saw us?"

She nodded.

"Saw us . . ." He looked right, then left, and satisfied no one was listening, quietly said, ". . . *kissing?*"

Another nod.

She looked miserable. Embarrassed. Scared.

And he shared every emotion.

Because what she was going through, what she might yet have to go through, was all his fault.

CHAPTER SEVENTEEN

Half a dozen times as they made their way west on I-68, Phillip said he was sorry. He'd said it silently, with his amazing sapphire eyes. By dry-washing his hands, as if the action could cleanse his conscience of some abstract sin.

Now, he lowered his voice to say, "I more or less knew that doctors shouldn't get involved with their patients —"

"Phillip. Please stop doing this to yourself. It's as much my fault as yours. *More* mine than yours, to be honest."

His gaze shifted from Gabe's peacefully sleeping face to her eyes. "How do you figure that?"

From the driver's seat, Pete had leaned slightly right, making it easier for him to hear every word. Later, Emily knew, he'd get her alone and, whether she asked for it or not, share his opinion about Phillip's sincerity.

"Pete's listening," she mouthed, then said aloud, "Maybe we can find a quiet place to talk about it, once we get Gabe settled in at home."

"Sure. I get it." And with that, he leaned back, arms crossed over his chest. "Bet you'll be glad to get home."

"Good thing we don't have pets, right?"

"An animal in the house? With Sarah Baker in charge?" He chuckled. "No way."

"Oh?"

"She was raised by the Old Amish code. Don't get me wrong, she takes good care of her goats and geese, the cow and horses, even the chickens."

"But they have a purpose, to pull plows or buggies, provide food."

"And stud services. If you have a good bull or stallion . . . Let's just say there's a lot of money in it."

"No pets indoors seems a reasonable rule, considering everything else she does."

"Yes."

Did his one-word reply mean he'd grown tired of Sarah being in control of his home, of his son?

"Was your mother very upset when you stopped behaving . . . Amish?"

"At first. But over time, she got used to it. So did the others."

"What others?"

"The bishop. The elders. My sister and her family. Just about everyone in Pleasant Valley."

"It must be difficult, living among people who disapprove of your choices."

"They were there for me when my father died, offering kind words and help with the chores. The same was true after my brother's funeral. And when I lost Rebecca? The entire community rallied round — not too close, just close enough that I understood that if I needed anything, they would provide it."

Was he trying to convince her? Or himself?

"In between the bad times," Phillip continued, "I tried to repay the favors. Small things, like repairing storm-damaged roofs, helping erect barns or round up runaway cows."

He seemed to have found reasons to stay, good reasons. Pleasant Valley was more than just his and Gabe's home. His friends lived there, too.

"I suppose," he said quietly, "if it sometimes seems they disapprove, it's because they want what they believe is best for me."

"If your roles were reversed, how would you behave toward *them*?"

"I don't know." He shrugged again.

"When they do my job and pay my bills . . ."

"Sometimes, though, don't you think it's just easier to go along with things?"

"Amish rules, you mean?"

Heart pounding, Emily whispered, "Yes." She cared about this man, and wanted him to be happy . . . even if it meant —

"Tried that," he said, "and walked around angry all the time."

"Well, bending to the will of others is never easy."

"But . . . ?"

"But neither is living with the distance you've put between yourself and . . . just about everyone."

"Except for Gabe." He turned slightly to face her. "And you."

It all made sense now. At first, she'd thought Gabe's condition had encouraged their . . . friendship. And while that might partially explain their closeness, it was clear that loneliness played a role, too.

"So there is no dog or cat waiting for you at home?" he asked.

Home . . .

"No. Just a few houseplants." And the once-glossy leaves were probably drooping and dull by now. She'd left in such a hurry that there hadn't been time to ask a neighbor to water them. Well, there might have been, if she'd given it a moment's thought.

If you can't plan ahead well enough to protect philodendrons, ferns, and palm trees, how do you hope to mother a sickly little boy and his brokenhearted father?

Gabe took Pete by the hand and led him inside, straight into the parlor, where Sarah sat, adding a square to the quilt on her lap. The minute she saw the boy, she stuck the threaded needle into an apple-shaped pincushion, eased the coverlet into the basket at her feet, and stood up. Her eyes filled with tears as she drew Gabe into a gentle hug. Then she held him at arm's length. *"Laat me je bekijken!"*

"*Grossmammi,* you have looked long enough!" Gabe teased.

"Ah, *du gucksht gut! Du moosht beheef dich. Unt die froher nacht for de Chrischdaag!"*

The boy looked up at Pete. "*Grossmammi* is excited to see us. That is why she speaks the German, and speaks it so fast." Wrapping his arms around her waist, he said, "I do not just look good, I feel good, too. You are right . . . I behaved. And being home again makes me *happier* than on the night before Christmas!"

She threw her head back and laughed. *"Ik*

282

van je hou!"

"I love you, too." He turned to Pete. "This is *Grossmammi.* If you were Amish, like me, you would know that means grandmother." Looking up at Sarah, he added, "This is Pete, *Grossmammi.* He is Dr. White's brother. He drove the ambulance that took me to the first hospital. And he drove the ambulance that took me to Baltimore. He saves lives, too, but in a different way than Dr. White."

Pete whipped off his baseball cap, sent her a quick nod. "Pleased to meet you, ma'am. You've got a terrific grandson here."

Emily had never seen the woman happier. And was it any wonder, with her home filled once again with the men in her life.

"Yes," Sarah said, "he is truly a gift from God." Lifting a corner of her apron, she dabbed at her eyes. "There is coffee on the stove. Come to the kitchen. I will pour for us a cup."

Like a litter of well-trained pups, the foursome followed her.

"*Zitten,* all of you!" she said, pulling out the nearest chair.

But instead of sitting, Emily went to her. "How can I help, Mrs. Baker?"

She didn't answer right away, then after pointing to the cupboard on the opposite wall, said, "Everyone needs a mug." Sarah pulled Emily into a hug. *"Hartelijk dank,* Dr. White. *Bedankt."*

Almost word for word what the young Amish wife had said after Emily threatened to report the abusive husband. "No thanks needed." She stopped herself from saying "Just doing my job" because it would only have been half true. Going the extra mile had been as much for Phillip — and herself — as it had been for Gabe.

Sarah opened the round-edged refrigerator and removed a pitcher of milk.

"Is it from your own cow?"

"From Buttercup. Yes. She is a Black Angus."

"An odd name for an all-black cow," Emily said.

"She has an almost yellow spot, right here." Sarah touched a finger to Emily's chin.

"Maybe later, you can show me."

"Maybe Phillip can show you instead," Sarah replied.

Hands clasped on the table, he said, "It'd be my pleasure."

"Mind if I tag along?" Pete asked.

"And me too?" Gabe said.

"You will rest after your long drive, Grandson." Sarah gave a dismissive shrug. "The rest of you can do as you please. But you might as well make yourselves useful." Sarah tapped the handle of a rough-hewn basket. "Bring in my eggs. But first, *koffie.*" She filled Phillip's mug with one hand, slid a plate of cookies onto the table with the other. "And *koekjes.*"

"I have not had cookies in days and days and *days*!" Gabe said, helping himself to a sugar-topped treat.

Emily took the seat beside him and helped herself to a cookie, too. "The quilt you're working on, Mrs. Baker . . . it'll be lovely. Is it for your own bed, or Gabe's?"

"Oh no." She sat opposite Phillip. "Much too colorful for me. It will be sold at Hannah's shop. The Englishers, they go *zijn gek op* for such things. But if you ask me? I think they should 'go crazy' for living Plain instead." Using her cookie as a pointer, aimed at her son, she winked. "Who knows. They might like it enough to do it for a lifetime."

A subtle invitation for Emily to at least consider what it might be like, taking up residence here on the Bakers' humble farmette? If Phillip's grin was any indicator, the answer was yes. She warned herself not to read too much into Sarah's comment . . . or Phillip's face. The woman had spent a lifetime "speaking Plain." More than likely, she'd referred to *all* Englishers. And Phillip? She didn't quite know what to make of his hopeful expression.

When the cookies were gone and their mugs empty, Sarah got to her feet. "Come with me, Grandson. It is time you had a rest in a bed that does not change into a chair."

He followed dutifully, but not before saying, "If you must leave before I wake up, Pete, will you come back and see me sometime?"

"Why sure. I'd like that." He winked at Sarah. "Especially if *Grossmammi* bakes more cookies."

Phillip stood in the open doorway. "Now, how 'bout that tour?"

"Duer dicht! Je laat de vliegen binnen!"

"No flies are getting in, *Moeder.* And we have English guests, so why all the German today?"

Chin high, Sarah looked from Emily to Pete and back again. "Since they will spend much time here, they need to learn."

Words, Emily told herself. *Just words . . .* Or were they yet another hint that Sarah might give her blessing, should things progress between herself and Phillip? Now that her grandson had been returned to her, his future prospects so much brighter, would she be more open to the world outside Pleasant Valley?

Now, Sarah shooed them outside and left the room.

A warm breeze swept through the tidy yard, rustling tree leaves and bobbing the flower blossoms. A sturdy gust lifted the cap from Pete's head, and he zigged left and zagged right as it bounced and rolled across the lawn. It stopped on the white-painted wooden porch of a small, tidy outbuilding located about thirty yards from the house.

"Is that your workshop?" Emily asked.

Phillip followed her gaze to the white crossbuck door. "It is. Would you like to look inside?"

Walking beside him, she said, "But there isn't a sign."

"A sign?"

"You know, to let people know what sort of business you're in."

"My business is built from repeat customers and word of mouth." He opened the door, and as she entered, said, "If I had a sign, what should it say?"

She looked around at the well-worn surface of the workbench and the tools — screwdrivers, hammers, handsaws, rasps, and wrenches — hanging in order by size on the pegboard above it. On the opposite wall, steel shelves held power tools, paint cans, and stacks of cleaning rags, while jugs of motor oil gleamed in the sunbeam that slanted through the front window. Overhead, fan belts, V-belts, and grooved belts hung from hooks that Phillip had screwed to the rafters. Tidy and dust-free, the shop smelled of fresh wood shavings and gasoline.

"Something simple, I'd think. 'Baker's Engine Repair.' " Forefingers and thumbs forming a square, she squinted. "With a descriptive subtitle, like 'Big or Small, We Fix 'Em All.' "

Reaching up, he straightened the clock that hung beside a pair of tin snips. "I need to move this thing. Every time the door closes, it tilts a bit." He peered through the window. "Look at your brother out there. . . ."

Emily moved closer and stood on tiptoe. She saw a calico kitten walking figure eights around Pete's ankles, then giggled like a child as it jumped up and stuck itself to his right jeans leg. "Have you ever lassoed a cat?"

"As a matter of fact," he drawled, "I'm right handy with a lariat. You know the old saying, 'Jack of all trades, master of few.' Man has to teach himself how to do many things on a spread like this."

How had he learned to imitate Old West cowboys? Had he read a Zane Grey novel or watched an old John Wayne movie? Had it been on the sly, or with the permission of the elders?

"So tell me, Cowboy Phil, how big is your ranch?"

"Just shy of forty acres now. My great-grandfather bought the land back in the twenties, and it's been in the family ever since. Started out with hundreds, but nature can be cruel. Storms, drought, weevils, deer herds, field fires . . . over the years, we had to sell a parcel at a time to make ends meet."

"That's a shame." A question came to mind, and she considered keeping it to herself. "Another reason you're not exactly devoted to God?"

In place of a direct answer, he said, "Want to meet Buttercup?"

"That sounds great." If he preferred not to discuss specific reasons for his anger with the Almighty, so be it.

A moment later, she found herself balancing on the middle board of a split-rail fence, stroking the cow's forehead. "Aren't you a pretty girl!" she cooed. "I'll bet your milk is as sweet as your disposition."

A long pink tongue swiped from Emily's

chin to her forehead, leaving a swath of spittle that smelled like a cross between damp dirt and freshly mowed grass.

"Well, you're welcome, Buttercup!" she said, hopping down from the fence.

Phillip slid a red paisley bandanna from his back pocket, and their fingers touched when he handed it to her. The brief contact reminded her of the time when her older brother told her to test a nine-volt battery. She'd asked how, and Joe said, "Touch your tongue to the terminals. You'll know!" She hadn't enjoyed that mini-jolt at all. But this one? Emily wouldn't mind another pulse!

What's wrong with you! Her imprudent decisions were directly responsible for the Barbara-inspired report that, by now, had probably passed throughout the ethics board. *You need to go home. Go to work. Leave Phillip and his lovely family alone. Period!*

"Sorry she upset you," he said, taking back the bandanna. As he oh-so-gently wiped her face dry, Phillip said, "Don't look that way."

"What way?"

"Embarrassed. You're a city girl. Cow spit isn't a regular part of your days."

If letting him believe that Buttercup's kiss was the reason for her distress made it easier to distance herself, Emily saw no reason to correct him . . . even if it did make her look like a whiny, spoiled brat.

"Does this mean I don't get the rest of the tour?"

" 'Course not." He wadded up the bandanna and tucked it back into his pocket and pointed. "The goats are over there."

"Hey, you two, wait up!" By the time Pete caught up with them, the kitten had snuggled deep into his shirt collar. "So Phil," he said, "any tips for discouraging the affections of a pretty young girl?"

"Sorry, Pete. My knowledge about girls — old, young, or four-legged and furry — is seriously lacking."

"Then I might just have to bring this one home." As if it understood, the cat climbed onto Pete's shoulder and rubbed her cheek against his. "Aw, now, aren't you a sweetheart?" She was purring loudly when he said, "How much do you want for her?"

"You're kidding, right? After all you've done for Gabe and me? If you want her, she's yours. Why, I'll throw in her littermates if you'd like."

"Well then, looks like I need to read up on the care and feeding of felines." He smiled at Emily. "You 'bout ready to hit the road?"

Phillip's disappointment dulled the blue of his eyes. "I was just about to introduce her to the goats. And the chickens." He gestured toward the small field behind the barn, where two cinnamon Morgans grazed contentedly. "Nimblewill and Goldenrod, too." He faced Pete. "With your work schedule, you might want to think about making her into an inside-only cat. All you'll really need is litter, and a box to put it in. Some treats to reward her when she uses it. Some dry food. Bowls that won't tip over easily. A brush. And clippers to trim her nails."

He paused, looked at Pete. At Emily. "What . . . ?"

"I thought your mother disapproved of animals in the house. How did you learn all that?"

"My wife." He turned his attention to Pete again. "She found a kitten, sort of the way you found this one. And like this one, it wouldn't let her be." Another shrug, and then, "She sent me into town for a book about caring for cats. Sent me back again after she'd read it. For food and . . . all the things I just told you about. Named him Trouble, 'cause he climbed everywhere, got into everything." Phillip hung his head.

But hadn't his wife died several years

earlier? Her own mother's cat had lived to be eighteen. Trouble should still be alive. "Where is he now?"

"Don't know. Last time I saw him was the day we buried Rebecca."

The rational side of her brain told her that neither she nor Pete had anything to do with the sadness in his eyes. But the other side, the side that wished she hadn't started falling for him, wanted to ease his discomfort. In a way, by getting too close to him, she had caused his misery. Some of it, anyway.

Change the subject, you ninny, before you start blubbering like a baby.

"Mind if I ask why you named your beautiful horses after weeds?"

A half grin brought some of the light back into his eyes. "After they were weaned, both were picky eaters. Wouldn't touch grain. Wouldn't even eat oats. But for some reason, they gobbled up nimble will and goldenrod. Turns out it was good for them, too, so . . ." He shrugged. "Made sense at the time."

"Makes sense now, too," Pete said.

Phillip ignored the compliment. "What'll you call that li'l gal on your shoulder?"

"Not Callie, that's for sure."

"There's no rush. Just keep an eye on her for a couple days. See how she behaves. If she has habits, that'll give you insights into her personality. That's how I chose Gabe's name. He was three months old, and we were still all calling him Baby Baker. That didn't seem right. Or fair. So I watched him. Listened to him. He hardly ever cried. Smiled all the time. I kept thinking, he's such a little angel. But I wanted him to grow up strong. Take control of his life. I didn't want him to ever feel powerless. Then I remembered that Gabriel was God's messenger. A mighty warrior." His eyes lit up a bit more. "Made sense at the time."

"Makes sense now, too," Pete said again.

Emily didn't want to leave. At least, not just yet. "That big-box store in town is open twenty-four hours. We have time to meet the rest of the menagerie and buy a few things for your little friend, there."

"She's a barn cat," Phillip said. "If you wait a while to leave, you might find out she's wandered off again."

"I don't know much about cats, but seems to me if she was going to wander off, she wouldn't be up here, purring like crazy."

"Have it your way." Phillip turned, started walking toward the goat pen beside the barn. "My mother enjoys these guys. Refuses to name them, though."

She leaned over the gate and held out her hand, and as they nibbled at her fingers,

Emily said, "Why?"

"As a girl, she lived through some hard times. Hard enough that her father was forced to kill her pet goat. A piglet, too. One of the milk cows. She understood why he had to do it, but I don't think she ever got over it. Giving names to things, in her mind anyway, only makes it harder to deal with things like that."

Emily couldn't imagine a scenario in which Phillip would let things get so out of hand.

"I've told her, over and over, that I'd never do anything like that." He patted a goat's head. "They give us milk, and after they're sheared, my mother weaves the hair into yarn."

"And the sheep, too?"

"Yep, the sheep, too."

"She's very industrious."

"I'm lucky to have her."

"She's lucky to have you, too. Don't try to deny it. I won't let you."

"Oh, you won't, huh."

A statement, Emily noted, not a question. But this didn't seem like the time or place to explain why she believed in him, admired him, cared about him . . . and *for* him.

"The chickens," he said, making his way toward the coop across the way, "have two purposes."

"Let me guess: eggs, and meat for soups, stews, and the roasting pan."

"You catch on fast."

"That surprises you?"

"You're a doctor. With who knows how many college degrees and awards. There's no doubt in my mind that you're smart. *Book* smart. People smart, too, to give credit where it's due. But you're a born 'n' bred city girl. A place like this should seem as foreign to you as Egypt or Thailand." He blew a two-note whistle. "Yet there you stand, your used-to-be pink sneakers covered in muck and mud and dung, looking like you don't mind it a bit. Almost like you were born to this life."

That shouldn't have stung, but it did. And as he had that day in the hospital hallway, Phillip tucked a curl behind her ear. She resisted the urge to grasp his hand, bring it to her lips, press a kiss to its calloused palm.

"You're not wearing a bonnet. Or an apron. If you'd been born here, you wouldn't be wearing those blue jeans or that pretty pink blouse." He wrapped a tendril of her hair around his forefinger, then gently tugged, and watched as it slowly slid free and once again dangled near her shoulder. "You'd look fine in a long, plain skirt, in high black boots and a white cap." He took a step closer, then another step. "Ah, but Emily, what a shame it would be to hide that glorious, womanly figure beneath —"

"Uh, hello?" Pete waved his free hand between their faces. "I'm. Still. *He-e-re.*"

If disappointment made noise, it would probably sound a lot like Pete's interruption. It took concentrated effort to end the intense eye contact that linked her and Phillip, just as surely as their embraces had connected them when . . .

When you broke the rules and made a mess of everything for Phillip, for yourself.

She looked at Pete. "Yes, you're here, all right, aren't you?"

He scowled. "I'm beat. I need a shower and a good night's sleep." He stroked the cat's head. "And so does little Clinger here. We want to go home."

"Clinger. I like it," Phillip said. "It fits. I'm glad you chose a name while you were still here."

"Speaking of leaving . . ."

"But Pete, we can't go yet. I said I'd gather eggs for Phillip's mom, remember?"

"Aw, she knows you won't."

"What! Why?"

"For one thing," Pete said, "you don't have anything to put them in. For another, when was the last time you stuck your hand under a hen and, from her point of view, kidnapped her babies? You think she's just gonna sit there and let you get away with that?"

It wasn't like Pete to behave this way. She chalked it up to being away from home for so many days, sleeping in a strange bed, spending countless hours in waiting rooms and behind the wheel, maneuvering the ambulance through highway traffic.

"Ten minutes. I'll make good on my promise, and we'll leave. You have my word."

Pete's shoulders slumped as Phillip said, "There's a box in my workshop. We'll wad up newspapers to soften the bottom. It'll do. You'll see."

"Good grief," Pete said. "Well, you two have fun. Clinger and I will be over there, enjoying the breeze under that tree. If we doze off, don't wake us." Snickering under his breath, he started toward the big oak, then slowed and said over his shoulder, "Don't do anything I wouldn't do, you two."

Phillip shook his head. "Something tells me *that's* a short list."

Mimicking his grin, Emily said, "When you get to know him better, you'll realize Pete personifies the 'all bark, no bite' cliché. Believe me, he's the most straitlaced person

I know."

He slid an arm over her shoulders as if he'd been doing it for years. "I like the sound of that."

It seemed the most natural thing to wrap her arm around his waist, and together, they walked toward his shop.

Once inside, he gripped the side rails of a narrow ladder. "There should be a couple of boxes in the loft," he said, one big booted foot on the first rung. Then, up he climbed, his movements upstairs causing miniscule granules to rain down from between the floorboards.

"What do you keep up there, sand?" she teased.

"Sort of. I use sawdust to soak up gasoline, oil, and grease spills." He leaned over the wobbly railing, balancing a two-by-two-by-two-foot cardboard carton on one shoulder. "Stand back," he said, and tossed it.

It tumbled end over end and landed upside down at her feet, and as she righted it, she heard him say, "You'll find some newspapers in the bottom drawer of my desk."

Not very many, as it turned out. "Are you saving these for any reason?"

Beside her now, he said, "Why do you ask?"

"Well, they're so old, the paper is crisp and yellow." She placed the editions onto the desktop, upsetting a two-inch-thick stack of bills. Crouching to pick them up, Emily groaned. "I'm such a klutz sometimes. Sorry, Phillip." She pretended not to notice familiar return address labels . . . a credit card company, providers of electricity, propane, and telephone services. Two statements had skidded under his desk chair, and she didn't recognize either. She reached for them, but he grabbed her wrist.

"Emily. Just . . . stop. Please," he ground out.

His hand was trembling as he accepted the mail, and she decided that telling him not to feel embarrassed would only make this proud, independent man feel worse. If not for Gabe's illness, he would have taken time to pay these bills. And then it struck her: It would take a while for the hospitals' billing departments to charge Phillip for the room, for the boy's surgery, medications, tests, lab results, and more. She made a mental note to look into ways to secretly help reduce those charges.

She balled up a sheet of newsprint and tossed it into the box. "Have any advice for me? For when I gather up the eggs, I mean?"

Phillip put his mail into the desk's shallow

center drawer and slammed it. "No quick moves," he said, wadding up a ball. "Talk quietly." The gruff tone had left his voice, but clearly, the incident wasn't behind them yet. "And once you start, don't stop or you'll get pecked."

"Can their beaks break the skin?"

"I suppose they could, but I've never seen it."

They continued in silence, crumpling sheets and tossing them, until the paper balls covered the box bottom.

"That oughta do it," he said. "My mother will be pleasantly surprised."

She noticed the ink on his palms. On hers, too. "Is there someplace I can wash up before I touch the eggs?"

"No need for that. Eggs aren't exactly, ah, pristine when they exit the hens."

Emily decided she'd find out soon enough what that meant.

"There's a bathroom back there," he said with a jerk of his head. "Nothing fancy — nothing around here is, because, well, Amish." One shoulder lifted, dropped. "At least it's clean."

Emily closed the door behind her and looked around. The room was tiny and, as her grandmother would have said, clean enough to eat from the floor. She glanced out the window and noted that his attention to detail, like a painter's signature, was written on low-mowed hills and deeply shadowed valleys reminiscent of the Irish countryside. White triple-board fences that ran straight and true kept the livestock safe, and stately trees, planted at precise intervals, provided places for them to escape blistering sun, sideways rain, and the often-fierce Allegheny Mountains wind. The crimson barn beamed bright against the blue sky, and every corner of Sarah's chicken coop had been perfectly mitered. None of this, she knew, had happened recently. And none of it was the result of nature's hand. *Phillip* had preserved the parcel that had been home to four generations of Bakers. He had every right to feel pride in all he'd accomplished, in everything he'd protected.

He hadn't come right out and said it, but painful events of the past led him to believe he'd find happiness and contentment far from this place, these people, this *life.* But nothing could be further from the truth. She'd liked and respected the almost shy, doting father and son she'd met at the hospital. But here, his steps were surer, his back straighter, his words more confident, and she *loved* the man he'd become.

"Thought I'd have to pick the lock," he

said when she returned to the workshop. "Are you okay?"

"I'm more than okay," she said, walking to the open door. "I'm fine, really fine."

The words made a strange, tinny echo in her head, because she'd said almost the same thing in Gabe's hospital room . . . in Alex's presence. Was the faraway look on Phillip's face proof that he remembered that moment, too?

She'd made him uncomfortable, yet again, and didn't like the feeling one bit. So she wiggled her fingers and sent him a wide, silly grin. "Ready when you are, Mr. Baker."

Moments later, they stood, shoulders touching in the chicken coop, a space not much larger than the workshop's bathroom.

"Did you build this yourself?"

He gave her a look that said, *Who else?*

"It's a construction marvel. Places for them to roost and nest, an enclosed space to keep foxes and raccoons out while they run around, special feeders and watering pans . . ."

"The wire mesh keeps out the crows and hawks, but I have to check the caulking every few weeks, make sure there aren't gaps where snakes and rodents can get in."

"Sounds like a lot of work. Who fed and watered the chickens while you were away?"

"Hannah. She brings the boys over twice a day and lets them help. Eli wants to build a coop just like this one, and they'll need to know how to take care of things. How to clean up the poop and feathers and shells."

"Twice a day?"

"Eggs are fragile. Even a slight crack in the shells can allow bacteria inside. And as a doctor, you know what that means."

"Salmonella, for one thing."

"Yup." He mimicked her earlier gesture and wiggled his fingers. "Watch," he said, "and learn."

The hen flapped her wings and cackled quietly as he slid a hand beneath it. Seconds later, he withdrew the hand, and after placing the egg into the box, said, "Your turn."

"There are more under there?"

"Just one. And once you have it, you'll move on down the line. And when we're finished, I'll show you how we wash them, and where we store them."

She took a step closer to the nesting box.

"Remember now," he said softly, "slow and steady, but sure and quick, even if she sets up a fuss. And just so you know, it'll be warm under there, and the egg will feel a little wet. That's the bloom. It helps keep bacteria from getting in."

Twenty minutes later, the box held nine

eggs . . . eggs she'd gathered and washed herself.

"You're a fast learner."

Together, they entered his enclosed back porch.

"A good thing, I suppose, since there's so much to learn around here!"

"Does that mean you want to come back?"

"You bet!"

He was smiling as together, they transferred the clean eggs to a small refrigerator.

"Hannah will come by later and get them."

"To sell in her shop . . ."

"And we'll take these last two inside."

"For cooking and baking."

"Yep, you catch on quick, all right."

She was proud of herself. More important than that, *he* was proud of her, and it showed.

"Want to come upstairs with me, check on Gabe?"

"You bet," she said again, and followed him up the steps.

"Oh, just look at him," she whispered from the foot of Gabe's bed. "He looks like a sleeping angel."

"Sleeping like a baby, thanks to you. And Dr. Williams, of course."

"Of course."

They walked softly all the way to the

kitchen.

"Where's your mother?"

"She could be any one of a dozen places. With her goats. In the basement doing laundry. Out back hanging clothes. In the parlor, sewing . . ." He took her hands in his. "Disappointed that she isn't here, are you?"

Emily couldn't help but feel impressed. He'd read her mood and recognized that she wanted Sarah's approval.

"I should go."

He kissed her fingertips, one at a time. "I wish you didn't have to."

"Pete's waiting."

He kissed her right palm. And the left. "Let him."

"But he's anxious to leave, so we can stop on the way home, to buy supplies for Clinger."

Now, he kissed the inside of her wrist, let his lips linger there, as if counting her pulse beats. "Have you ever been driving along the highway and passed one of those billboards that says, 'If you lived here, you'd be home now.'?"

She had, but Emily didn't trust herself to admit it.

He gathered her close, inhaled deeply. "Emily, Emily, Emily," he breathed into her hair. "What are you thinking?"

That there are so many reasons I can't stay, so many reasons this . . . this thing between us is a bad idea.

"That any minute now," she fibbed, "Pete will burst in here and say, 'Let's hit the road!' "

"Let him."

She felt his lips graze her cheek, press against her temples and chin.

Earlier, she'd acknowledged that he behaved differently here. Emily felt different here, too.

Because right or wrong, she'd given her heart to Phillip Baker, Amishman.

Doug Becker seemed to love his position as chairman of the Ethics Committee, and as if to prove his clout, he'd worn a three-piece suit and silk tie today.

The conference room could easily accommodate all thirty members, each representing the hospital's various departments, from nursing to social work to clergy. The number of empty chairs surprised her. Not even Garrett Regional's legal representative had shown up. A good thing or a bad thing? Emily wondered. Just as surprising was the grand display of pastry trays that ran the length of the table. There would be leftovers, lots of them, and Emily intended to commandeer as many as possible for the lab techs, nurses, and aides whose dedication made her life and the lives of patients so much easier. Even Barbara's coworkers would receive some treats, because they couldn't be held accountable for the petty jealousy that had inspired this meeting.

The chairman stood, cleared his throat, and knocked on the tabletop to silence the quiet murmuring of those present. Barbara, seated across from Mike, smiled sweetly at Doug, while Phillip, in the chair beside Pete's, stared at his hands, folded tightly on the table.

"As you're all no doubt aware," Doug began, "the purpose of this hearing is to consider, debate, and possibly take action on the issues revolving around Dr. White and her alleged relationship with her patient's father, Phillip Baker."

He returned to his seat and scribbled a quick note on the tablet in front of him.

"Let me begin by thanking Ms. Barbara Evans for the wide array of refreshments."

Nods of approval and quiet thank-yous floated around the room, and Doug knocked on the table again.

"Let me state for the record that this is *not* a legal proceeding. It's a hearing, the sole purpose of which is to determine whether or not Dr. White's actions toward Mr. Baker caused harm to her patient . . . Mr. Baker's son."

The woman beside him, who'd been typing notes into a laptop, stopped when he paused.

"Are you getting all of this, Myra?"

She answered in a dull monotone. "Yes, Doug. I'm getting all of this."

"All right then. Let's begin with Ms. Evans." He swiveled his chair to face her. "Barbara, is it your contention that Dr. White initiated a sexual relationship with Mr. Baker?"

"I, well, I saw them kissing. Twice. And both times, it was pretty passionate. If they'd do that in a hallway, outside his little boy's hospital room, where any Tom, Dick, or Harry could see them, I can only imagine what goes on in private."

"Do you have reason to believe the relationship is sexual in nature?"

"Well, I can't be sure, but —"

"What harm came to the patient as a result of this . . . kissing?"

"Well, I'm, I, I'm just as concerned about Mr. Baker's well-being. He's Amish. And the Amish are innocent of things like this. Plus, he's naturally lonely, what with being a widower and all. That makes him vulnerable, as well. And Dr. White knew all that, but she took advantage of his innocence and vulnerability."

Emily couldn't bear to look at Phillip. Barbara had forgotten to say that the Amish were private people, too. He'd probably hate her when this was over, for putting him on display, like one of those fancy pastries!

"Thank you, Ms. Evans." Turning to Pete, Doug said, "Mr. White, you are Dr. White's brother, is that right?"

Pete sat up straighter, shot a wink in her direction. "Yes, and I'm proud of it."

"What, to your knowledge, is the relationship between your sister and Mr. Baker?"

"I guess I'd have to classify it as . . . friendly associates. I've never witnessed anything untoward. And, might I add, I spent a lot of time with them going to and from Hopkins, before and after Gabe's surgery. Spent a good deal of time with them before the trip. After, too. But like I said, I, uh, I don't think I've ever seen them so much as hold hands."

Doug said, "Thank you, Mr. White."

Pete sent the thumbs-up sign to Emily. "Love you," he mouthed. "Bunches."

Until that point, she'd kept a tight rein on her emotions. But Pete's words and gestures reminded her that, despite crazy things like this hearing, she was blessed to love and be loved by a brother like him.

"Mr. Shaffer. It's my understanding that you have strong opinions about these charges?"

Mike got up, leaned both fists on the table, and glared at Barbara. "She's a jealous, vindictive gossip. If, God forbid, I ever end up as a patient in Garrett Regional, I do *not* want a woman like her assigned to my room! Here's the gist of things: She developed a crush on me, but I wasn't interested."

Barbara pounded her fist onto the table. "That's only because *she* had you wrapped around her pinkie!" she shouted.

"Ms. Evans," Doug warned, "please don't make me dismiss you from a case you initiated."

"Ever since then, Barbara has had it in for Dr. White," Mike concluded.

Now it was Phillip's turn, and Emily wished she could leave the room. She wouldn't call him shy, exactly, but he'd never seemed comfortable as the center of attention, either. If he was still speaking to her when this was over, she'd consider herself lucky.

"Were you aware of Ms. Evans's antipathy

for Dr. White, Mr. Baker?"

Mike sat down, and Phillip stood up. "I did notice something. And I once overheard her talking with one of the other nurses about Dr. White. I asked Pete about it and he told me pretty much the same story we've just heard from Mike."

"And what about your relationship with Dr. White? Did you feel targeted by her?"

"No sir, I did not." He was looking directly at Emily when he said it. Looking . . . and smiling just a little.

"But there was . . . kissing."

"Yessir. And I initiated it, not Dr. White." Now *he* scowled at Barbara. "I'm Amish, that much is true. But I'm neither innocent nor vulnerable."

"Dr. White? Do you have anything to add?"

"Only that I'd never do anything to jeopardize a patient."

Doug made another note on his tablet, then looked around the room. "I suggest we take a vote. If you believe we should send today's notes on to the medical board, write a *K* on the Post-it in front of you. If not, write a *V.*"

"*K* for kiss and *V* for vindicated?" Myra asked.

Doug didn't answer, and no one else

weighed in, either. And after a moment of paper-rustling and clicking pens, the notes were passed to Myra, who shuffled, then opened each, and read the vote aloud. "Sixteen *V*s," she said, "and one *K.*"

"Well then, that settles it." Doug pulled back his sleeve to check his watch. "Sorry to have wasted your time. Thank you for participating, in any case."

"Wait. You mean to tell me it's over, just like that?"

"Yes, Ms. Evans, just like that."

"This is an outrage. She kissed Mr. Baker. Who will she take advantage of next? You have to send the information on, if for no other reason than to make the medical board aware what she's capable of."

Emily trembled with rage and burned with shame . . . for Phillip and herself. *You should threaten to sue her for defamation!* She wouldn't of course, because she didn't have time for such foolishness, and neither did Phillip. Plus, it would be unfair to put him through yet another "because of Emily" ordeal.

"Show of hands," Doug said. "Who's in favor of sending a notification to the board?"

No one spoke. No one moved, until Barbara huffed, picked up her purse and notebook, and slammed out the door.

"Thanks again, everyone," Doug said.

"Myra," Emily said, "I wonder if Barbara would mind if you shared all these delicious leftover pastries with the staff? It seems a shame to let them go to waste."

"I'm surprised a big-hearted gal like her didn't suggest it, herself." Myra's sarcastic joke inspired quite a ripple of chuckles from other board members.

The room emptied quickly, and on his way toward the elevators, Mike high-fived Emily. "I'm glad things ended the way they did. Maybe she'll quit Garrett, see if she can find work at a shrink's office." He laughed.

"I'm glad it's over, too. And I'm sorry you got dragged into this."

"I wasn't dragged. I volunteered." Walking backward, he tacked on, "Think I'll take the stairs. Winning energizes me!"

"Have a good day, Mike."

"I will." Then, "Hey! Now you two can do the whole full disclosure thing. Be happy, guys!"

The door to the stairwell drifted shut as Pete hugged her from behind. "I'm proud of you, Em. You handled yourself like a champ in there. In your shoes, I probably would've said some things I'd pay for later. But you?" He moved to her side. "You're strong and brave, and I hope when I grow up, I'll be just like you."

"Stop it, you goofball. You're making me blush."

He looked at Phillip. "Tell her how cute she looks, all pink-cheeked."

Phillip nodded. "She's cute, even when she isn't blushing."

"Know what? I'm taking the stairs, too. 'Cause Mike's right. Winning *is* energizing." Pete jogged toward the stairs. "Gotta pick up a few things at the grocery store before I head to work. 'The hurrier I go, the behinder I get,' " he said, quoting Alice's rabbit.

"Just be careful, you speed demon. I owe you a dinner, remember?"

"Don't worry, I remember. And hey, you two should listen to Mike. Do some disclosing!" he said as the door drifted shut behind him.

"He can be a little nutty sometimes, but I love him to pieces," she told Phillip. "He's a best friend and brother, all rolled into one, and I don't know what I'd do without him."

"He's a good man. And gave us some good advice."

"What advice?"

"The whole full disclosure thing."

But Phillip, she wanted to say, *we can't disclose what doesn't exist.* She loved him

— or thought she did, anyway — but admitting it was a far cry from making a "we're a couple!" announcement.

Emily said, "We have a lot to discuss, that's for sure."

"When?"

"When what?"

His quiet laughter almost soothed her rattled nerves.

Almost.

"What's so funny?"

"You are." He caressed her cheek, let his fingers linger, and as his thumb drew lazy circles on her jaw, the elevator opened. They waited for several doctors in scrubs and a nurse or two to exit, and when the doors closed again, he hit the Close Door button. "I never would have pegged you for a 'fraidy cat."

"A . . . a what?"

He backed her into the corner and effectively trapped her there by pressing his palms to the wall to the right and left of her head. "We haven't known each other very long, but Emily, *we know* each other. People don't go through what we just went through without seeing deep into each other's souls. I learned a lot about you, watching and listening as you took care of Gabe. And I'd like to think you learned a lot about me, too."

She started to tell him that their experience wasn't unlike every other that families endure, every hour of every day, in hospitals all around the globe, but he silenced her with a kiss. A lengthy, loving kiss that left her feeling breathless and rubbery-legged.

"Do you think there are cameras in this elevator?"

He glanced around. "Good question. But it's okay. A gathering of your peers just cleared you of any wrongdoing. And who knows? Maybe when the pictures are circulated, it'll save us the trouble of making our . . ."

". . . public disclosure," they said together.

Their moment of laughter ended with another slow kiss, and a line from a verse by Walt Whitman flashed in her mind. *"There we two, content, happy in being together, speaking little, perhaps not a word . . ."* She hadn't truly understood the words during that English Literature class, because poetry had never been her forte. Too many abstracts. Not enough clarity. But she understood the words now. If only she could continue living them.

Now, Phillip backed up, just enough to meet her eyes. "I know you have questions.

I do, too. And naturally, we both have some personal things to sort out, logistical things to figure out. Big stuff. Small stuff. But we'll get it done. We have to get it done, because Emily — although I tried hard not to — I've fallen —"

Her cell phone rang, interrupting him, and providing her with the perfect excuse to break the intense eye contact.

"Sorry," she said, hitting the Accept icon. "I have to take this."

He pressed the Open Door button. "I know, I know. You're a doctor. I need to get used to the fact that other people need you, too."

"Em . . . it's me . . ."

"Pete? What's wrong? Why do you sound so —"

"Accident," he choked out. "Bad one. Ambo . . . T-boned me."

"Omigoodness! Where are you?"

"Out front. They're . . ."

Something cut off his sentence, and she looked at the phone, hoping the call hadn't dropped.

". . . taking me into ER now."

"I'll be down in five minutes."

She hung up, dropped the phone back into her bag. Phillip read her face, then pulled her into a sideways hug. "You're trembling. What happened? Is Pete all right?"

"I don't know. It doesn't sound good. He's in the ER." This time, it was Emily who pressed Close Door, holding the G button at the same time.

"What're you doing?"

"Making sure the elevator won't stop until it reaches the ground floor. Pete showed me this. . . ."

He'd taught her how to control the elevator, saying people like them — doctors and EMTs — never knew when a trick like that might come in handy. That day, he'd put it into action because an extra-large, extra-toppings pizza was waiting for them at Tominetti's. Tears filled her eyes as she leaned into Phillip.

"Aw, *lieverd, het komt wel goed.*"

He must have seen that she hadn't understood a word, for he quickly said, "Don't worry, sweetheart, he's tough and strong. He'll be all right."

"He has to be. . . ."

The instant the doors opened, she ran full out toward the ER, and Phillip ran right beside her.

He has to be all right, she thought, racing into the trauma center. *Because if he isn't, I'll never be all right again.*

CHAPTER EIGHTEEN

Phillip was standing beside Emily when she found Pete's cubicle, where a team of gloved, green-garbed doctors and nurses had surrounded the gurney. There was blood. A lot of it. On the gurney. On the floor. On the gloved hands and scrubs and shoes of every team member. It wasn't Phillip's first experience with this much blood. Cows and horses routinely sustained deep gashes, brushing against barbed wire, giving birth . . . and when they were slaughtered for market. But this, *this* was different. It didn't matter to him that as a doctor, Emily was familiar with the blindingly bright lights, the flurry of activity, the urgent shouts. He wanted to protect her from it, because the guy on the table was *Pete,* her beloved brother.

"Get her outta here!" a burly doctor bellowed.

"That's Emily White," someone said.

"She's one of us."

"Why are you here?" the loud man demanded.

"That's her brother. Pete. He's an EMT."

"Paramedic," Pete wheezed. "There's a difference."

"But this isn't the time to talk about it," the loud man said. Aiming a scowl their way, he said, "Get out. Both of you. Right now, or I'll call security."

Emily seemed rooted to the spot, and it took considerable effort to move her. "They'll come find us just as soon as they stabilize him. Meanwhile, how about some coffee?" Phillip suggested in a quiet voice.

"I'm already shaky enough." She plopped onto the barely cushioned faux-leather seat of a waiting room chair. "You must have a dozen chores waiting for you. I'll be all right. You don't have to stay."

"I know that. I *want* to stay."

"But . . . Gabe. And your mother . . ."

"I'll call Hannah, let her know I'll be home just as soon as someone brings us good news."

They'd only stood in Pete's cubicle for a few minutes, more than long enough to imprint the ghastly image on Phillip's brain. The sight reminded him of the day a tourist had brought a gaggle of rowdy youngsters into Hannah's shop. The youngest grabbed an Amish doll, screamed, "She doesn't have a face!" and ripped the toy limb from limb, spewing its sawdust innards across the rough-hewn floor. It took Hannah several hours to repair it — longer, she said, than it had taken to sew the doll in the first place — but when she finished, it looked good as new. Phillip hoped the doctors and nurses could work the same miracle on Pete's broken, battered body.

Emily, shuddering beside him, said, "I'd go to the chapel, but I'm afraid the doctors will want to talk to me while I'm gone."

"God can hear you just as well, right where you sit."

"Yes, that's true, isn't it?"

He told her what he'd learned about the colossal Jesus statue that stood beneath the domed ceiling of Hopkins's administration building. Told her about the elderly woman he'd met, and her story of the way people rubbed its toes, and begged God for a miracle.

"Too bad there isn't something like it here," she said, her voice cracking.

"Close your eyes," he said, guiding her head to rest on his shoulder, "and picture it, arms extended and hands open to accept prayers."

"I remember it well." Eyes closed, she spoke the words carved into its base. " *'Kommer til mig,'* Danish for 'Come to me.' "

" 'Come to me,' " Phillip continued, " 'all you who are weary and heavy burdened, and I will give you rest.' "

During those dark days after Rebecca's funeral, how many times had members of the community pummeled him with Matthew 11:28? *Too many.* But here, with Emily so close, seeking his strength, Phillip finally found comfort in the verse.

A quiet voice said, "Emily?"

In the time it takes for a shooting star to vanish into the inky sky, Emily was standing in front of a middle-aged woman.

The nurse said, "He's asking for you."

Like an obedient child, Emily followed. "I should gown up, put on a mask."

The woman shook her head. "Honey, I think he'd rather see your pretty face."

Phillip read between the lines: Germs can't hurt Pete now. More than ever, he wanted to be nearby, in case Emily needed him. So he walked a few steps behind them, hoping to discourage any attempts to shoo him away.

He saw right away that the team had done a fair job of cleaning Pete up. They'd raised the top half of the gurney slightly, no doubt to ease his ragged breathing.

"Shouldn't he be on a respirator?" Emily asked.

"He refused it," said the nurse.

"He refused? But . . . but why?"

The change in her expression, from hopeful to stony, told Phillip that after one look at Pete, at the monitors that beeped and hummed all around him, Emily knew exactly why. A breathing machine, like protective garb, was pointless now. At times like this, he supposed, what she'd learned during years of doctoring delivered more grief than comfort.

"Stand closer," Pete rasped, and held out one hand.

She took care not to put too much pressure on the needle that penetrated the big vein on the back of his hand.

"Thought I told you to be careful," she said, forcing a smile.

"Looked both ways," he gasped, holding up his right hand. "I swear." He took a moment to inhale. Exhale. "Ambo came outta nowhere."

She looked across the gurney and into the worried eyes of the woman who'd brought her here. "Where is the ambulance crew?"

"They're down the hall. We're working on them, too."

"Does anyone know what happened?"

"Only Pete, here. He's been saying the same thing over and over since he got here: The ambo came out of nowhere."

"Em," Pete said, waving her closer, "you . . . will you . . ."

"Anything, Pete. Just name it."

"Clinger . . ."

"Don't you worry. I'll take good care of her until you're able to do it yourself."

"No. This is . . . it's bad, Em." He wheezed again. "I'm not gonna . . ."

"Shh," she said, a finger over his lips. "Stop talking nonsense. You'll be fine."

Emily met the woman's eyes again. "How soon before they take him up to surgery?"

Phillip's heart ached when, in place of an answer, she shook her head, slowly.

"But you took X-rays, right? A blood panel?"

"Yes."

"I want to see the films. The lab reports."

She made a move, as if to walk toward the computer against the wall, but Pete winced and held on tight.

"Now who's . . . talking nonsense?" One side of his mouth lifted in a faint smile. "You're a doctor." He grimaced. "I'm a parame—"

"Yes, we know. You're a paramedic." It was

a feeble attempt at humor, but Phillip gave her points for trying.

"So . . . Em, we both know . . ."

"Peter Edward White, stop talking that way. Stop it, right now."

He closed his eyes, and the weak smile vanished. Yet again, he waved her near. She dropped the side rail and leaned in close. "That's right. Be quiet, so your poor beat-up body can start healing."

The dim smile was back, but Pete's eyes didn't open.

"I love you, you big goofball. You'd better pull yourself together, because . . ."

She bit her lower lip, whether to keep it from trembling or to stifle a sob, Phillip couldn't say.

". . . because I need you."

One eye opened, but just barely. "You're tough." He rested for a second. "Strongest person I know." Another pause. "You're . . . gonna be fine." Pete lifted his head, scanned the room, and when he saw Phillip, he smiled, this time, with both sides of his mouth. "Gonna be fine," he repeated, " 'cause . . . that . . . big oaf . . . will take . . . good care . . . of you."

For the first time since she'd entered the partition, Emily met his eyes. Tears clung to her lashes and glittered like diamonds under the harsh overhead lamps. She extended her free hand, and like iron slides toward a magnet, he went to her.

"Phil . . . ?"

"I'm right here, Pete."

"I know you are. I'm a mess . . . but . . . I'm not . . . *blind,*" he said on a one-note chuckle. And then, his features relaxed and his voice faded further still. "You two . . . good for . . . each other. So . . . so don't . . . be stupid and . . ." His eyes bored into Phillip's. "She's stubborn. Won't . . . admit it but . . . she's gonna need you . . ."

"I'm not going anywhere," Phillip said, wrapping his free hand around Pete's. "You've got my word on that."

Now, Pete zeroed in on Emily's face. "When . . . when you tell . . . Dad and the . . . the others . . . Spare them . . . the gory details." He squeezed her hand. "Okay?"

"Okay."

"Promise?"

"Promise."

"By the way?"

"What . . ."

"Love you, too."

Pete's hand was cold, his skin a pale, eerie shade of gray.

He struggled to lift his head, and this

time, the nurse helped him. "Don't say . . . don't say I . . . didn't warn you," he said to Phillip. "Em is . . . stubborn."

Then the monitor went crazy, its ear-piercing beeps pulsing so fast that it almost sounded like one continuous note. The noise incited a whole new burst of activity, more shouted orders, additional personnel gathering around Pete's bed. They asked her to move, and when she didn't, *told* her to leave. But Emily wouldn't budge. Refused to let go of Phillip's hand, either. "Pete wants me here, so I'm staying. And Phillip," she said, looking up at him, "is staying with me."

"We won't leave you, Pete."

Eyes closed and lips slightly parted, Pete's once animated face was now devoid of all expression.

The nurse muted the monitor's sound, but the bright golden line that had tracked Pete's heartbeats was still visible, pulsating so quickly now that it reminded Phillip of Gabe's very first drawing — thousands of sharp up-and-down *V*s placed so close together that the blue crayon all but blotted out the white paper. More than three hundred beats a minute, the glowing numbers announced.

Thirty seconds passed. A minute. And

then? The line stopped moving, split the monitor's screen in half.

"Flatline," said one of the nurses.

"Time of death?" said another.

"Eleven oh-five," said the first.

Through it all, Emily stood, silent and statue-still, squeezing Phillip's fingers so tightly that the tips had turned white.

The nurse stepped up beside her. "You know the routine, Doctor."

"Yes," she said on a heavy sigh. "I know the routine." And meeting the woman's eyes, Emily asked, "What's your name?"

"Lauren."

Nodding, she said, "Thank you, Lauren, for . . ."

Until that moment, she'd held it together. Now, the floodgates opened.

Phillip guided her to the far side of the room, taking care to put her back to Pete's bed and the now-whispering team. When Rebecca had died, they'd said, "You can stay with the body for a few minutes. Before we bring her down to the morgue."

He hadn't stayed. Hadn't wanted to. Why would he, when, for his whole life, he'd been taught that upon a person's death, the soul left the body, and began the remarkable trek to Paradise. But his choice needn't be Emily's.

Spying a tissue box on a cabinet beside them, she helped herself to one.

"Um . . . Lauren? Do you need me to sign anything, or . . . or anything?"

"No, not right now. You work here, so it isn't like we don't know how to find you. If you want to leave, go ahead."

She looked up, her teary eyes locked to his, and said, "Can you take me home?"

"Yes. Of course. I'd be happy to. Sure." Phillip would have added, *It's my pleasure,* but he thought he already sounded enough like an idiot.

One arm across her narrow shoulders, the other around her waist, he guided her to the exit. He'd parked on the far side of the lot, to save having to pay for a space in the garage. "Why don't you wait right here while I get the truck."

"No. I'll be alone soon enough." Linking her arm through his, she fell into step beside him. "Thanks for being here. Don't know how I would have gotten through that if you'd left, when I suggested it, I mean."

If he remembered correctly, she lived minutes from the hospital. Once he got her home, he'd borrow her phone and call Hannah. After explaining what had happened, he was sure that his sister would volunteer to go to his house, keep an eye on their mother, and on Gabe, too. For the first time in a long time, he felt blessed to have easy access to a loving family. If he made good on his silent threat to leave Pleasant Valley, he'd have to give that up, along with the farm, and the workshop, the beautiful Alleghenies — and Backbone Mountain — visible through all seasons, right from his front porch.

Emily hadn't said a word. Not as they crossed the broad parking lot. Not as she settled into the pickup's front seat. He hated to interrupt whatever thoughts were tumbling around in her pretty head, but he needed her address.

"Is it easy to find your place?"

"Very," she said. A sob had thickened her voice. "Follow Third Street to Lake. I'm the third house on the left."

She'd praised him, back in his workshop, saying she'd never known a more clean and organized man. When they entered her home, he could have paid her the same compliment. Plus, her taste in colors and furnishings was pleasing, soothing, and completely opposite from Rebecca's. But then, his wife had spent her whole life Amish, and Emily, well, Emily personified the term *Englisher*.

"I'm gonna fix us a cup of coffee. Unless

you'd rather have tea."

She stood in the middle of her living room, elbows cupped in her palms, nodding. "Coffee sounds good. There's ham and cheese in the fridge, if you're hungry."

"I'll eat, but only if you'll join me."

He'd anticipated another agreeable nod. A "make yourself at home" comment. Instead, she half ran across the room, flung herself into his arms, and wept.

Never in his life had he heard anyone cry this way. It seemed the sobs started all the way down in her feet, then swelled up, up, until they poured from her lips.

Phillip guided her to the couch, positioned her on the center cushion. She surprised him again, because instead of curling up beside him, she climbed into his lap. And there she stayed until the tears stopped. He felt honored that she'd trusted him enough to shed some of her grief, right here in his arms. He'd promised coffee. A sandwich. But she'd dozed off, and to keep that promise, he needed to move her . . . the last thing he wanted to do.

So there he sat, alternately stroking her hair and pressing kisses to her temple, listening to her soft breaths and very much aware that her loving heart was beating against his chest.

He'd stay until dark — until morning — if that's what she needed.

Who are you kidding? he thought. *It's what you need, too.*

Phillip had barely crossed the threshold when Sarah said, "You are late."

Yes, he was. *Hours* later than he'd said he'd be.

Fists resting on her generous hips, she said, "Well?"

"I was in the elevator, ready to leave the meeting when Emily got an emergency call on her cell phone."

"What meeting?"

Oh. That's right. He hadn't told Sarah that, after seeing that kiss, a nurse had filed charges against Emily.

"Nothing important." And it wasn't . . . anymore.

"She had to rush away to care for a patient?"

"No. It was . . . personal." Very personal, he thought. "Her brother was in an accident. A bad one." Relating the information in such a casual tone sounded cold. Sounded wrong. And reminded him that he should check in on the paramedics who'd collided with Pete's car, in case Emily asked how they'd fared.

"He seems like a nice young man. Very handsome. Not as handsome as you, but I am sure he has turned a few heads in his day." She filled a mug with hot black coffee and put it on the table. "Sit. I will warm up your supper."

"Thanks, *Maemm,* but I'm not hungry."

Frowning, she clucked her tongue. "Did you have a restaurant meal with Dr. White? That sort of spending needs to stop, Phillip. The hospital bills will begin arriving soon, and we cannot afford such extravagances."

"You're right, of course. But we didn't eat in a restaurant. Didn't eat at all." He sat down, wrapped his hands around the mug, and struggled to get the words out. "Pete is dead, *Maemm.*"

Eyes wide, she laid a hand against her bosom. "Oh, that is a terrible thing. I pray he did not suffer."

As a matter of fact, his last minutes had been pure torture. Phillip had seen that glassy-eyed look too many times. In his father's eyes. His brother's. Horses and cows, and even a goat or two. Rebecca, thankfully, had slipped away peacefully. He'd seen a book in town once, with the picture of a beautiful, sleeping princess on its cover. Rebecca's last minutes had always reminded him of that.

"It is sad, but sometimes, God's will is like that." She poured herself a mug of coffee and sat in the chair beside his. "How is Emily taking it?"

"Not well." He thought of the way she'd clung to him. The warm tears that had seeped through his shirt were dry now, but if he concentrated, he could still taste them on his lips.

"Will you attend the funeral?"

He was a little surprised that she even had to ask. "Yes, definitely."

"And the burial?"

Again, he said, "Yes, definitely."

"Will you allow me to attend?"

That she wanted to go surprised him so much, he was left speechless for a moment.

"If you like."

"Then it is settled."

"I'm sure Emily will appreciate seeing you there."

"She is English by accident of birth, but I like her. And not only because she saved Gabe."

Coming from his mother, that was high praise.

She finger-dusted the stains on the front of his shirt, and when they remained, Sarah said, "You eased her tears?"

He sipped his coffee and she shook her

head. "Pretty girl like that does not need mascara. I hope it will wash out in the laundry."

Sometimes, he was astonished by the way her mind worked. It seemed she believed that if a thought came into her head, she should free it, immediately, even if it caused ruffled feathers or hurt feelings.

"I suppose there will be flowers in the funeral parlor."

"Pete was a well-liked guy. So yes, I'm sure his friends will want the family to know how much he meant to them. Especially those who live too far away to attend the services."

"The Plain way is the better way."

Phillip wasn't so sure, but she didn't need to know that. It seemed sad that loved ones weren't allowed to express their grief through eulogies, by singing the deceased's favorite hymns, and decorating otherwise sad and bleak chapels with colorful floral sprays to celebrate the transfer from earth to Paradise. He pictured Rebecca's marker, carved from sandstone of the same height and width of the others that stood behind the church, identical, so that no one would get the idea that her life — or her loss — meant more than anyone else's:

REBECCA BAKER
WIFE OF PHILLIP BAKER
BORN MAY 5
DIED NOVEMBER 21

"I will need to take an iron to my mourning dress and bonnet ribbons."

By his count, she'd worn it eleven times. After Pete's funeral, he hoped, she could hang it behind her other dresses — six in all, sewn from pale shades of gray, blue, yellow, and pink — for a long, long time.

Phillip noticed her latest quilt project, neatly folded in a wicker laundry basket near the parlor entry. "That'll bring in two hundred dollars or more," he said. "But life is short, *Maemm.* Why don't you make one like it for your bed and for Hannah's?"

"It saddens me that you even have to ask. The designs are too bright, the fabric too fine to lay upon an Amish bed."

He'd heard it all a hundred times before. One of his fondest wishes was that sooner, not later, she'd admit he was right, and that she deserved to warm herself with something that *wasn't* plain. At least once in a while . . .

Phillip doubted it would happen.

She claimed to be happy, living without color, forgoing ruffles and lace, avoiding makeup and stylish hairdos. But he'd often asked himself . . . if the Plain life was as satisfying and fulfilling as she professed, wouldn't she laugh and smile and enjoy herself *more*?

Yet while he was with Emily, he'd come to a stunning conclusion: Yes, there were some unappealing elements to the Amish way of life. But if he walked away, he'd have to leave the good with the bad. The realization was eye-opening, because for the first time, he considered the possibility that others in the community felt exactly as he did — perhaps felt it even more deeply. The difference? They'd carried the load without complaint, without talk of quitting, like a spoiled child. He thought again of what he'd told Emily, about the way the community always rallied round, anytime a member was in need. They were connected by faith in God. Almost as important, they were connected by an invisible family bond. He loved Emily, but left to choose between her and this life?

His mother's whispered prayer penetrated the fog of his thoughts. Sarah prayed for him and Gabe, for Hannah and her family, for other members of the community. Prayer, he decided, was where she found joy and solace. He'd often entered a room and found her at the sink, at the stove, at a window, eyes closed and lips moving as she talked with God. Once, he'd come home early, and overheard the bishop scolding her for spending too much time with her Bible. "Too much study can make you arrogant or confused," Fisher had said. "I know too many people who decided to leave the church after reading something they did not understand. Better to bring your Bible to church, where the elders and I can guide you." Phillip had wanted to applaud when she replied, "And how am I to know that *you* are the teacher God has chosen for *me*?" Fisher left in a huff, and he'd never second-guessed Sarah again.

Sarah whispered, "Amen," then said, "I prayed a special prayer for you today, Phillip."

"Oh?"

"I asked God to change you back into the faithful follower you were before Rebecca died. I do not care what clothes you wear or whether or not you shave. I only want to know that my son is right with his Maker."

They'd had this discussion five times, ten, even. But she refused to accept that *death after death* had shattered his faith long before he'd lost Rebecca.

"It would make me happy to see you get

rid of those leather belts and Englisher caps, and go back to looking and talking like one of *us.* But if this brings you comfort, so be it."

"*Maemm,* I'll always be one of you, no matter what I wear or how I talk."

"Have it your way, then. Your stubbornness is teaching me patience, if nothing else."

Smiling, he quoted from the book of James: " 'Be patient, therefore . . . See how the farmer waits for the precious fruit of the earth? . . . you also be patient . . .' "

"My son the Bible scholar." She blew him a kiss. "A word of warning . . . do not let Bishop Fisher learn that you have memorized verses!"

CHAPTER NINETEEN

The funeral director had to open the partition separating Pete's viewing room from the one beside it. As the staff set out chairs and arranged vases and potted plants on the tables, Emily stood, transfixed by the digital photo display her sister had put together. Pete chewing the railing of his crib. Painting his face, hair, and high chair with spaghetti sauce. Crouched by the Christmas tree, mouth agape as he unwrapped a Superman costume, that year's had-to-have-it gift. Then, Pete in his Little League uniform and playing the sax with the junior high brass ensemble. On horseback. Riding the too-big-for-him bicycle that it took him two summers to grow into. Cap and gown. Paramedic uniform. Suit and tie for a homecoming dance. Jeans and a plaid shirt, chopping wood for their dad's fireplace. Orioles cap and Cal Ripken shirt at Camden Yards. White tux as a groomsman in Mi-

randa's wedding. Her sister had pro-
grammed his favorite song into the slide-
show, and Louis Armstrong's raspy version
of "What a Wonderful World" played softly
in the background. Emily's tears flowed
freely.

"Did the guy ever frown?" Phillip asked,
dropping a hand on her shoulder. "That
smile . . . it followed him all through his
life, didn't it?"

"I'd be hard-pressed to cite a time or
place when he wasn't happy." Plucking a
tissue from one of the end tables, she
dabbed at her eyes. "Well, that isn't entirely
true. He cried buckets when my grandparents died. And when we lost our mom."
Just then appeared an image of Pete, arms
around the neck of a big fuzzy dog. "What
a mess he was when the vet diagnosed
Stinker with Cushing's disease!"

"Stinker?"

The memory made her ask herself . . . is
it possible to feel joy and melancholy at the
same time? "Let's just say that pup had a
very sensitive gastrointestinal system."

Phillip turned in a slow circle and took
her with him. "Looks like a flower shop in
here. Smells like one, too. And you know?
Every petal could represent a moment in
Pete's life. A moment when he did or said

something that touched another person's life."

"If I believed in reincarnation, I'd say you're Hemingway, come back to life."

Phillip pointed. "Is that your dad?"

She followed his gaze to where her father stood, shaking hands, smiling, doing his best to console the friends and coworkers who were there, supposedly to comfort *him.* Emily took Phillip's hand, led him across the plush, flowery carpet.

"Dad, there's someone I'd like you to meet. Dutton White, this is Phillip Baker. Phillip, this is my dad."

Dutton held out his hand. "Ah, the father of the little boy Emily sent to Hopkins."

Phillip returned the greeting. "Yes. Gabe. And thanks to your daughter, he's doing fine."

"Good, good. Glad to hear it."

"Where are you and the rest of the family staying while you're in town?"

"Emily's place. It's like we've gone back in time . . . three or four kids to a room, shoulder to shoulder seats at the table, always empty milk and juice jugs . . ." A quiet sigh escaped his lungs. "Pete would have loved it."

"Until bedtime," Emily said.

Dutton laughed. "Oh man, you're right!

I'd almost forgotten how grumpy he could get if anyone interrupted his sleep."

"Miranda," Dutton said, "have you met Phillip?"

Emily's sister stood between her and Phillip and, placing a hand on his arm, said, "No, but we all heard about you. A *lot* about you."

"Yeah. If your ears have been ringing lately," Joe said, "blame Pete. He went on and on and *on* about you."

"Uh-oh. Hope he didn't let any cats out of the bag."

Miranda's husband and Joe's wife joined them, and they all shared "Pete told me this" and "Pete told me that" stories he'd shared about Phillip. And about Gabe. And Clinger the cat.

"How's that li'l ruffian doing?" Joe asked. "Last time we FaceTimed with Pete, the crazy thing had climbed up the curtains and perched on top of the rod." The memory brought a tear to Joe's eye, and he dried it on the back of his hand.

"She's fine," Emily said. "But she misses Pete."

"How can you tell?" Miranda wanted to know.

"Because she walks around, sniffing everything, meowing, as if she expects Pete to show up and scratch under her chin."

"But . . . they were only together for, what, a couple of days?" Dutton pointed out.

"True," Phillip said. "But once in a while, good things happen fast. Real fast."

The family thanked him for coming, then one by one meandered through the room, talking with visitors, admiring flower arrangements and reading the cards attached, and reminding folks to sign the guest book.

"I haven't seen Sarah or Gabe in a while, have you?"

"They're downstairs, in the lounge. My mother believes Gabe needs to spend as much time off his feet as possible. So they're down there, sipping lemonade and eating stale cookies. Which, might I add, she insisted on bringing with her."

"That's good. I'm glad they decided to come with you."

"Gabe thought the world of Pete. He would have pestered me nonstop if I'd left him home."

"You don't think it'll upset him, seeing Pete this way?" She glanced at the gleaming mahogany coffin, where a three-foot cross made of black-eyed Susans — the only flower Pete knew by name — leaned on an aluminum easel.

"I know it sounds a little crazy, but Amish kids are exposed to death at a very young age. This isn't the first time Gabe has attended a funeral, although, it's the first time seeing someone he cared about."

"It's his first outing since his surgery, too. He hasn't admitted it — not to me, anyway — but I think he was afraid he might not make it."

Guilt darkened his eyes. "I hadn't thought of that. I can be a real idiot sometimes."

"Don't beat yourself up, Phillip. He's here, right downstairs. Doing great, and getting better by the hour. And I know you well enough to say that's how he'll stay, if you have anything to say about it."

"You're something else, you know that? Here you are, comforting *me* at your brother's viewing."

"At times like these, it's good to shift your focus."

"Well, take it from me. Don't go near Pete right now. Not until everyone but immediate family has left."

"Why?"

"Because that's when you'll hear thoughtless, hurtful things, things said with all good intentions . . . things that will sting when you think of them, even years from now."

He'd lost several close relatives, so if

anyone ought to know about a thing like that, it would be Phillip.

"Things like what?"

He tapped the tip of her nose. "If I tell you, that'll make *me* one of those well-meaning but thoughtless, hurtful people, now wouldn't it? Years from now, I don't want one of those stupid things to come to mind."

Years from now . . . as if he believes we could actually build a life together . . .

The family decided to meet for supper at Tominetti's, Pete's favorite restaurant. They asked for his favorite pizza toppings in his honor: spinach, goat cheese, and banana peppers on a bed of extra sauce. When the waitress heard the order, she asked why he wasn't with them.

"There was an accident," Joe said. "Pete . . . I'm afraid Pete didn't make it."

"Oh no, I'm so sorry." Bea dropped a hand on Emily's shoulder. "You two have been coming in here for, like, *ever.* You guys got along so great, like best friends. It made me jealous, 'cause my brother an' me can't spend five minutes together without finding something to bicker about." Tucking the pencil behind her ear, she said, "When did it happen?"

"Few days ago," Joe said.

347

Bea dropped the order pad into her apron pocket. "I'll be right back."

Minutes later, when she returned with their drinks, she said, "Tonight's on the house. Boss's orders. Said Pete could always make him laugh."

"Be sure to thank him for us." Emily couldn't imagine coming here ever again. Even good memories wouldn't be easy from now on.

They went through the motions, doing their best to keep the conversation light as the food disappeared. But despite their best efforts, the family couldn't hide their grief. Now and then, tears choked off a "Pete story."

Back at the house, it took hours to get everyone settled down for the night, but after making sure they were comfortable in their makeshift beds, Emily carried a mug of herbal tea and a fuzzy lap robe onto the back deck. After lighting a citronella candle, she dropped onto the padded seat of a wood glider and stared out into the yard. Moonlight shone from dewdrops that clung to every blade of grass and the midsummer breeze rustled the maple leaves. Cricket chirps harmonized with cicada songs, and somewhere close by, an owl hooted. A week or so ago, she'd seen a fox scamper alongside the back fence, and the week before that, her neighbor had warned her to "keep an eye peeled," because he'd spotted a trio of coyotes trotting across the road. Just last week, Pete had told her how lucky she was, living in a virtual wildlife habitat.

The French doors squealed quietly, telling her that one of her houseguests was up. Emily turned toward the familiar sound and smiled. She couldn't think of anyone she'd rather share her quiet time with than her dad.

"Sorry you got stuck with that lumpy sofa bed, Dad."

He joined her on the glider. "Aw, it isn't so bad. But to be honest, the mattress isn't the reason I can't sleep."

Miranda had always been daddy's little girl, and because Joe's engineering degree gave him the skills to work for Dutton's company, he and their dad quickly became more closer, even, than father and son. Pete, the always playful adventure seeker who'd dropped out of college to become a paramedic, never had much in common with Dutton. Emily and Pete talked often about that disconnect, and how she'd felt it, too. Once, she admitted that the gap was the very thing that connected her to Pete, and Pete to her. And he'd responded with "Two lovable mutts on the same leash."

"I miss him, too, Dad."

"That li'l waitress was right. You two always were tight as a drum. Life's gonna feel different, real different without him."

It was going to feel like moving through life wearing a high-heeled shoe . . . on just one foot.

"He knew your mother loved him. She told him all the time. That, and how proud she was of him. I hope he knew I felt the same way."

She reached over, gave his forearm a light squeeze. "He knew. And he loved you, too, Dad."

Once, after a family get-together, Pete confessed that he believed their father saw him as a major disappointment, because he'd chosen the fire department over a college education and the family business. She'd cited examples that the opposite was true, but when he and their dad were together, Emily could see that Pete's opinion had never changed. But their father would never hear the story from her.

"Tell me, honey, what's with you and that Baker guy?"

"He's nice, isn't he?"

"Seems so. But I only talked with him for a few minutes. To judge his true character,

I'd need to see how he reacts to hard times, disappointment, if he gets up every time he falls, the way Pete did."

His words reminded her of a plaque she'd seen while browsing a craft show: "Say *I love you* today, because tomorrow isn't promised." *Another "if only" for the books . . .*

"His little boy was the one wearing short pants and suspenders? And the mother wore the long black dress?"

Despite the beautiful June weather, Sarah had worn a long-sleeved black dress. Its hem nearly touched the toes of what Phillip called "nun shoes," and the long brim of her hat cast a shadowy veil over her face. At the invitation of Old *and* New Order patients, Emily had attended several Amish funerals, and it had been her experience that only the deceased's widow wore traditional head-to-toe Anabaptist mourning garb. If Sarah had hoped to underscore how different the Amish and the English were . . . *Point well made, Sarah,* she thought.

"He's adorable, don't you think?"

"Hmm . . . sounds to me like you set the 'don't get emotionally attached' bar pretty low for this case."

"Not Phillip," she said. "I meant *Gabe* is adorable!"

"I knew who you were talking about.

Question still applies . . ."

Emily sighed. She'd never developed a talent for evading his questions and saw no reason to give it one last effort tonight. "I tried not to get involved, but . . ."

"What's that old movie quote?"

Emily sent him a sad smile as together, they recited, " 'Do or do not, there *is* no try.' "

Pete. That's who they should be talking about. Not Phillip and Gabe. And certainly not *her.*

And yet she said, "Phillip is easy to like."

"Aha. So it's Phillip, is it? Sounds like I was right. You set the bar low when it came to Gabe *and* his dad."

She could recite hospital ethics codes, but why confuse things?

When it became obvious that Emily didn't intend to discuss her feelings for Phillip, Dutton got to his feet. "Well, honey, I suppose we should at least try and catch a few z's. Tomorrow's gonna be another long, hard day."

"Truer words . . ." she said.

Yesterday, when she'd let herself into Pete's condo to retrieve Clinger, Emily couldn't help but notice his will, spread out on the coffee table. The handwritten note beside it began, "Hey, Family. My job can be dangerous, so I decided to act like a grownup . . ." He'd spelled everything out, from which suit to bury him in to the Scriptures and songs for the service. Ironically, he'd signed it just four days before the accident. She'd followed every instruction to the letter . . . the funeral home and cemetery, even the restaurant that would spare the family the trouble of preparing what he'd called the "Relax, the worst is behind you meal." Tomorrow would *not* put the worst behind them. That would come every time she heard a song or watched a movie he'd loved, each time she saw an emergency vehicle speeding down a highway.

"Think I'll stay out here for a few minutes more." She got up, too, and walked with him to the door. "At least it isn't supposed to rain tomorrow. Pete would have hated being the reason people got wet."

"Truer words . . ."

When Dutton hugged her, Emily felt his tears on her own cheek. And as he disappeared into the darkened house, a quote from another craft shop plaque came to mind: "In the end, we only regret the things we left unsaid."

Any uncertainties revolving around her relationship with Phillip dissolved instantly.

Emily knew what she had to do.

And tomorrow, she'd do it.

Emily looked around at the thirty or so people seated in the restaurant's small banquet room and admitted that Pete had been right about everything, even the "worst is behind you" line from his note. The tears had ended, and in their place, the smiles and laughter summoned by "That Pete was something!" stories. And it did her heart good to hear that every man aboard the ambulance that crashed into Pete's car had been labeled stable.

"Emily? Are you holding up all right?"

She'd recognize that voice anywhere. Turning, she said, "I'm surprised to see you, Alex."

"Surprised? But why? We still have friends in common. And when I heard . . . well, knowing how close you and Pete were, I had to come."

No, he didn't have to, and she wished he hadn't. "Your flowers were lovely. Even my dad commented on them." *Leave it to Alex to send the biggest arrangement known to man,* Dutton had said. *The only thing bigger,* Miranda agreed, *is his ego.*

"Sorry I couldn't get here sooner."

She wanted to shout, *Relax. Not one*

person said, "Where's Alex?" Instead, she watched as two of Pete's firefighter pals hugged Dutton and quietly said, "Pete would have loved this get-together."

Alex took a step to the left, blocking her view of them. "Take a ride with me."

Emily met his eyes. "What? *Now?* You're kidding, right?"

"I have something to tell you. To ask you, to be more precise. And I need to get back to Baltimore tonight. Surgery tomorrow."

"I don't know, Alex. There's so much to do. And the family is heading back to Baltimore today, too, so . . ."

"Surely they can spare you for a few minutes."

Of course they could. But that wasn't the point. Who did he think he was, waltzing in here at the eleventh hour, trying to make her feel guilty for doing the right thing?

"You know me, Emily. I don't give up easily."

Memory of the flood of texts, e-mails, and voice mail messages he'd left after the breakup proved it. If she gave him five minutes now, she could spare herself hours of nuisance calls later.

"Let me tell the family that I'm stepping out for a couple of minutes."

"There's m'girl!"

First chance she got, Emily intended to find just the right phrase to let him know she was *not* his girl . . . and wipe that self-satisfied smirk from his face.

Minutes later, they stood on the restaurant's back deck, overlooking Deep Creek Lake. Forecasters had predicted rain this evening, but from the look of the looming steel-gray clouds, it would arrive earlier than expected.

"What's on your mind?" she asked him.

"You look marvelous. Even on a day like this, with your eyes all puffy from crying, you're a knockout."

Always the charmer, eh, Alex? Even on the day of my brother's funeral? "I told the family I'd only be gone for a minute or two."

"Sit with me," he said, pointing to a table near the deck rail.

"I'm fine right here." If he didn't get to the point soon, she'd leave him out here, alone.

"I miss you, Emily."

Even after all this time? Wow, I must have been some catch!

"I was an idiot."

Was?

"Never should have let you get away."

"What kind of surgery?" she asked, hoping to change the subject.

"What kind of . . ." He chuckled. "Oh. Tomorrow. Bypass. Why? You want to assist? We made a great team, working on your friend's kid."

His skills in the OR were unparalleled; few people could argue with that. Knowing what needed to be done and issuing the orders that would make it happen were just two of his well-honed skills.

She looked at her wrist, tapped an imaginary watch face. "Tick-tick-tick . . ."

"Good gravy, Em, I know this is a tough day for you, but have a heart. I'm trying to tell you that I'm sorry. That ending things was a mistake. That I want you back."

Emily could remind him who'd *ended things.* Could remind him *why* and admit that if she hadn't thrown herself into work, his persistence would likely have paid off: They'd still be a couple . . . and she'd still be miserable.

"Sorry," she said, "but in my opinion, traveling back in time only succeeds in sci-fi movies."

"Aw, kid, you're breakin' my heart."

She didn't believe it. Not for a minute.

"I have an idea," she said. "As long as you're in town, why don't you pay Gabe a visit. You know . . . my friend's kid? The one you operated on? I know he'd love to

see you, and I'm sure his dad and grandmother would appreciate hearing the great
Dr. Alex Williams say that Gabe is doing
fine."

"Is he here?"

"He's *four,* Alex, and only came home
from Hopkins a few days ago. Why would
he be here?"

"I just thought . . . It seemed that . . ."
He shook his head. "Sure. Okay. I'll check
in with the kid . . . with Gabe, I mean. On
one condition."

Oh, how like him to attach a stipulation.
"Which is . . . ?"

"You'll go with me. To Gabe's house. We
were a team in that OR, so it makes sense."

He smiled. The engaging, flirty smile that
had attracted her to him in the first place.
The same smile he'd no doubt aimed at the
half dozen — that she knew of — women
he'd graced with his companionship while
engaged to Emily.

"All right."

"Excellent! I drove the new Porsche. Just
wait till you hear that baby purr!"

Emily wouldn't hear it, because she had
no intention of riding to Phillip's house with
Alex.

"I'll give you directions and meet you
there. That way if one of us gets an emer-

gency call, the other won't have to worry about getting back to their car."

Winking, he tapped his temple. "Always thinking, aren't you?"

"I'll just let the family know where I'm going."

"Shouldn't you call the boy's father? Let him know we're on the way?" Alex thumped the heel of his hand to his forehead. "Oh, you can't, can you? Because the Amish don't have phones."

He'd find out soon enough that the Oakland community followed New Order rules.

"Give me your cell phone," she said, holding out her hand.

Alex hesitated, but only for a second.

She called up his maps icon, typed in Phillip's address, and returned the device. "If the system misdirects you, just remember, it's 219 North to a right on Paul Friend Road, then left on Pleasant Valley. There's a big black mailbox at the end of the drive that says Baker. You can't miss it."

After enduring a series of good-natured *woo-hoo*s and *Cupid must be in town*s from Joe and Miranda, Emily left the restaurant. With a little luck, she'd reach Phillip's house before Alex, to deliver a "Heads up, trouble's a-comin' " warning.

But, as luck would have it, Alex was

already unfolding himself from the front seat when she pulled into the drive. Phillip must have heard the sports car's engine, because he was on the porch, feet shoulder-width apart and arms crossed, watching.

When Emily stepped up beside him, he said, "Everything go well this morning?"

"As well as can be expected." *What a trite thing to say,* she thought. "Alex thought that since he was in town, he should check on Gabe."

Phillip welcomed the surgeon with a hearty handshake. "Good to see you again, Dr. Williams." Then he opened the screen door and invited them inside. "My mother just took a pound cake out of the oven. Would you like a slice now, or after the exam?"

"After," Emily answered, "so Gabe can join us." Later, she'd apologize for not waiting for an invitation to lead Alex upstairs. Between now and then, she hoped to make him so uncomfortable, he'd leave without taste-testing Sarah's cake.

"Gabe's room is right down this hall."

"Come here often?" Alex teased when they reached the landing.

His implication came through, loud and clear, and she chose to ignore it.

They found Gabe on hands and knees,

mimicking a train whistle and pushing a hand-carved engine car across the polished hardwood.

"Dr. Williams!" he said, sitting back on his heels.

Alex crouched, picked up the engine, and spun its wheels. "Cool train."

"My dad made it."

"Talented man." Straightening, he smoothed his trousers' creases. "How are you feeling?"

"No dizzy spells. No fainting. No pal . . . palpi . . ." Sighing with frustration, he rolled his eyes. "My heart beats like it is spozed to. Good work!"

Alex crossed to the bed and, patting the mattress, said, "How 'bout hopping up here for me, so I can have a look at your incision."

Gabe did as he asked, even lifted his shirt without being told to. "*Grossmammi* says it doesn't need a bandage anymore. And that it will heal faster if the air can get to it."

"She's right. It looks better than I expected."

He'd worn his stethoscope into the house, and when Gabe noticed it, he said, "Do you wear it all of the time, *everywhere*?"

Laughing again, Alex said, "I take it off to sleep. And shower."

"And eat, right, because if you got food on it, then you would get food on your patients."

"Right!" He returned to Emily's side. "I'm glad to see that his cheeks have pinked up a little. And it looks like he's put on a pound or two. He's right. Good work!"

"His dad and grandmother deserve some of the credit. They're the ones who've been taking such terrific care of him. Gabe deserves some credit, too, for being so cooperative."

"And there it is . . . the self-deprecating side that made me fall in love with you."

Gabe's eyes widened and his eyebrows disappeared under thick blondish curls. She held her breath, wondering what he'd say.

It wasn't like Alex to come to her rescue. Or anyone else's, for that matter.

"Not that kind of love, Gabe. Emily . . . Dr. White and I are old friends. Went to medical school together."

"I wish I could go to medical school."

"Hard work, that's what earned me the scholarships I needed for college tuition. Then more hard work to pay for med school. That's how I could afford the things I wanted." He sat beside Gabe again and, scrolling through the photos on his cell phone, showed off his sailboat, the house in

362

Myrtle Beach, a shiny Harley, and of course, the Porsche.

"They are very nice," Gabe said, "but Dr. Williams . . . you do not understand. Amish boys are not allowed to go to college."

"What? No!" On his feet again, he said, "That's ridiculous, and just plain *wrong*. A boy as smart as you could become anything you wanted. An astronaut. A doctor. A —"

"Dr. Williams? Will you tell me again about my device? I have tried to remember what you said, but I forgot."

Flustered, Alex dropped the phone into his shirt pocket. "The ICD is about this big." He made an *O* by connecting his thumb and forefinger. "It's like a tiny computer and runs on a battery. Wires connect it to your heart."

"And if my heart starts beating funny, it will shock me, and make it beat right again, right?"

"Exactly. That's why Em . . . Dr. White is going to keep a close eye on you. On the ICD. She'll be able to read the information it collects, to make sure it's working properly."

Until Gabe's eyes filled with tears, Emily had thought Alex handled the questions perfectly. Sitting on his other side, she pulled him close. "What's wrong, sweetie?"

"I could still die, even with the ICD."

He was right, but the chances of that were slim. Very slim. She'd never liked lying to patients, but in cases like this, the truth really *could* hurt.

"You're not going to die, Gabe."

But he wasn't convinced. "Pete was big and strong. I am small and weak. If *he* died . . ." A sob interrupted his sentence, but he quickly added, "I will miss him."

"Everyone who knew him will miss him," she admitted. "But listen to me, Gabriel Baker. You are *not* going to die. Not for a long, long time, anyway. Why, you'll have a white beard by then, a beard so long that it'll touch your toes!"

"But . . . but in the hospital, after my operation, I had a dream. My mother came to me. She did this . . ." He stretched out his arms, wiggled his fingers. "I know why. She wants me to come to heaven, to be with her."

"No, that can't be right. She wouldn't want you to leave your dad or grandmother. I'll bet she was just excited about how much fun your life is going to be from now on." She pulled him closer. "You've been thinking about this for days and haven't told anyone?"

Staring at his tightly clasped hands, he

shook his head.

"Not even your dad?"

Another shake.

"Well, you stop worrying. There's absolutely no reason for you to be afraid. Because you're not going to die." She met Alex's eyes. "Isn't that right, Dr. Williams?"

"Yes. Yes, of course. Everything is healing nicely, and you look good, too."

Gabe knuckled the tears from his eyes. "Can we go downstairs now and have cake now?"

Laughing, Emily said, "How'd you know about that? Can you see through the floor?"

He pointed at the heating grate under the window. "No, but I can hear through it!"

Tears stung her eyes. Tears of relief and absolute joy. She kissed his cheek. "Oh, my word. I love you to pieces, you silly li'l nut!"

"If you don't have any more questions," Alex said, "I should go." He stood in the doorway. "Will you walk with me, Emily?"

She kissed Gabe's forehead. "Meet you in the kitchen, okay?"

Outside, Alex walked around to the side of the house, out of sight of doors and windows. *This isn't good,* she thought, following him. *Not good at all.*

"Gabe opened my eyes to something," Alex said. "Time is precious. And it's a sin to waste even a minute of it."

"I don't think anyone would disagree with that."

"What I'm trying to say is . . . I came here hoping to get you back. But now . . ." He looked up, as if hoping to read the rest of his comment on the darkening clouds overhead. "But now, I have to come clean. You deserve honesty.

"I came here hoping you'd agree to see me now and then. On weekends. For short vacations. Stolen nights here and there. I can see now that if I had made that proposal, you would have turned me down flat."

"Alex, what *are* you talking about?"

"An affair, Emily. I wanted to ask you to be my" — he licked his lips — "my mistress."

"You're kidding. *Right?*"

He shook his head. "I don't want any of that now. You deserve better. I'm engaged, and she . . . she deserves better. Hell, even *I* deserve better."

"You wanted me to be your . . . your mistress?"

"Yeah," he ground out. "Sorry."

"You have everything now. A house — *two* houses — cars, boats, a successful career, a fiancée . . . I'm happy for you. I really am. Why aren't *you* happy for you?"

"Guilt, I guess. Didn't think I'd earned all that good stuff."

"But now you're going home. To become the guy who *did* earn it. All of it. You're going home to the woman who will truly share your life. No more sneaking and cheating and lying. Is that what you're saying?"

"That's exactly what I'm saying."

Arms crossed over her chest, she said, "And Gabe led you to this . . . confession?"

He nodded.

"From the mouths of babes, huh?"

Another nod. "Gabe is a great kid. You're gonna be a great mom." He looked around the yard, his gaze traveling from the barn to the chicken coop and workshop, the house and beat-up truck parked in the driveway. When his eyes met hers again, he said, "That Phillip, he's —"

"He's what?" Phillip wanted to know, coming up behind them.

"A lucky man." Alex hugged her. "Sorry about Pete. If you ever need anything, call me."

Emily and Phillip stood side by side, watching the gray-white dust cloud kicked up by the Porsche's wide tires. When it turned onto the road, he said, "What was *that* all about?"

She linked her arm through his. "How

'bout we go inside and I'll tell you all about it . . . over cake and coffee."

CHAPTER TWENTY

"That pound cake smells heavenly," Emily said as they entered the kitchen, helping herself to a mug of coffee. "Can I pour both of you a cup?"

Sarah looked at Phillip. "Has she fallen? Thumped her head?"

"Not that I know of," he said.

"Where's Gabe?"

"Still in his room, I suppose."

"Will you call him? I have something to say, to all three of you."

Phillip made a move toward the back stairs, but Sarah stopped him. "I will go," she said. "You stay with Emily."

When she was out of sight, Emily said, " 'You stay with the crazy lady.' "

"Well, you *are* behaving a little . . ." He drew invisible circles beside his temple.

He was almost afraid to ask what, if anything, Alex Williams had to do with it.

"What did he say to prompt your . . . mood?"

"Nothing. Everything." She went to the cupboard, took four plates from the shelf, and distributed them around the table. Opening and closing drawers until she found the flatware, Emily added forks and napkins to the setting. "Milk for Gabe," she said, filling a tumbler. She met his eyes. "For you, too? Or would you rather wash down your cake with coffee?"

"Coffee, I think. But I'll get it."

"What about your mother?" Emily was still holding the milk pitcher when she asked, "Think she wants coffee or milk?"

His mother walked up to the table and said, "Anyone who knows me can tell you that I never drink milk."

"*Grossmammi* does not like it."

"I have a lot to learn. We'll start the list with 'who likes milk and who doesn't.' "

Emily found a big knife and proceeded to cut the pound cake. "Thick or thin?" she asked Phillip.

"Medium."

Smiling, she served everyone a mid-sized slice. "It doesn't feel right, inviting you to sit in your own kitchen, but please. Won't you all have a seat?"

"She is scaring me," Sarah whispered.

Me too, Phillip thought, *a little.*

Once everyone had settled around the table, Emily sat beside Gabe.

"I think you all know how much I loved my brother. Pete was one of the brightest lights in my life, and I'll miss him, terribly."

"We are sorry for your loss," Sarah said, "but he is with God, as was His will. Do not be sad anymore. You can rest assured that Pete is happy."

It was his mother's clumsy way of offering consolation. He hoped Emily would understand.

"Life is so fragile. But I don't need to tell you that. You've both lost loved ones. Losses like that . . ." She took a deep breath. ". . . they teach us to value every day, every second with family and friends."

"Emily, what can I get for *you*?"

"Nothing just yet, Mrs. Baker."

"Not even coffee?" Phillip asked.

"In a minute. I want to say this. I have to say it. I haven't sorted it all out yet, but . . . It appears Pete left everything to me. His house. His car. All the money in his bank accounts."

"And Clinger," Gabe put in.

"Yes, and Clinger." She met Phillip's eyes. "Once everything is liquidated, I'll have more than enough money to buy some land.

371

I know just the place. There's already a house on it. A shed, too. And a small garage." She waved a hand in front of her face. "But I digress . . ."

"Digress? What does that mean, Dad?"

Grinning, he said, "It means Emily distracted herself and thinks it's time to get back on track."

"Yes, yes, that's it, exactly!" Hands clasped under her chin, she said, "Here's what I've been thinking. . . ."

"Uh-oh," Sarah said, and eyes turned heavenward, she added, "Lord be with us . . . for here it comes."

Gabe used the back of his hand to wipe away his milk mustache. "Here comes what?"

"Trouble, I think."

Phillip didn't know what Emily had been thinking about, or if it was, as his mother believed, trouble. But he'd take it. Seeing her this happy, this enthusiastic, was a beautiful thing. And it was contagious.

"I've made some phone calls," she continued, "conducted some online studies, and guess what?"

"We are not mind readers," Sarah said.

"Oh, Mrs. Baker, you can be so funny when you set your mind to it!"

"It was not a joke." But she was smiling

when she said, "Call me Sarah."

"Sarah," Emily echoed. Then, "After all my research, I found out that I have more than enough money to pay cash for the property. I'll sell my house in town, of course, and when I add the proceeds to what Pete left me, I'll have more than enough to open a medical clinic. . . ."

"A clinic," Phillip echoed.

". . . where anyone who can't afford — or doesn't want — insurance can come, for antibiotics, vaccinations, examinations . . ."

"And I thought we Amish were the only ones that believed in 'shuns.' "

His mother's joke struck a chord with Emily, who laughed until tears filled her eyes.

"It was not that funny," Sarah muttered.

When the giggles subsided, Emily sighed. "We're so blessed, all of us. We have our health, safe places to live, plenty to eat, and each other."

Sarah nodded. "True. Yes."

"Which brings me to the other reason I wanted to talk with all of you. Oh! And before I forget . . . Phillip! There will be more than enough to bring all your bills up to date, too!"

"Oh, now there's where I have to draw the line. I can't let you —"

"You can, and you will. But hush, and let

me finish. I promise, I'll explain that, after . . ."

Gabe scratched his head. "After what?"

Emily patted her lap. "Will you sit with me, Gabe?"

Eyebrows high on his forehead, he sent Phillip an "I don't get it" look.

Once he'd done as she asked, her arms went around him. "I love you to pieces. You know that, right?"

"Yes . . ."

"Now, I want to make sure you understand that I'd never try to replace your mother. In fact, I'll do everything humanly possible to help you remember and honor her, always. But . . ."

"Uh-oh," Sarah said again. "What did I tell you? Here comes the trouble!"

". . . but I'd love it if you'd let me be your *substitute* mom."

"If I say yes to that, wouldn't you and my dad have to get married first?"

She pressed kisses all over his face, and while he squinted and giggled, Emily said, "That's a very good question." Reaching across the table, she grasped Phillip's hand and, eyes on Gabe again, said, "That's what this whole long announcement has been about, you sweet boy, you! Do I have your permission to ask him to marry me?"

Gabe's eyes widened and his mouth formed an *O*. Then he threw his arms around her neck and squealed, "Yes! Ask him!"

"What about you, Sarah? Do I have your blessing to marry your son?"

The older woman's eyes filled with tears and, with one hand over her heart, she said, "But Emily, you are not Amish."

"Remember when I said I'd done some research? Well, that's one of the things I looked up. Marriage between people of our varied backgrounds isn't the norm, but it's acceptable to New Order Amish . . . as long as I cooperate fully. Allow the bishop to baptize me. Put on the bonnet and the apron, so to speak. And promise never to stand in the way of . . . well, for lack of a better word . . . *our* ways."

"You would do all of that? The clinic? Leave the English world behind? You will respect our ways? All of that, for us?"

"Yes, Sarah, I would. Definitely I would. But not just for all of you. For me, too."

"There's still the matter of the bills," Phillip said. "I can't let you —"

"Once we're married, Phillip, we'll be partners, in all things, in all ways. What's mine is yours, what's yours is mine." She winked. "Just so you know, I might just paint the chicken coop *pink*."

Sarah gasped. "You would not do that!"

"All right, lavender then."

When their laughter quieted, Phillip got up, motioned for the rest of them to do the same.

"Oh, if only Pete could see us now," Emily said.

"He'd be happy?"

"Yes, Phillip, he'd be happy. Very happy."

"Group hug, then," he said, and once they'd all gathered close, he met his mother's eyes.

"I'm gonna need a pin, *Maemm*."

"A pin? What for?"

"To pop this big fat head of mine, so it won't get stuck in the doorway."

She rolled her eyes. "Ach! Emily's 'crazy' is contagious!"

"My head swelled right up," he explained, "when the most beautiful, talented, big-hearted woman in the world asked me to marry her."

Sarah chuckled. "And your answer? What will it be?"

When he shrugged, three voices groaned.

"Will it be an Amish wedding?" Sarah wanted to know.

Emily beamed. "Of course. But you'll have to teach me how it's done."

"Ach," Phillip said, *"Ik ben gezegend."*

"What does it mean? I forget, Dad."

"It means, 'I am blessed.' "

Sarah began to cry, and when Gabe asked why, she said, *"Ik ook."*

"I know that one! It means 'me too'!"

"Will you and Phillip have more children?" Sarah asked.

Phillip nodded. *"Als dat Gods will is."*

"This mother's prayers have been answered!" Sarah exclaimed. Then, "You can take the man out of the Amish, but you cannot take the Amish out of the man. Praises to Him!"

"I cannot wait," Gabe said, jumping up and down. "I will have brothers and sisters!" He paused, then added, "If it is God's will . . ."

Phillip stepped away from the group, but only long enough to draw Emily into a fierce hug.

"Ik van je you," she said.

"Amish?" he asked. "You're kidding me."

"Told you I've been studying!"

"Now then, how might I stop you from telling us everything *else* you've learned?"

He read the message that glowed in her eyes, and he kissed her.

EPILOGUE

"There," Phillip said. "Your sign is fixed."

Last week's storm had blown it from the hangers and split it right down the middle.

"You didn't just fix it, Phillip. You made me a brand-new one!"

"No wife of mine will hang a shingle that looks . . . unkempt."

"It's beautiful. Even better than the first one."

Emily stepped back to admire it. BAKER FREE CLINIC, said the bold black letters. Beneath them, Phillip had fashioned a smaller sign of balsa wood, one that could be turned from OPEN to CLOSED.

"You're amazing, and I love you to pieces."

"*I'm* amazing? Says the woman who walked away from a prestigious position at the hospital? Sold her house and everything in it to buy this house and lot, which just so happens to abut Baker land? Who works tirelessly to provide neighbors, friends, and family with the best medical care they've ever had — even the few who can't afford to pay for it?" He drew her close. "*You* are the amazing one. And I love you for it."

She snuggled close and felt the unmistakable thump of their baby's feet against his stomach. Phillip took a half step back, pressed a palm to either side of her swollen belly.

"He's an active little fellow, isn't he?"

"Could be a *she,* you know."

"Yes, I know."

"So if it's a girl, you won't be disappointed?"

"Disappointed! A miniature Emily would be a grand addition to the Baker family." He kissed her, then nodded toward her desk, where she'd started a list of baby names. "Have you decided what we'll call him . . . or her?"

One hand resting on her stomach, she said, "Yes, as a matter of fact, I have. Petra for a girl, Peter for a boy."

"Good, strong names. Pete would be proud. And I'm proud to bestow the name in his memory." Placing his hand atop hers, he said, "Are you happy, Emily?"

"Ecstatically. Deliriously. Madly happy."

It's what she always said when he asked the question, and more than anything, she hoped he believed her, every time.

"But Em, you've experienced so many changes. The sacrifices have fallen on your shoulders alone."

"I haven't sacrificed anything. My life is better than it has ever been." She kissed his chin. "Besides, you sacrificed your bachelor life to become my husband."

"Ah, yes. My oh-so-active bachelor life."

She'd never grow tired of hearing him laugh this way. It told her that *he* was happy, right here where he belonged, surrounded by the Plain people and lifestyle he loved.

"Be honest now," he said. "You don't mind wearing skirts and aprons?"

"Not a bit. The clothing is actually quite liberating."

"And the shoes?"

"Very sturdy. Very supportive. Even after a long day on my feet."

He tucked wayward curls from her ears, as he'd been doing almost from the moment they'd met. "Make me a promise."

"Who knew you could be so greedy! I've already promised to spend the rest of my life beside you. Promised to spend it here, in Pleasant Valley, living the Plain life. Promised to give you children. And you want more?"

He grinned. "Well, when you put it that way . . ."

Giggling, Emily stood on tiptoe, and after kissing him, said, "For you, I'll promise anything. *Anything.*"

"You're right. I *am* greedy. Because the truth of it is . . . *you're* all I'll ever need."

She'd heard it said that the human heart could overflow with love, but until she met Phillip, Emily hadn't believed it. He'd brightened every dark corner of her life, bringing laughter and fun in ways that only he could.

"Promise me you'll never hide your beautiful hair under a bonnet."

"But Phillip! What would Micah Fisher say about that!"

He did his best to imitate the bishop. "Obey your husband, woman. If he says do not cover your hair . . ."

The baby kicked again, and bending at the waist, Phillip kissed her belly. Straightening, he said, "Promise?"

"All right. Here at the clinic, and in the privacy of our house, I won't wear the cap. But in church and when we're —"

"That's m'girl."

A lifetime ago, when Alex had spoken those very words, she'd wanted to bellow, "I'm *not* your girl!" But now, standing in the protective circle of Phillip's arms, Emily thought they were almost the most beautiful words in the English language.

"I love you," he said.

Those . . . *those* were the most beautiful words, and she'd never tire of hearing — or saying — them.

ABOUT THE AUTHOR

Once upon a time, best-selling author **Loree Lough** literally sang for her supper, performing before packed audiences throughout the United States. Now she'll croon a tune or two for the "grandorables," but she mostly writes. She and her husband divide their time between Baltimore and the Allegheny Mountains.